Roberta Grieve had her first story published in 1998 and since then has had many stories and articles published. She is secretary of the Chichester Writers' Circle and editor of the Chichester Literary Society's quarterly newsletter. She enjoys painting and walking. Roberta lives in Chichester, which is the setting for *Abigail's Secret*.

ABIGAIL'S SECRET

Abigail Cookson's mother disappeared when she was a small child, and her father is the town drunk, but at last she finds happiness when she meets and falls in love with handsome sailor Joe. She gets a job at a large department store, and her troubles seem over. But Joe goes off to sea and Abby's employer is not as respectable as she thought. Then Abby discovers she is pregnant, and it seems things can't get any worse. The start of World War Two gives her the chance of a new life, but can she ever forget Joe?

Books by Robert Grieve
Published by The House of Ulverscroft:

A HATFUL OF DREAMS
THE COMFORT OF STRANGERS
THE CROSS AND THE FLAME
SEA OF LOVE

ROBERTA GRIEVE

ABIGAIL'S SECRET

Complete and Unabridged

ULVERSCROFT
Leicester

First published in Great Britain in 2008 by
Robert Hale Limited
London

First Large Print Edition
published 2009
by arrangement with
Robert Hale Limited
London

British Library CIP Data

Grieve, Roberta.
  Abigail's secret
  1. Single mothers- -Fiction. 2. World War, *1939 – 1945*- -
Social aspects- -England- -Fiction. 3. Large type books.
I. Title
823.9′2–dc22

  ISBN 978-1-84782-628-2

Published by
F. A. Thorpe (Publishing)
Anstey, Leicestershire

Set by Words & Graphics Ltd.
Anstey, Leicestershire
Printed and bound in Great Britain by
T. J. International Ltd., Padstow, Cornwall

This book is printed on acid-free paper

PART ONE

1938–1940

1

Abby Cookson woke from a troubled sleep and tried to stand, wincing as she flexed her cramped limbs. The events of the previous evening flooded back and she raised her eyes to the ceiling. With a bit of luck her father was still sleeping off his latest boozing spree.

Pain coursed through her bruised body as she bent to pick up the hair ribbon which had come off in the struggle. She tied back her springy chestnut curls and prodded her cheek gently, hoping the bruise wasn't too obvious.

The knocking which had woken her came again, sharp, impatient. She'd have to answer it. Mr Skinner wouldn't go away until she did. Friday was rent day and she'd already missed last week. If she wasn't careful she and Dad would be out on the street. The two up two down in shabby Tanner's Court wasn't much, but at least it was a roof over their head.

Abby went to the door, her feet crunching on broken crockery. Glancing towards the stairs, she retrieved the rent book and money from behind the skirting-board. At least Dad hadn't been able to force her to reveal her latest hiding-place.

She opened the door, ready with excuses, promises. But it wasn't the rent man. Holding a hand to her bruised face, she attempted a smile. 'Oh, it's you, Mr Leighton. I thought it was old Skinner.' She held up the rent book.

'He'll be along soon,' Dan Leighton replied. 'I'm just finishing my round, wondered if you needed any milk.'

'No thanks,' Abby said quickly. Paying the rent was hard enough, let alone buying luxuries like fresh milk.

'It'll only go to waste.'

Abby hesitated. 'No, really.'

'You'd be doing me a favour, my duck. I hate tipping it down the drain.' He grinned. 'If you don't need it you can always give it to the cat.'

She couldn't help smiling, although it hurt her jaw. 'We haven't got a cat.'

Dan laughed. 'Never mind, Abby, fetch your jug.'

She got the blue-and-white striped jug from the dresser behind the door. At least Dad hadn't broken that.

Glad as she was of the milk, she hated accepting charity — even from Mr Leighton, who'd always been kind to her. She could tell he'd noticed the bruise although he hadn't mentioned it.

Abby followed him to the end of the twitten, the narrow alleyway leading to the half-dozen cottages that made up Tanner's Court. While he filled the jug, Abby stroked the horse's smooth neck.

'Here you are, my duck.' Dan's voice roused her and she looked up, taking in the row of flint and brick cottages across the road, the poor but clean children playing hopscotch on the cobbles. Over the rooftops she caught a glimpse of tall trees turning gold in the autumn sunlight, the spire of Chichester Cathedral towering over the little market town. The sun rarely penetrated the gloom of Tanner's Court and not for the first time Abby wished her father were in regular work so that they could afford to rent one of the houses in George Street, with their neat front gardens and brightly painted front doors. But these days he was lucky to be in work at all.

Dan touched her arm. 'You all right, Abby?' He held out the jug.

'I'm fine,' Abby said. She thanked him for the milk, blushing a little with shame. She knew he'd guessed what had happened and she wanted to leap to her father's defence, explain that it wasn't his fault. But that would mean admitting what he'd done.

The jug was full to the brim and Abby

carried it carefully through the twitten and into the cottage. She set it down on the draining board in the scullery and covered it with a clean cloth.

She went to the foot of the stairs, listening for the rhythmic snores from upstairs that told her Wally Cookson was still sleeping. If only she had a father like Mr Leighton, Abby thought, wondering why he'd never married. He'd have made someone a good husband. He wouldn't steal the rent money for drink. Nor would he beat his child for some imagined slight before sinking into a drunken stupor and missing yet another day's work.

Dan Leighton watched the girl disappear into the gloom of the twitten and took up the horse's reins. 'Come along, Gertie, old girl. Time we was heading back to the farm,' he said. Before turning the corner he glanced back at the entrance to Tanner's Court and sighed. It would take more than a jug of milk to brighten that poor lass's life, he thought.

At the end of George Street he saw one of the Misses Crocker tending her little front garden. He raised his cap and wished her good morning.

'What a lovely day, Mr Leighton,' she said. 'I do hope it will stay fine for the fair. The young people do so enjoy it.'

Dan glanced up at the blue sky. 'Well, it

seems set fair for the moment, Miss Thomasina.' As he turned his cart and set off towards Fishbourne he couldn't help chuckling. People hereabouts couldn't tell the Crocker sisters apart until they opened their mouths. Miss Hortense barely acknowledged him. How could two people so alike in looks differ so much in temperament, he wondered. Well, Miss Hortense had lost her fiancé in the war, and as the years passed she'd become more and more embittered.

The Great War had ruined as many lives as it had taken, his included. And twenty years later people were still suffering. If it wasn't for the war he might have been a contented married man with a daughter just like Abby, he thought.

As he reached Westgate and the open fields beyond the city walls, Dan recalled the bruise on Abby's face. How he'd stopped himself rushing into the house and confronting Wally Cookson, he didn't know — except that it wouldn't have helped her. Rage tightened his fists on the reins and the old horse faltered. He loosened his grip at once. 'Sorry, Gertie, old girl,' he muttered, breathing deeply of the fresh country air. But his anger didn't lessen. Nor did the pain in his heart.

Each time he saw Abby she seemed to grow more like her mother. At eighteen, apart from being so painfully thin, she was the image of Carrie. From her wild chestnut curls to her vivid blue eyes and the sweetness of her smile, it was like seeing the Carrie he'd loved and lost all those years ago.

No use dwelling on the past, he told himself. It was his own fault and he'd almost learned to live with the mistakes of his impetuous youth. Knowing that he did all he could to make Abby's life a bit easier helped a little. He wished now he'd slipped a few coppers into her hand so that she could go to Sloe Fair and have a bit of fun like other lasses her age. But he knew she'd have refused. Proud, just like her mother, he thought.

★ ★ ★

Abby put her foot on the bottom stair. She ought to wake Dad up, try and get him to show his face at the factory — that's if he still had a job to go to. He'd got the sack so many times in the past few years and she wondered what they'd do if he lost this one. This was his second spell of employment at the Shippam's paste factory and he'd been lucky to get another chance, with unemployment so bad everywhere. If it wasn't for Alf Jones the foreman, who'd served with him in the Sussex Regiment at Verdun, he'd have been tramping the streets begging for work like so many others.

If she had a job herself, things wouldn't be so bad, Abby thought, pouring some of the creamy milk into an enamel mug. She drank it down, rinsed the mug under the cold tap and replaced it on the shelf.

Better get washed and tidied before Mr Skinner knocked on the door. Then she'd have to spend her last precious coppers on some food. There was nothing in the larder and she'd been banking on Dad giving her some housekeeping money. But as usual he'd gone straight into the Star when he left the factory and not come home till he was thrown out.

He'd seemed quite amiable when he staggered through the door last night — until Abby had tentatively asked him for money. She'd hardly eaten anything all day and was hoping the chip shop in Northgate was still open.

Wally turned on her with a snarl. 'What have you done with the last lot I gave you?' He snatched at the red ribbon in her hair. 'Spending it on fripperies, I suppose. If you've got money to waste on rubbish like this, you don't need housekeeping from me.'

'But, Dad, we owe two weeks' rent and I haven't got enough put by.'

'Old Skinner can whistle for his money. He's got a nerve anyway, expecting us to pay rent on this dump.' His eyes narrowed. 'Did you say you've got some put by? Holding out on me, girl, eh?' He held out his hand. 'Come on, then, where is it?'

'It's for the rent, Dad. I've put it away.'

'You've no right to keep money from me,' he shouted. 'Where is it?' He thrust his hand into the jug on the dresser, pulled out the drawers and emptied them on to the floor. His hand swept along the shelves, sending cups and plates crashing to the floor.

Abby tried to grab his arm. 'Don't, Dad. Please.'

He pushed her away and she fell against the dresser, hitting her face. She curled up, covering her face, sobbing as he aimed a kick at her ribs with his heavy work-boots.

'Don't worry, I'll find it.' Wally clumped up the stairs and a minute later she heard him crashing about in her room. She sniffed back her tears and gave a nod of satisfaction. He won't find it up there, she thought.

At last it went quiet and Abby tried to get up. But she could hardly breathe for the pain in her ribs and, with a sigh, she wrapped herself in the crocheted blanket from the wooden armchair. It wouldn't be the first time she'd slept on the cold floor, too exhausted and frightened to climb the narrow stairs to her room.

* * *

Now, she washed her face at the sink in the scullery and tidied her hair, peering at herself in the tiny mirror. The bruise didn't look too bad and if anyone asked, she'd tell the truth — she *had* fallen. No one need know the reason.

She tucked her blouse in and smoothed her skirt, satisfied that she looked reasonably presentable. At least she'd managed to get herself a few decent clothes while she'd worked for Lady Grisham. If only she was still in service at the Manor. Being a kitchen maid was hard work, but at least she'd been well treated and never had to worry about going hungry. And her employer had understood when she needed time off to look after her sick father. The war, which had ended just before she was born, had left its mark on millions, and Lady Grisham, who'd lost a son in the trenches, had been sympathetic — until Dad had stormed up the drive and hammered at the manor door demanding to know why his daughter hadn't come home on her half-day, bringing her wages with her.

Abby sighed, remembering how she'd pleaded to be allowed to stay, trying to explain that it was the sickness that drove her father to drink, that he didn't mean to offend anybody.

'But I can't have him turning up here, upsetting my guests, not to mention the other servants. He quite terrified poor Letty when she opened the front door.' Lady Grisham was kind but firm. 'I'm sorry my dear, I'll have to ask you to leave. I will, of course, give you an excellent reference. And I wish you well in finding another position.'

But it had proved impossible to find another job. Chichester was still a prosperous market town compared with many places. But even here the depression had hit some of the small factories and work was scarce. What jobs there were went to men with families. Besides, once word of her father's trouble-making got round, no one would even give her an interview.

It hadn't been too bad through the summer. She'd managed to get some seasonal work tomato-picking in the nurseries to the south of the city and, later on, apple picking. But that had finished and all she could look forward to was a winter of cold, wet manual labour in the potato and sprout fields.

Her father was still asleep when Mr

Skinner knocked on the door. She paid a week's rent and a couple of shillings off the arrears, promising the rest next week. He appeared to be satisfied and Abby sighed with relief. You didn't have to get far behind to run the risk of being evicted and, although the workhouse across the main road had closed down years ago, the building still stood as a stark reminder of what happened to people who didn't pay their way.

Abby shivered and ran through the twitten into the sunshine of George Street. She hurried along, head bent, hoping no one would stop and speak to her. Living in Somerstown was almost like living in a village. Everyone knew what went on and gossip was rife. And of course, Wally Cookson's reputation had spread beyond the small suburb into the city itself.

Not for the first time, Abby thought about running away — to Portsmouth maybe. With Lady Grisham's reference she could get a live-in job at one of the big houses on Southsea Common. No one would know her — or her father — there.

But no matter what he'd done, she couldn't leave him. He needed looking after. It wasn't his fault he was this way. People said it was his experiences in the trenches that had changed him. But Abby's early memories were happy ones. It was after her mother left when she was only seven that the drinking got out of control.

If Mum hadn't run off with her fancy man, they'd still be a normal family, Abby thought, as she turned the corner into Cross Street on her way to the grocer's in High Street. A sharp voice broke into her thoughts and brought her to a halt.

'Well, my girl, aren't you going to say hello?' Aggie Thompson was leaning on her front gate, duster in hand.

'Gran, I didn't see you,' Abby said. She'd hoped to get past her grandmother's house unnoticed. But Aggie was always out the front, pretending to clean her windows or polishing her brass knocker. Little of what went on in Somerstown escaped her eagle eye.

'If you're going to the shops you can get a few bits for me while you're at it.' Aggie turned to go into the house without waiting for a reply. 'Come in a minute, while I find me purse.'

Abby hesitated before following her up the short front path. She put a hand to her cheek. As soon as Gran saw the bruise there would be questions, followed by a tirade of abuse against her father. She should be used to it by now.

She waited on the doorstep while her

grandmother fumbled in the depths of her black handbag and brought out her purse.

'I want a small bag of flour — plain, not self-raising, mind. And if you're going into East Street you can get me a nice pork chop from Elphick's. Make sure it's not all bone and not too fatty. I can't cope with fat at my age . . . ' She turned to hand the money to Abby and stopped abruptly. 'What happened to you, girl?'

Her hand covering her cheek again, Abby avoided her grandmother's eye. 'I fell,' she mumbled.

'Fell, my hat. He hit you, didn't he?' Aggie pulled Abby's hand away and inspected the bruise. 'He could've had your eye out. Oh, if I could get my hands on him . . . '

Abby almost laughed at the image of the tiny woman facing up to big Wally Cookson. But it came out as a strangled sob.

Aggie's demeanour changed in a flash. 'Come on, lovie. Sit down and tell me what happened.' She drew the girl into the shabby, cosy kitchen and pushed her into the armchair in front of the range. 'A nice cup of tea, that's what you need. And I bet you haven't had breakfast either. What's got into him taking things out on a slip of a girl?' She bustled around, pushing the kettle on to the hob, taking down cups and saucers from the dresser, buttering a thick floury home-made scone, muttering all the while.

Abby leaned her head against a cushion and closed her eyes. It would have been so easy to stay there and let Gran look after her. But her eyes flew open at the old woman's next words and the familiar anger flooded back.

'I always said my Carrie was too good for him. But she waited for him all through the war, even when she thought he wasn't coming back. She could've had any man she wanted. But she had to go and fall for that drunken wastrel.'

Abby had to protest. 'But, Gran, he wasn't like that before. He only started drinking after she left.'

'How do you know? You were too young to understand.' Aggie's lips thinned to a hard line. 'How can you defend him when he does things like that?' She gestured at Abby's bruised face.

'I told you — I fell.' Now the anger boiled over. 'Anyway, why shouldn't I defend him? He's my father. Besides, going off and leaving your child is far worse . . . ' She choked back the angry tears.

'Well, maybe. I don't condone what she did. Besides, she knew I was here to look out for you.'

'Gran. I'm sorry — didn't mean to upset you.' Abby tried to put her arms round the old woman.

Aggie pushed her away. 'It's been a long time, girl — eleven years. Maybe we should just accept it and get on with things.'

'But I can't help wondering where she is now and why . . . '

'No use upsetting yourself.' The familiar no-nonsense Gran was back. 'Now, are you going to drink that tea and get to the shops? All the best chops will be gone by the time you get there.'

Abby drained the cup, but she only picked at the scone, although she'd had no breakfast. There were so many questions she wanted to ask, to help her understand. But this was the closest her grandmother would ever come to showing her feelings. If she didn't talk about it, she could pretend her daughter wasn't a wicked woman who'd left her war-scarred husband and gone off — probably with another man — abandoning her only child.

That's what everyone in Somerstown thought. And, as a staunch member of the Methodist Chapel, Aggie Thompson was still finding it hard to live with the scandal that had erupted when Carrie Cookson had disappeared eleven years ago. Never mind the scandal, Abby thought, as she said goodbye to her grandmother. She was the one who'd had to live with the pain of being abandoned by the mother she adored.

★ ★ ★

Back in Tanner's Court, Abby cleared up the broken china from the night before. Gran had asked her to stay for dinner but there was only the one chop, so she'd made the excuse of needing to cook for her father. Not that there was much to cook.

She'd crept into the house and up the stairs, relieved that Wally had gone — not to work, that was certain. Probably spending the last of his wages in the Rainbow now that he was no longer welcome in the Star. The room was strewn with clothing, the bed rumpled and smelling of stale booze. She straightened the bedclothes and picked up the dirty shirt and vest from the floor, gasping as something rattled to the floor. She pounced on the single shilling, glanced round furtively as if Dad might still be in the room.

That would go towards the rent arrears, she thought. She'd hide it in the tin behind the skirting board. He'd never miss it, the state he was in last night. Even so, she felt guilty for hiding the money. The minister's booming voice echoed in her head. *'Thou shalt not steal*'. But it wasn't stealing. Dad lived here too, why shouldn't he pay something towards the rent?

She tried not to think about it as she stuffed the dirty washing into the copper in the scullery, draped the blanket over the armchair to hide the gaps in the upholstery and dusted the dresser. Finished, she put her hand in the pocket of her skirt, feeling the coppers that Gran had given her as thanks for doing the shopping.

'Go to the fair this evening, girl. Enjoy yourself for once,' she'd said.

Abby had intended to put the money aside. But, returning from shopping, she'd heard the noise of the fair being set up in Oaklands Park, the throb of the motors that powered the roundabouts and the big dipper, the music, the shouts of the brawny gypsy-looking men, dogs barking, children screaming. A thrill of excitement had gone through her, as it did every October when Sloe Fair came to town.

She carried the broken crockery out to the dustbin and stood for a moment, enjoying the feel of the autumn air on her face and bare arms, wrinkling her nose as a breeze brought the smell from the row of lavatories on the far side of the cobbled courtyard. Not all the inhabitants of Tanner's Court were as scrupulous as she was. The sounds of the fair

19

came to her and she decided she'd go after all. She didn't have to spend any money.

★   ★   ★

The noise was deafening and the air was filled with the mingled smells of hot engine oil, candyfloss and fried onions. But that just added to the excitement of Sloe Fair. It seemed as if everybody from Chichester and the surrounding villages was there to enjoy the highlight of the year. Usually it rained and the field outside the city walls became a sea of mud — not that it stopped people enjoying themselves. It looked as though they'd be lucky this year. The ground was bone-dry after the long hot summer and, although it was October, the air was balmy and still.

Abby pushed through the crowds, hoping for a glimpse of her friend, Rhoda, who worked as a parlour-maid in one of the big Georgian houses in St Martin's Square. She didn't get much time off and Abby seldom saw her these days. But if she'd managed to slip away she'd be flirting with one of the fairground lads. Rhoda was what Aggie Thompson called 'flighty'. But then Gran disapproved of most things other people called fun.

Abby couldn't help smiling, but she was worried too. The fairground people weren't like the lads they'd grown up with. She hoped Rhoda wouldn't do anything silly.

But when Abby eventually caught sight of her friend she was arm in arm with a young gypsy-looking man, laughing up into his face. As she approached, the couple disappeared behind the stall.

Disappointed at having no one to enjoy the fair with, Abby found it hard to enter into the spirit of things. She knew she shouldn't have come. Her head ached from the noise and the smells and, as she stumbled across the rough field, unwelcome memories began to intrude. It was on Sloe Fair night, all those years ago, that her mother had disappeared.

A sob rose in her throat as she replayed that last memory, Mum laughing as she tried the coconut shy, Abby waving from the carousel.

The music seemed louder now and other memories came — Mum laughing as the hoopla man held her wrist, helping her to flick the rings over the hoops, as she tried to win a doll for Abby. Then laughter dying as Dad rushed at the man, fists flying, blood. When Abby burst into tears, Dad swept her up in his arms.

'It's all right, my duck. No one's going to hurt you.' He stroked her hair, glaring over her shoulder at the man. 'You leave my wife alone, you hear?'

Mum had run off into the crowd and Dad had taken her to Gran's house. She never saw her mother again.

Lost in thought, she didn't notice the three youths barring her path until one of them grabbed her arm.

'On your own? Want some company?' He glanced at his companions and sniggered. 'We'll make sure you have a good time.'

Abby swallowed, nervous of the way he was looking at her. 'I must get home. My father's not well . . . '

His hand tightened on her arm. 'Well, Daddy's going to do without his little girl tonight. You can look after us instead.'

'Let go.' Abby tried to prise his fingers away, kicking at his shins.

He laughed harder. 'Wildcat, eh? Grab her, lads. We don't want her getting away.' They dragged her towards the shadows at the edge of the field.

She screamed and the leader clamped his free hand over her mouth. She bit down and he let go. The other one still had her arm and she kicked out again.

A figure loomed out of the shadows and she screamed again as hands reached for her. 'It's all right. Don't be frightened. What's going on?'

The man looked down at her, his face

creased in concern. Abby glanced round to see the lads running off.

She took a shuddering breath. 'I'm OK, really.'

'You're sure? I thought I heard a scream.'

'I'm fine now, honestly.'

'Were they bothering you?'

'I don't think they meant any harm.' Now they'd gone it was easy to believe they'd just been larking around.

'Let me walk with you — get you home safely,' the young man said. 'You live in Somerstown, don't you?'

Abby nodded, still a bit nervous. He looked a bit familiar but she was sure she didn't know him. He was tall and well-built, with a shock of straw-coloured hair which refused to lie flat, even when he ran his hand over it as he did now, his face creased in a frown.

'Look, there's no need to be nervous. I only want to walk with you.' He laughed. 'We have met before you know. I'm Joe Leighton — '

'Are you related to Dan — the milkman?' Abby interrupted.

'He's my uncle. I sometimes help on the round, when I'm home on leave.'

She remembered him now, although she hadn't seen him for some time. 'I'm Abby,' she said, suddenly shy.

'I know,' he said, taking her arm and

guiding her through the crowded fairground towards the gate. 'I've seen you when I've been on the milk round with Uncle Dan.' As they walked, he told her he was in the navy, now based at Portsmouth. 'I usually stay with Dan when I'm on leave,' he said.

Abby gradually stopped shaking and began to enjoy being with him. In the shock of the attack she'd forgotten that she'd hardly eaten all day, her only thought to get home and bolt the door. But now the smell of frying food made her feel faint and she stumbled a little.

Joe gripped her arm more tightly but she pulled away. 'I was going to get some chips,' she said.

'Good idea.' He went up to the stall and ordered two portions of cod with a generous helping of chips.

As they walked towards the little streets of Somerstown they shared the greasy food, chatting as if they'd known each other for ever. They were almost at the entrance to Tanner's Court when Joe spoke abruptly. 'What were you doing at the fair on your own?' he asked.

'I was looking for my friend.'

'And those louts — what were they up to?'

'They're boys from round here. They were trying to scare me, just joking around.'

Joe pursed his lips and she was sure he

didn't believe her. 'Well, if you have any more trouble, let me know. I'll deal with them,' he said.

'Don't worry, my Gran will sort them out. She knows their parents,' Abby said, although she'd no intention of mentioning the incident to her grandmother. She had enough trouble already.

But Joe burst out laughing. 'Well, knowing your Gran, if I was them, I'd be shaking in my shoes.'

Abby couldn't help laughing too. Everyone round here knew that Aggie Thompson, despite her size, could be quite fierce when the occasion demanded. She ate the last chip and screwed the paper into a ball.

'Thanks for walking me home. I'm all right now,' she said, stopping at the mouth of the twitten.

'I ought to see you right to the door,' he said.

But Abby didn't want him bumping into her father and insisted he left her there.

Reluctantly, he said good night. 'Maybe I'll see you around. I don't go back to Portsmouth till Monday,' he said.

Abby nodded, not sure what to say. She watched him turn the corner, wishing he'd made a definite arrangement to see her. Still, he was home for a few days — and he knew where she lived. She felt her way across the dark courtyard. No light shone from the house and she wondered if Dad had managed to get hold of some beer money. Too much had happened this evening and she didn't think she could cope with another confrontation.

But Wally was sitting in the dark, staring into the glowing coals of the range. He looked up as Abby opened the door.

'Hello, love. Had a good time?'

Abby didn't answer, furious that he was pretending nothing had happened. How could he forget his behaviour of the night before? But, as she lit the gas and noticed his haggard face and bloodshot eyes, her heart softened. She knew he drank to forget her mother and what she'd done. And it was always worse at Sloe Fair time.

'Had any supper?' she asked.

He nodded.

Abby went through to the scullery and filled the kettle. 'Want a cup of tea?' she called.

'No thanks. I'm off to bed now. Got to get up for work in the morning.'

'Did you go in today?' Abby couldn't help asking.

He shook his head. 'Alf Jones came round. Said he put in a word for me but if I don't turn up tomorrow I won't have a job. I tried to tell him I was ill but he wouldn't listen.'

Abby came into the room and put the kettle on the range, bending to rattle the poker between the bars of the fire. Wally hadn't moved from the armchair.

'But you are feeling better, Dad?' she said, trying not to sound impatient. Sometimes it was hard to keep up the pretence that Wally's frequent absences from work were the result of some unspecified war disability and not the effects of the previous night's boozing.

'Not too bad,' Wally said. 'Though I might wait till Monday.'

Abby got the teapot down from its shelf and measured a small amount into it, poured on the hot water. 'But Mr Jones said — '

'I know what he said — that's why I'm going to work tomorrow. Don't worry, I won't get the sack this time. And I'll try to keep off the booze, I promise.' He sighed and dropped his head in his hands. 'Abby, love, I can't help it . . . '

She sat on the hard chair opposite him. 'Dad — it's all right. I understand.' She touched his arm. 'I'll get another job too. But there's nothing here. I've been thinking of going to Portsmouth. Why don't we both go? There's work in the dockyard. Mr Leighton's nephew told me they're building lots of new ships. We could make a fresh start, away from the memories . . . '

Wally leapt from the chair. 'I can't leave here. This is my home.' He waved his arms wildly. 'You don't understand. I can't leave this house. Your mother . . . ' His voice trailed away. His eyes were red-rimmed, haunted.

The door to the stairs crashed behind him and Abby heard his stumbling footsteps in the room above. Poor Dad, she thought. How could she leave him too? Even after all this time he still loved and missed her mother. She did understand. The love remained even when you were feeling hurt and angry. Maybe he hoped she'd come back one day — and he had to be here just in case she did. Abby felt the same — her own hope had never died either.

She followed him up the stairs and got into her own bed. But she couldn't sleep. The noise from the fairground continued late into the night. And, like the chair-o-planes whirling faster and faster, Abby's thoughts whirled in a confusion of images. But, as she eventually slipped into sleep it was the image of the straw-haired sailor who looked as if he'd be more at home on a farm cart than on one of His Majesty's ships that filled her mind.

2

Joe Leighton walked through the narrow streets towards the cathedral, then out of town across the fields to the farm. The full moon and the brilliant stars in the clear sky reminded him of being at sea again. It was beautiful and sometimes he wondered why he'd ever left his home town.

But his uncle had taken him to the Navy Review at Portsmouth when he was ten years old and the sight of the ships had set his pulses racing. He knew that one day he'd be on one of them, sailing the world, seeing strange new places and customs. After all, there was nothing to keep him here. He had no family other than his uncle. The only prospect before him on leaving school was to join Dan on his small dairy farm or get a job on the production line at Shippam's. Neither appealed to him. There were other jobs in the town — the brewery or tannery. But they seemed equally dreary to a lad yearning for adventure.

Uncle Dan had tried to dissuade him. 'I look on you as my son. I always thought you'd take over from me one day,' he'd said.

29

Joe felt bad about disappointing him, but he didn't change his mind. And when he reached his fourteenth birthday, off he'd gone to Portsmouth thinking he'd be straight off round the world on one of those gleaming new destroyers. It hadn't worked out quite like that — there'd been months on the training ship at Gosport which wasn't a ship at all, although it was called HMS *St Vincent*. And even when he'd been assigned to a ship it hadn't sailed anywhere, just sat there in dry dock while the ratings cleaned and polished every inch of her. But when at last he left Portsmouth *en route* to join the China Fleet, it was everything he'd dreamed of. He couldn't imagine settling down on land. Now he was back in Portsmouth and set to stay for a while. But he still loved the life. And there was always the chance he'd be off again one day.

The farmhouse was in darkness and Joe crept up the twisting stairs to his room, trying not to disturb Dan, who had to rise at four to oversee the milking and get the churns loaded on to the cart by six o'clock.

Joe was up not long after his uncle, despite being unable to sleep. He stumbled downstairs, rubbing his eyes and yawning. The large kitchen was cosy in the glow of the oil lamp hanging from a beam in the centre of the room. The smell of rising dough filled his nostrils, making his mouth water.

At the range the housekeeper, Hannah Knowles, looked round and smiled, her eyes almost disappearing into her rounded cheeks. 'Night on the tiles, eh, young Joe? Oh, well, there's always a few sore heads round this way after Sloe Fair.'

Joe grinned. 'I only had a couple of beers. I was going to come home early but . . . ' he stopped himself from mentioning Abby Cookson. Hannah had worked for his uncle for years, had practically brought him up after his parents died. She was always on at him to find a nice girl and settle down instead of gallivanting off round the world. Usually he didn't mind her teasing but Abby was different.

Hannah gave him a knowing look but he was spared further comment when Dan came in with Wilf Knowles, bringing a blast of cold air and the smell of the farmyard with them.

Dan rubbed his hands. 'Chilly out there. Looks like our Indian summer's over.' He sat at the table and turned to Joe. 'You're up early, lad. Thought you'd have a bit of a lie-in this morning.'

'Couldn't sleep. Besides, I promised to help on the round this morning.'

'Plenty of time. Got to get those churns

down to the station first, and pick up the empties from Deanery Farm.' He rubbed his hands again. 'Breakfast first.'

They sat at the scrubbed kitchen table, Dan and Wilf eating with the silent concentration of men who'd been hard at work for hours, Joe less hungrily. He was thinking about Abby, a child last time he'd seen her, now matured into a lovely young woman. For the first time in his life he was reluctant to return to his ship. He had to see her again before he went back to Portsmouth.

Hoping he sounded casual, he asked Dan if he still delivered in Somerstown.

'Yes, I do the station first, then the big houses, Somerstown last.' He pushed his plate away and stood up. 'Right, I'll start loading the churns,' he said.

Outside, the sky was pearl grey, a nip of frost in the air. In a few weeks it would still be dark at this time and Joe shivered at the thought. As he coaxed Gertie out of the stable and between the shafts of the cart, he wondered why, on the farm, he so hated getting up and starting work in the dark. Yet, on board ship, he loved being on deck throughout the night watches, even when the wind was tearing at his coat and the rain trickling down his neck. He just knew that being at sea was all that mattered.

By the time Dan and Wilf joined him he'd hitched Gertie to the cart and loaded the full churns, anxious to get going. The sooner they got the main deliveries over, the sooner they could start on the local round. He'd hated helping his uncle when he was a boy. But now, the prospect of seeing Abby Cookson again was worth being on the receiving end of Aggie Thompson's caustic tongue or Miss Hortense's icy stare.

Joe wasn't the kind of sailor who had a girl in every port. He'd had a couple of brief flings, forgotten as soon as they were over. But Abby wasn't like any girl he'd ever met. He couldn't wait to see her — and if he did, he prayed he wouldn't make a fool of himself in front of Dan.

★   ★   ★

Abby's first thought when she woke was of Joe Leighton coming to her rescue. She told herself she'd been quite capable of dealing with those bullies herself. They'd only been larking about after drinking too much. And if anyone knew how to deal with drunks she should. But being looked after felt good, she thought, smiling.

Her mood changed when she thought about her father. Did he really mean it this time? Would he really give up drinking? She sighed, wanting to believe him but knowing it was unlikely. He was always sorry and ashamed after one of his sessions and for a while he'd stay sober, work hard, pay the rent. But then something would happen to start him off again.

It all came back to her mother. If Carrie hadn't run off and left them, he wouldn't get in this state. The familiar anger boiled up and she swung her legs out of bed. She couldn't let the bitterness spoil her life. It was like Gran said, she had to move on and accept what had happened.

Downstairs, Wally was already washed and dressed, a pot of tea on the table, the range stoked up and glowing behind the bars. 'Here's your tea, love. I'm just off. Don't want to be late after I promised old Jones.'

Abby smiled, relieved. 'You'll be home at dinner time?' The factory stopped work at noon on a Saturday.

Wally nodded, his lips twisted in a wry grin. 'Have to come straight home, won't I? No beer money.' He pushed back his chair and stood up, grabbed his cap off the back of the door.

When he'd gone Abby set about cleaning the house. It might be a shabby run-down place — some might say a hovel — but at least it was clean. As she worked, she dreamed of living in a cosy cottage with doors and windows that didn't let in the draughts, and maybe a gas or electric cooker to replace the smoky old range that always needed black-leading and made such a dust every time you took the ashes out.

It didn't take long to make the beds, sweep down the stairs and wash the scullery and living room floors. Unlike the other houses in Tanner's Court, Number Four had wooden floorboards covered in lino instead of cracked and broken flagstones. Wally had done it himself, he boasted, wanting to make the place nice for his family. Whenever Abby polished the floor she told herself her father wasn't all bad.

The dishes were washed and arranged on the dresser, the rag rug beaten outside the door and replaced in front of the range. Abby had done her best but it wasn't as cosy as she remembered it before her mother had left. Most of the ornaments and trinkets that used to adorn the mantelpiece and dresser were gone — either broken in Wally's drunken rages or pawned when times were really hard.

She washed her hands and face and tidied her hair, noting with relief that the bruise on her cheek was less noticeable today. She retrieved the hidden money, deciding to spend the shilling she'd found in Dad's room. With the pennies left over from the fair last night, she'd have enough to buy something nice for dinner and a few provisions to last until his next pay-day.

Before she went out Abby used up the last of the milk Dan had given her to make a rice pudding. She put it on the bottom shelf of the oven where it would cook slowly while she did the shopping. It was Dad's favourite and would maybe help to keep him in his present good mood.

At the entrance to Tanner's Court, Abby hesitated. She could cut through Cross Street to High Street and do her shopping there. The long way round into town was a pleasanter walk and she was less likely to see her grandmother. The bruise might be fading but it was still visible and she hated having to lie.

As she turned the corner she heard her name called. 'Abby, wait a moment please.'

One of the Misses Crocker was standing at her front door. Abby wasn't sure which of the sisters it was and she almost walked on. Miss Hortense was sure to give her a lecture on the evils of drink when she spotted the bruise — as if she didn't have first hand experience of the problem.

But Gran had brought her up to be polite

to her elders and she stopped at the gate. 'Good morning, Miss Crocker.'

'My dear, I hope you don't mind me asking — I wondered if you'd be kind enough to get me some darning-wool from Wheelers?'

It was Miss Thomasina — the other one wouldn't call her 'my dear'.

The old lady gave her the money and Abby ran down the garden path, thankful she hadn't remarked on the bruise. The elder sister would have made some comment. She hoped it was gone by tomorrow. Gran insisted on her going to chapel now she was living back home and she couldn't bear the knowing looks she was sure she'd get from all those nosy old biddies.

Abby couldn't stay down for long. Her father was in a good mood and she'd met a nice young man at the fair. If she could find a job too, she'd be happy. She turned the corner and almost bumped into Mr Leighton.

He was filling a jug from the churn on his cart. 'Did you enjoy the fair?' He grinned.

'It was all right.' If only she didn't blush so easily.

Dan opened the vicarage gate. 'Can't stand here chatting — vicar wants his milk.' He walked quickly up the path.

Abby wished she'd summoned up the nerve to ask if Joe was around. She so wanted to see him again. Was she being silly? They'd only spent a short while together but she knew he was special.

She shivered in the chilly wind and moved closer to Dan's horse, stroking the silky neck, enjoying the warmth. Gertie blew through her nose and nuzzled at Abby's shoulder.

'You're a lovely girl, aren't you?' she said.

'She's not the only one.'

The voice made her jump and this time she felt the blush all over, right down to her toes. 'Hello, Joe. I didn't expect to see you . . . ' she stammered.

Joe ran his hand through his mop of hair. 'Still here,' he said. 'Helping Uncle out. Back to Portsmouth on Monday.'

'Oh.' Abby didn't know what to say, wished she was as confident as her friend Rhoda.

Joe smiled. 'It's strange coming back on leave. Most of my mates have moved on, or they're courting or something. Usually I can't wait to go back. But . . . ' He fidgeted with the horse's bridle, looking at the ground. 'Would you go out with me?'

Abby wasn't sure if she'd heard right. 'Go where?'

'Anywhere. The pictures. Or we could go for a walk. I could show you the farm.'

She couldn't afford to go to the cinema and she didn't know him well enough to let him pay for her. She'd like to see the farm though. Still, she didn't want to sound too eager. 'I'm busy today. But we could go for a walk tomorrow — after service.'

Joe's eyebrows shot up. 'Don't tell me you're a churchgoing lass?'

'What's wrong with that? Besides, my gran likes me to go with her — the Wesleyan chapel in Broyle Road. You can meet me afterwards if you like.'

Abby hid her face in the horse's mane, holding her breath for his answer. When he said, 'All right,' a smile lit up her face.

'See you, then.' Abby ran off down the road before he could change his mind.

She loved going in to Wheelers, the large department store in South Street, called The Emporium. It sold everything from pins and darning-wool to ready-made ladies' and menswear, as well as upholstery and curtain fabrics, table linen and bedding. Abby seldom had a chance to shop there and she loved seeing the rolls of silks and satins piled up on the shelves and the rainbows of knitting wool in their pigeon holes. She would have liked to work there if it wasn't for the owners — Ernest Wheeler, a lay preacher at chapel, who scared the youngsters with his fire and brimstone sermons, and his stout, pompous wife.

Today she didn't linger, her mind full of her

next meeting with Joe Leighton. Gran wouldn't approve, of course. But then she wouldn't approve of any boyfriend who wasn't a chapel member. But Joe was from a decent family and she'd known his uncle ever since she was a baby.

After delivering Miss Crocker's darning-wool, she unpacked the shopping, putting the scrag-end of lamb she'd bought into the meat safe on the scullery wall. That would do for tomorrow. She glanced at the cheap clock on the mantelpiece. Dad would be home soon. She'd better peel some potatoes and get the sausages on. Busying herself between the scullery and the range in the living room, she couldn't stop thinking about Joe Leighton.

She'd heard the expression 'a girl in every port and a port in every girl', as well as 'you know what sailors are', usually accompanied with a wink and a nudge. But she didn't believe Joe was like that. She'd always been fond of his uncle and felt sure he was of the same character. She sighed. She'd just have to wait and see how he behaved when they went out tomorrow — that was, if he turned up.

★   ★   ★

Sunday dawned with clouds and threatening rain. Abby hoped it would hold off until after her walk with Joe. She'd put on her best Sunday frock, a sky-blue cotton with white collar and cuffs, and she didn't want to cover it up with her shabby raincoat. As she brushed her wayward curls and pulled her blue felt hat on over them, she knew she was looking her best, despite the fading bruise on her cheek. She was tempted to try and cover it with a little powder, but her grandmother would have a fit if she turned up at chapel wearing make-up.

She'd probably have a fit anyway, if she caught sight of Joe, but Abby didn't care. For the first time for months she felt happy. Her father seemed to be keeping his promise. He'd stayed in last night, reading his paper and dozing in the armchair. Abby, sitting opposite doing her mending, had glanced at him from time to time, basking in the unaccustomed contentment. If only it could always be like this. Wally's good mood had continued this morning and he'd waved her off to chapel with a grin instead of his usual sneering comments.

She hardly dared admit that the main cause of her happiness was the prospect of seeing Joe again. As she turned the corner into Cross Street her face broke into a smile and she almost skipped up the path to her grandmother's house.

The front door opened abruptly and Aggie stood there, prim and respectable in her long black coat with the fur collar, the black hat with its curled feather, clutching her Bible. 'What are you looking so pleased about, my girl?' she snapped.

Abby's smile faltered. 'I was just thinking how nice your garden looks, the asters are gorgeous, and I love those browny-coloured chrysanthemums.' She couldn't say they were the same colour as Joe's eyes.

Gran looked her up and down. 'A new dress I see. Where did you get the money for that, then?'

'I bought it when I was working at Lady Grisham's. I've been saving it for a special occasion.'

When Aggie asked what was so special about going to chapel with her, Abby could have bitten her tongue out. She stammered something about the weather and not being able to wear summer things much longer.

'You youngsters spend far too much time thinking about clothes and how you look. Frivolous, that's the word.' Aggie set her lips in a grim line and strode out briskly.

As Abby hurried to keep up with her her pleasure in the bright morning was somewhat dimmed. If she'd turned up for church in her old jumper and skirt that would have been wrong too. Sometimes she couldn't please her grandmother, however hard she tried.

Her spirits rose when the first hymn was 'Eternal Father, Strong to Save' and she sang more fervently than usual, a lump clogging her throat when she came to the words, 'Oh hear us when we cry to thee, for those in peril on the sea.' She pictured Joe in his uniform and hoped he'd be wearing it when he came to meet her.

Guilty day-dreams relieved the boredom of the minister's droning sermon until at last they'd intoned the last prayer and she was free to run outside into the October sunshine. Gran was talking to the minister in the porch and she made her escape.

Joe stood by the gate, his hands in the pockets of his brown corduroys, looking as handsome in his working clothes as he did in the navy uniform. Trying to look casual, Abby slowed her steps and strolled down the path. When she got near, she glanced up as if noticing him for the first time. 'Oh, you came then,' she said.

He scuffed his toe in the dirt. 'Sorry I couldn't make the service. I was helping Uncle Dan in the dairy.'

Abby guessed he was just making excuses. Most of the lads she knew wriggled out of church or chapel if they could. She grinned at him. 'You didn't really want to come, did you?' she asked, hoping he'd answer honestly. She really liked him and she didn't want any secrets between them — even one so seemingly trivial.

He laughed. 'You're right. You have to attend church parade in the navy unless you're on watch. Caps off, stand to attention — seems like hours sometimes while the padre drones on. Can you blame me for opting out when I don't have to go?'

'No.' Abby giggled. 'Your padre can't possibly drone on more than our minister. The sermon seemed even longer this morning.'

'Well, you're free now. Where shall we go?'

Abby glanced back at Gran and the chapel ladies. They were indulging in their usual Sunday gossip, looking like a flock of crows in their unrelieved black, feathered hats nodding as they shredded someone's reputation.

When Gran glanced at her Abby grabbed Joe's hand, pulling him round the corner. 'I don't care where we go, so long as it's away from here.' She didn't want Gran asking questions about her new friend.

Walking up the hill away from the town, they branched off and took a path through the fields. They leaned against a farm gate, looking down at the inlets of the harbour spread out below them like the fingers of a hand, sparkling in the sun.

Abby turned to Joe and smiled. 'Don't you miss all this when you're away?' she asked.

'Not really. I couldn't wait to get away. I wanted to see the world before I settled down,' Joe said.

'And what have you seen?' Abby asked with a teasing smile.

'I've been to lots of places — China — all over. They called us back when there was all that trouble — you know, when we thought there'd be a war. But now Chamberlain's sorted it all out I expect we'll be off again.'

Abby didn't like to think of him going off to the other side of the world. Why did he have to go away? She tried not to think about it, to just enjoy being with him as their walk took them past the new housing estate and across the main Portsmouth road. They followed a narrow lane to where the little River Lavant ran down towards the harbour. After the long hot summer there was no water in the riverbed and Joe took Abby's hand and ran down the bank across the gravel bottom and up the other side. At the top of the bank, Abby stopped short in alarm as she came face to face with a herd of cows.

Joe laughed. 'They won't hurt you,' he said. 'Just keep walking.' He kept hold of her hand

and started briskly towards the gate that led into the farmyard.

She wanted to run as the cows bunched together and started to follow. But then she'd have to let go of Joe's hand and she didn't want to. Besides, the cows weren't so scary with the warmth of his hand enfolding hers. Just as she was thinking how nice it felt, he let go her hand and waved.

'There's Dan.'

By the time they joined Joe's uncle Abby had convinced herself that the hand holding hadn't meant anything. But she was beginning to wish it did, just like she wished he didn't have to go back to his ship the next day. By the time he came home on leave again he'd have forgotten all about her.

Dan threw the last of the corn into the feeding trough and straightened up. 'Just in time for dinner,' he said. 'You are stopping, aren't you, Abby?'

Abby glanced at Joe. He'd said nothing about staying for dinner. She'd left a stew simmering on the range, so she didn't have to hurry back. Dad could help himself. But she didn't want to seem too eager.

Dan didn't wait for a reply, shouting through the open back door, 'One extra for dinner, Hannah. Set a place, would you?'

Hannah, wispy grey hair escaping from its

bun, her face red from the oven, came to the door wiping her hands on a snowy white cloth. 'No need to shout, Dan Leighton. I saw the young lady coming across the fields so there's a place already set. Just get those muddy boots off and wash your hands and I'll dish up.'

Her warm smile belied the harsh tone and Abby smiled as the little woman greeted her. 'Come in, Abby. Nice to meet you.'

At her questioning look Hannah said, 'I knew your mother — and you're just like her.'

Abby followed her into the farmhouse kitchen, eyes widening at the sight of the huge joint of beef on its platter at one end of the scrubbed pine table. A bowl of roast potatoes and a steaming jug of gravy graced the centre.

'Sit, sit,' Hannah said, gesturing to a chair at the other end of the table. She swept a saucepan off the stove, deftly strained it into a colander, then tipped the cabbage into another dish. She did the same with a pan of carrots and put both dishes on the table. By then, Joe and Dan had joined Abby at the table.

As Dan carved the meat, Abby realized there was another place set. She was wondering who else was joining them when Hannah went to the door again and yelled,

'Wilf Knowles, what's keeping you? There's good food going cold on the table and if you don't get in here quick, I'll give yours to the dog.'

Seeing Abby's expression, Dan started to laugh. 'Take no notice of Hannah, she likes to think she's in charge around here.' He carved off a couple of slices of beef and passed the plate to her. 'Help yourself to vegetables, lass and don't stint yourself. There's plenty to go round.'

Hannah sat at the table. 'I don't want good food going to waste after I've been slaving over a stove all morning.'

Abby felt a bit embarrassed. Maybe she shouldn't have stayed after all. She saw that Joe was laughing too. 'No chance of that with your cooking,' he said, his mouth already full. 'You could give our ship's cook lessons.'

At Dan's urging Abby took a good helping of potatoes and poured the thick gravy over them. The walk across the fields had given her an appetite and as she started to eat her shyness evaporated and she began to enjoy herself. She hadn't eaten a meal like this since she'd left Lady Grisham's. But it wasn't just the food, it was the company.

It didn't take her long to realize that beneath Hannah's gruff manner there was real warmth. She was plainly fond of Joe and his uncle and her nagging was a form of affection.

They were halfway through their meal when the back door opened again and a thin, stooped man entered in stockinged feet, his cap in his hands. 'Sorry I'm late, my dear. It took a bit longer to fix that fence than I thought.'

'I don't know what things are coming to, having to work on a Sunday,' Hannah said, setting a plate down firmly in front of him. She had dished up his dinner earlier and put it at the back of the range to keep warm.

'The beasts don't know it's Sunday, do they, my dear,' Wilf answered mildly.

'What's that got to do with it? I know the animals have to be fed and watered, the cows milked, whatever day it is. But other farm work can wait. It's the Lord's day, after all.'

Dan coughed. 'My fault, Hannah. I asked Wilf to do it today. Can't have the animals straying on to the railway line, can we?'

'Oh, well, you're the boss, after all,' Hannah said. 'Now then, Wilf, eat up. There's apple pie and custard to follow.'

Abby looked down at her plate to hide her smile. What had Hannah been doing all morning but working? She knew that her grandmother never spent Sundays in the kitchen. Chapel, Bible reading and cold meat was the Sunday rule in the Thompson household, a routine that Abby had been expected to follow as a child. Gran would be horrified to see her now, seated at a table groaning with food and listening to the laughter and banter of this close-knit family. For, although Abby knew that the Knowleses were not related to Dan and Joe, they felt like a family. Their bickering and arguing were a way of expressing their affection for each other. It was something Abby couldn't remember experiencing before.

When the meal was finished, Hannah pushed back her chair. 'Right, you men, into the parlour. I'll bring in a cup of tea in a minute. You've earned your rest.'

Abby stood up and carried some of the dishes over to the sink in front of the window.

'Come on, Abby,' Joe said, walking towards the door.

'Not you, young man. No canoodling in the parlour for you.'

Abby blushed and she saw that Joe had gone a bit red too. 'I'll help with the washing up,' she said quickly.

'And so will Joe,' Hannah said, wagging a finger at him as he started to protest. 'You got out of helping Wilf with the fence this morning so it's only fair you should do something. You youngsters can clear up here while I put my feet up with a nice cup of tea.'

'You deserve a rest too, after making that lovely dinner,' Abby said.

'I suppose you're right,' Joe said, picking up a tea towel. He turned to Hannah, grinning. 'You're a hard taskmaster — worse than my CPO. I can't wait to get back to sea.'

Hannah laughed and slapped him on the arm. 'Get away with you. And when you're done, you'd better walk Abby home. Her dad will be wondering where she's got to. And don't be late back, mind. It's an early start for you tomorrow. And you've got your packing to do.'

'Don't remind me,' Joe groaned.

Abby didn't want to think about it either and she plunged her hands into the soapy water, picked up a plate and began scrubbing at it, trying to blot out the reminder that soon she'd have to say goodbye to Joe.

'You'll wash the pattern off if you scrub that plate much harder,' Joe said, making her jump. She hadn't realized he was so close behind her. 'What were you thinking about?' he asked.

She could feel his warm breath on her neck and she felt the hot blush stealing over her. She took a deep breath. 'I was thinking that we'd better get on with the washing up before Mrs Knowles comes back.'

'And I was thinking that I want to kiss you and wondering if you'd object,' Joe said softly. He put his hands on her shoulders and turned her to face him, took the plate from her.

The door opened and he began wiping the plate furiously. Abby turned back to the sink and picked up another, her face burning.

'Don't think you've finished yet,' Hannah said sternly, setting the tray of teacups down. 'There's these to do and all.'

She looked from one to the other, her eyes twinkling, and picked up a pile of plates to put on the dresser. 'I can see you've been busy.' She arranged the plates to her satisfaction and came over to the sink where Abby was now scrubbing at a saucepan. 'Go on, love. You've helped enough. Get along while the weather's still fine. That rain won't hold off much longer.' She gave Joe a push. 'See the girl right to the door, mind, and get back in time for milking.'

Joe laughed. 'I don't know how you manage when I'm away,' he said.

'Well, you know what I think about that,' Hannah snapped, folding her arms across her chest.

Abby dried her hands. 'I'll just say goodbye to Mr Leighton and Mr Knowles.'

'They're both snoozing in the parlour.

Don't disturb them. My Wilf's not as young as he was and he needs his rest.'

'All right then. Thanks for the lovely dinner, Mrs Knowles.'

'Call me Hannah. And don't forget, you're welcome any time — even if young Joe's away. Not that you'd be here if it wasn't for him.' She chuckled, her smile encompassing both of them.

Alone with Joe once more, Abby tried to forget what he'd said before they were interrupted and she asked what Hannah had meant.

'She thinks I should have stayed home, instead of going to sea. After all, as she says, the farm will be mine one day, but I don't want to think about that.' Joe shrugged. 'She doesn't understand about the navy. It was something I just had to do.'

Abby didn't understand either. If she lived with such lovely people somewhere like Applegate Farm she'd never want to leave. 'Do you think you'll always be in the navy, Joe?' she asked.

'I've got a few years to do yet,' he said. They reached the main road leading into Somerstown and he stopped and looked back. 'I do miss it when I'm away, but I always wanted to travel — and the navy was my best chance to do it.'

Abby grabbed his hand. 'I wish you could stay,' she said, blushing at her boldness.

'I'm beginning to think the same.' He kept hold of her hand and swung her round to face him. 'I meant it, you know — back there, before Hannah came in.'

The tell-tale blush crept up her cheeks again. 'I wouldn't mind,' she whispered.

He pulled her towards him and his lips brushed hers gently. Before she could respond, he pulled away. 'I really like you, Abby, but I don't want to rush you.'

'I like you too, Joe.' She wished he'd kiss her again. But he was walking on.

'You might meet someone else while I'm away,' he said. 'I'll be off again soon and God knows how long I'll be away. It's not fair to pin you down. I'd like to see you again but if I can't get back, will you let me write to you? Then, if we still feel the same way when I come home again, we'll take it from there.'

Abby was disappointed but she had to admit he was being sensible — not that she wanted to be sensible. Feelings she'd never experienced before were coursing through her body since his lips had touched hers — exciting feelings but a little scary too.

When they reached the dark entrance to Tanner's Court, he kissed her again. This time it was no mere brush of the lips and she clung to him, enjoying the feel of his mouth on hers. She wished it would never end, but he pulled away and pushed her towards her front door. 'You'd better go in. I don't want your dad yelling at me,' he said.

'You will write, won't you?' she asked, tears trembling on her eyelashes.

'I promise,' he said and strode away down the narrow street. She waited till he reached the corner, hoping he'd look back and wave but he carried on walking.

When she got indoors she leaned against the closed door and let the tears fall. It had been the most wonderful day of her life and she couldn't bear the thought of the lonely days to come until she saw him again. Reliving those last moments in the alley she thought maybe it was just as well he'd pushed her away. If he hadn't she would have done anything he asked. Words echoed in her head, 'slut', 'trollop' and, worst of all, 'just like your mother'.

But this was different, she thought, as she dried her eyes. She'd only just met Joe but already she was in love. 'You're wrong, Joe,' she whispered, 'I'll never meet anyone else. It's you I love.'

★ ★ ★

Joe hardly noticed the three mile walk back to Applegate Farm, his thoughts on the girl he'd left. For the first time in his life he was in love, he couldn't ask her to wait for him — it wouldn't be fair. Although he was based in Portsmouth for the next few weeks, he knew that when they left port he might not return for two, maybe three years. Anyway, it was stupid to feel like this about a girl he'd only met a couple of days ago, especially as ordinary seamen weren't allowed to get married until they were twenty-five. How could he expect her to wait years for him?

He'd been looking forward to another overseas posting but now he was dreading it. His uncle still hadn't come to terms with his decision to go to sea instead of joining him on the farm. Now that he'd met Abby Joe was beginning to question that decision himself. Since he'd joined the navy six years ago he'd never been so reluctant to go back to his ship.

He quickened his steps. The least he could do was help with the milking one more time. At the farmhouse door he took off his boots, pausing with his hand on the doorjamb as he heard Dan's voice.

'I hope he's not mucking that girl around,' he said. 'I wouldn't want to see young Abby hurt. She's enough to put up with — '

Hannah interrupted him. 'Joe's a good lad.

He'll treat her right, don't you worry. Besides, I think he's really smitten.' She chuckled.

Joe felt himself reddening. She's right about that, he thought. He knew he shouldn't keep listening but he was too embarrassed to make his presence known.

'Maybe, but you know what they say about sailors,' Dan said.

'Joe's not like that,' Hannah said indignantly. 'Besides, what would you know about it, a crusty old bachelor like yourself?'

'Not from choice, you know that, Hannah. If things had been different I would have been wed with kids of my own. It were me own fault. I didn't have to join up, being a farmer and all. But me mates were all signing on and they said the war would be over by Christmas . . . '

'And when you got back Carrie had gone and married someone else.'

'That lout Cookson. God knows what she saw in him.'

Joe heard a loud thump and knew that his normally placid uncle had hit the table. It was no secret that Dan had once courted Abby's mother, but he hadn't realized he still felt the same after all these years. No wonder he was so protective of her daughter.

He opened the door and went in, hoping they wouldn't guess he'd been listening. He'd make sure Dan knew that his intentions towards Abby were entirely honourable. In the space of three days he'd fallen in love and he'd never do anything to hurt her. He just hoped she felt the same way and that she'd wait for him while he was at sea. He couldn't bear the thought of history repeating itself.

3

Abby lay awake, reliving the day she'd spent with Joe, wondering how she could feel sad and happy at the same time — happy that she'd met someone so special, sad that she might not see him again for ages. Still, he'd promised to try and get home again and if not, he'd write.

She woke next morning, still half-dreaming, feeling again the warmth of Joe's hand in hers, reliving that wonderful moment when their lips had met. The kiss had been all she'd dreamed of and she would treasure the memory for ever.

If only she could talk to him right now. For the first time she envied the rich Grisham girls who spent hours on the telephone arranging parties and picnics. They hadn't had to worry about getting a job, either.

She threw back the blankets and leapt out of bed, shivering as her feet met the cold lino. She pulled back the curtains to reveal a bleak, grey day — the golden autumn days might never have been. Better get used it, she told herself. The winters always seemed colder in Tanner's Court. Her thoughts flew back to the attic room she'd shared with two other maids at Grisham Manor. The work had been hard and the days long, but she'd been warm and well-fed.

If it hadn't been for Dad's drunken interference she'd still be there. But then she wouldn't have met Joe. As her grandmother was fond of quoting, 'God moves in mysterious ways'. Abby smothered a giggle, imagining Gran's scandalized expression at such a thought. Not that she'd tell Gran about Joe. It would be her secret for as long as possible.

She smiled and hummed a dance tune as she ran downstairs, stopping short at the sight of her father at the kitchen table, unshaven and bleary-eyed. His voice was surly as he looked up at her. 'Don't know what you've got to sing about, my girl. You should be out looking for a job. They won't come to you, you know.' He banged his fist on the table. 'And what about my breakfast, eh? The least you can do is look after your old dad, 'specially as you're not working.'

Abby didn't reply, but hurried over to the range and began to riddle the smouldering embers, rattling the bars with the poker. Anyone would think it was her fault she was out of work. But she didn't want to provoke him. At least he was up. Maybe he'd keep his promise to go to work today.

She got cups and plates down from the dresser and put the tin of condensed milk on the table. 'I'll have to go shopping,' she said, pouring hot water into the teapot.

'Well, don't ask me for any money — I gave you some the other day. Don't know what you do with it,' Wally growled.

She ignored him and said, 'Just tea and toast today, Dad.' She didn't tell him about the eggs Hannah had given her when she left the farm yesterday. They'd do for their tea tonight.

★ ★ ★

In town Abby scoured the shop windows for notices offering employment. She'd do anything — clean, scrub, run errands. Useless to try for another service job. Despite the reference from Lady Grisham, word of Wally's behaviour was sure to have spread. As for working in an office, she had no qualifications and no chance of going to evening classes to learn shorthand or typing.

She was just passing the Buttermarket when Hannah Knowles came down the steps, almost bumping into her. 'Abby, where are you off to?'

'I'm looking for work.' She choked back a

sob. 'I've tried everywhere. I don't know what to do next . . . '

'Don't worry, dear, you'll find something, a bright girl like you.' Hannah put a hand on her arm. 'Why don't you come to tea next Sunday? You never know, Joe might manage to get off.'

Abby felt better already. 'I'll come over after dinner. Now I'd better get on with job-hunting.'

As she walked away Hannah said, 'Creek End Farm are harvesting their potatoes. It's not much but . . . '

'I'll go out there straight away. Thanks, Mrs Knowles.'

Abby skipped down the street, her heart much lighter. Even casual work was better than nothing.

★   ★   ★

By the time she saw Joe again she'd been working at Creek End for several weeks. He hadn't been able to get off that first Sunday but when she got to the farm Dan and the Knowleses welcomed her like one of the family. And she'd been back several times since.

★   ★   ★

The weather during that November was exceptionally cold and wet and Abby's hands were cracked with chilblains, her back aching. But she was happy as she trudged along the main road to Applegate Farm, hands deep in her pockets, shoulders hunched against the wind.

She looked up at the piercing whistle and saw Joe striding towards her. As she ran into his arms, he swung her round, holding her tightly against his chest.

'You were miles away,' he said, laughing. 'I've been calling for ages. What were you thinking about?'

'You, of course,' she said, returning his kiss.

'Ooh, you're cold.' He took her hands and kissed them. 'No gloves?' He kept hold of one hand and put it into the pocket of his greatcoat, clasping it firmly. 'When that one's warm we'll swap sides,' he said. 'And now I know what to buy you for Christmas — a nice pair of gloves.'

'I'd have to keep them for best. The ones Gran knitted for me are all holes. Woolly gloves and muddy spuds don't go together.'

Joe laughed. 'Enjoying life on the farm, are you?'

'It's a job.' Abby shrugged. 'Anyway I want to hear what you've been up to.'

'You'll have to wait. I don't want to have to

go through it all again when we get indoors.' They had reached the track leading down to the farm and Joe gave her hand a tug. 'Come on, let's get out of this wind.' He started to run and she flew along beside him, laughing as Mollie, Dan's collie dog, came racing up the track, leaping around them and barking.

But although she was laughing, Abby felt a shiver of apprehension. Joe had news and that could only mean he was going away again. How could she bear it? But she had to be brave and not spoil the little time they had together with tears.

It was almost dark as they went through the gate into the farmyard. Lights glowed from the kitchen window and they could see Hannah bustling about. The farmhouse kitchen was warm with the smell of baking and Abby's mouth watered. The table was laid with plates of sandwiches and scones, a huge pat of butter and jars of home-made jam.

When they were seated round the table Dan gave Joe a nudge. 'Well, lad, what news?'

Joe grinned. 'We sail tomorrow . . . '

Abby gave a little gasp, her hand shaking so much the cup rattled in the saucer. Joe grabbed her hand. 'It's all right, Abby. I'll only be gone a few weeks. I might not be here for Christmas, though.'

Disappointment washed over her. Of course, she'd known he'd be off sometime, but she hadn't really faced up to it. While he was down the road in Portsmouth, with the possibility of time off, he hadn't seemed so far away.

Joe still held her hand under the table and she clung on desperately, hardly listening to the conversation around her.

'I've been transferred to a destroyer — the one they've been building at Portsmouth. She starts her sea trials tomorrow — we'll be gone six weeks at most.'

'But then you'll be off to the other side of the world again, I suppose?' Hannah said, with a sympathetic glance at Abby.

'Not sure where, though. But we'll probably have a week or so in port while they sort out any problems.'

Dan gave Joe a sly nudge. 'Time was, you couldn't wait to get back to sea,' he said.

'Well, I've got a reason for wanting to be home now,' he said, squeezing Abby's hand.

She felt herself reddening and took a sip of tea to hide her confusion.

Hannah passed the plate of scones. 'Help yourself, my duck. There's plenty more,' she said.

Abby took one, spread butter and jam and took a bite. But she could hardly swallow.

The meal came to an end at last. Dan and Wilf pushed their chairs back, put on their jackets and boots and disappeared to check that the animals were bedded down for the night. When Joe offered to help Dan waved him away. 'Time you were walking Abby home,' he said.

They strolled up the lane, their arms round each other, each of them conscious of their imminent parting. By unspoken consent they didn't take the shortest route back to Somerstown but walked up West Street towards the cathedral. The bells were pealing for evensong and the stained glass windows lit from within lent a fairytale enchantment to the scene. It was freezing but neither of them was in a hurry to reach Tanner's Court. In the shelter of the Cross Joe pulled Abby towards him. The warmth of their kisses dispelled the cold. Joe slipped his hands inside her coat and she strained towards him, enjoying the feel of his body against hers.

She had never felt like this before and she wished they could stay there for ever. But Joe abruptly took his hands away. 'Better get you home,' he said, his voice harsh.

'What's wrong?' She caught hold of his hand. 'Please, Joe — I don't want to go home yet.'

He shook her off. 'I don't want to either.

But we can't . . . ' he shrugged his shoulders helplessly. 'Look, Abby, you must know how I feel but — I'm a sailor. I have to be away for months at a time — if not years. It's not fair on you.'

'But, Joe . . . '

He groaned and pulled her towards him, burying his face in her hair. His voice was muffled. 'I love you, Abby. I want to ask you to wait for me but . . . '

'I will. I'll wait for ever.'

'You say that now, but what if some other feller comes along while I'm away? I can't expect you to be true to me when I've got nothing to offer you.'

At that moment Abby would have promised him anything. He loved her. Oh, she knew he was being sensible but she didn't feel very sensible right now — far from it. Feelings she hadn't known existed were churning her stomach and all she wanted was to be near him.

He took her hand and they started walking, reaching the entrance to Tanner's Court far too soon. In the shadows of the twitten, Joe stopped and pulled a package from his pocket. 'I was saving this for Christmas,' he said.

'Can I open it now?' Abby was already tearing eagerly at the wrapping. In the meagre light of the gas lamp at the end of the street, she saw the gleam of silver. She held it up — a tiny heart-shaped locket on a chain. 'Oh, Joe, thank you,' she whispered, reaching up to kiss him.

He took the locket from her and turned her round so that he could fasten it round her neck. She shivered at the touch of his cold fingers on her bare skin.

'I haven't got anything for you,' she said.

'Never mind,' Joe said. 'You're the best present of all.' This time their kiss was even more passionate than before. Abby knew she should push him away but her strength had deserted her.

As Joe's breathing became heavier and his hands more eager, footsteps rang on the cobbles. They sprang apart, Abby's heart racing from a mixture of fear and passion. A figure pushed past them in the darkness. Thank goodness it wasn't her father. But she knew she'd been recognized and news of her wanton behaviour would be all round Somerstown in no time, surely reaching her grandmother's ears.

'You'd better go,' Abby said.

'Forgive me, Abby — I got a bit carried away.' His lips brushed her cheek. 'Don't forget to write,' he said. And then he was gone.

★　★　★

On Christmas Day Abby went to chapel with her grandmother. During the long sermon she fingered the silver locket, which she kept hidden under her jumper. If only she'd been able to buy Joe something as nice. Shivering in the freezing chapel she warmed herself with day-dreams of what she and Joe would say to each other when they met next day. His ship was unexpectedly in port and he'd promised to try and get to Chichester on Boxing Day.

A sharp poke in the ribs made her sit up straight. Tight-lipped, Gran shoved the open Bible at her, pointing to he relevant passage. Mr Wheeler, the owner of The Emporium, was standing on the platform beside the minister, it being his turn for the reading that day. His wife and daughters sat in the front row, nodding as he read.

Abby bent her head, pretending to follow the verses in her Bible. It was a relief when they stood up for the last carol — at least they were more cheerful than the usual hymns. Abby enjoyed the stirring tune of '*Oh, Come All Ye Faithful*', but she was relieved when the service ended.

As they filed out into the chilly morning, she whispered to her grandmother, 'I'll go on ahead and put the vegetables on.'

Gran, waiting to shake hands with the minister, nodded and Abby slipped away. She hoped Dad had remembered his promise to stay sober and keep an eye on the joint of beef she'd saved up for. It had taken some persuading to get Gran to come to Tanner's Court for Christmas dinner and Abby didn't want anything to spoil it.

After dinner they exchanged small gifts, all any of them could afford. The casual work at Creek End Farm had come to an end and, despite her efforts, she hadn't been able to find another job.

With no money for Christmas presents she'd unravelled an old jumper and knitted scarves for Joe and her father. She'd also cut up an old dress and made an apron for her grandmother. She hated needle-work and making the gifts took her a long time. But keeping busy passed the long evenings.

Aggie thanked her and handed her a parcel wrapped in brown paper. No festive bows or coloured wrapping for her.

It was the expected pair of knitted gloves. 'Thanks, Gran, they're lovely. Just what I needed.' She didn't have to fake enthusiasm. She was grateful for the thoughtful present. She put a hand to her throat, felt the locket under her jumper. She didn't really need any more presents but she was touched that Dad had taken the trouble to buy her some scented soap and bath salts. He'd even got a small box of chocolates for his mother-in-law.

Abby had managed to save a little money from her farm work and, despite Dad's protests, she'd bought a wireless. They were looking forward to hearing the new king who'd been crowned the previous year.

'He's a good king,' Gran said, pleased that the new monarch was a married man with a family. She had no time for the newly created Duke of Windsor and his fancy woman.

Abby went into the scullery to wash up, smiling as she listened to her grandmother's forceful opinions. Good job Dad hadn't had a drink, otherwise he'd be starting a row. It was a relief when she heard him snoring and Gran joined her to help with the chores. But her relief was short-lived.

'I've been hearing things about you, my girl,' Aggie said. 'Taking up with a sailor and canoodling in dark corners. It won't do, girl. I've done my best to see that you know right from wrong . . . '

'I know, Gran. And I haven't . . . ' Gran wouldn't let her finish. Oh, why wouldn't she believe that her meetings with Joe were innocent? Not that she'd felt so innocent last time they'd met, even though they'd done nothing wrong.

'You'll go the same way as your mother if you're not careful.'

'You shouldn't say things about her — your own daughter,' Abby said. It was an old argument. 'You don't know that she went off with someone.'

'What other explanation is there?' Aggie's voice caught and Abby turned from the sink to see tears in her grandmother's eyes. She wasn't as hard as she made out.

'I'm sorry, Gran. Let's talk about something else.'

'This sailor? Dan Leighton's nephew, isn't it?'

Abby nodded.

'Well, they're respectable enough, I suppose. But, I'm not happy about your carryings on, mind.'

Abby told a white lie. 'He's gone to sea. He'll probably be gone for months.'

'He'll have forgotten all about you by the time he comes home again.'

Abby's heart protested. But she agreed for the sake of peace and quiet. By the time they returned to the living room, Wally was grunting and stirring in his chair.

Aggie put her coat on, saying she needed to get home to feed the cat, and Abby offered to walk with her — anything to get away from her father's increasing irritability.

As they turned into Cross Street, Aggie asked if she was coming to chapel that evening.

'No, I'll stay and keep Dad company,' Abby said.

Gran patted her arm. 'I know you're a good girl really. I just worry about you. Thanks for the lovely dinner, love. You'll make some man a good wife one day.'

Abby felt herself blushing, thinking of Joe. She came down to earth quickly as Gran gave her arm a little punch. 'And you can take that look off your face, my girl. I said 'one day' and I meant a long way off. You're too young to get serious.'

'I'm nearly nineteen,' Abby protested.

'No matter. Besides, you'll soon forget about sailor boy when he's been gone a while.'

I won't, Abby thought as she said goodbye to Gran and turned her steps towards home. Dad was still slumped in the chair and she crept up to her room where she poured her heart out on paper to Joe — just in case he didn't get home tomorrow.

★   ★   ★

The next day was cold and bright and Abby enjoyed the walk to Applegate Farm, although she felt a twinge of guilt at not spending the day with her family as usual. Gran disapproved but when she saw that Abby was determined, she said, 'Don't worry about your father. I've invited him round for dinner and, if he's too drunk to bother, I'll be quite happy on my own, especially now I've got the wireless for company.'

But really, Abby was too happy to care. She was seeing Joe today — she refused to believe he might not make it. Besides, he'd promised to phone if he couldn't get away, so at least she'd hear his voice.

When she reached the farm, Hannah was in the yard throwing scraps to the chickens. 'Glad you could make it, love,' she called, her brown eyes twinkling. 'It's all right — he's here. They're putting some feed out for the cows. They'll be in soon. Come in and get warm.'

Abby followed her into the house, feeling suddenly nervous and hoping things would be the same after their weeks apart.

The farmhouse kitchen was as warm and cosy as usual, the table in the middle groaning with heaped dishes. After her walk in the frosty air, Abby was hungry and the smell of roast goose made her mouth water.

'Sit down, love,' Hannah said, pointing to a chair beside the stove which was twice the size of the range back in Tanner's Court. Abby held her hands out to the glowing bars, noticing the big pot bubbling on top.

Hannah saw her glance and smiled. 'That's the pudding. Joe loves his Christmas pudding, so we saved it for today.' The back door opened. 'And here's the lad himself.'

Abby swung round, her face growing warm, her heart beating faster. He stood there in his old farm clothes, his cap in his hands, a big grin on his face. She couldn't move, shy of greeting him in front of Hannah, while he too seemed rooted to the spot.

'Well, come in, lad, you must be frozen.' Hannah broke the spell. 'Abby's just got here and dinner's nearly ready. I'll go and call the others.' Without waiting for a reply she bustled out of the room.

Suddenly they were in each other's arms, their kisses hungry. The weeks melted away as if they'd never been apart. How could she bear him going away again?

She smiled up at him as he ran a finger down her cheek, twined his hands in her hair, and drew her towards him for another kiss.

They were so engrossed in each other they didn't hear the door open. When Hannah coughed, they sprang apart and Abby blushed.

She pulled away and went to help Hannah dish up the meal. By the time Dan and Wilf came in she was more composed.

As the men began talking about the farm and a problem with one of the cows, she realized that she and Joe had scarcely exchanged a word beyond the murmured endearments while they were kissing. It was a good job Hannah had come in then, she thought. Where Joe was concerned, she wasn't the 'good girl' her gran thought she was.

She sat as close to Joe as she could get without touching him, unwilling to leave his side. Warm contentment stole over her as she listened to the murmur of their soft country voices. If only she could stay here, she thought. If only Joe didn't have to go away. But she wouldn't think about that. She had to live for the moment, store up memories to treasure for the future.

As on her previous visits to the farm, she and Joe were left alone in the big kitchen to clear up after the meal. The job took twice as long as it should have, interrupted by frequent hugs and kisses. Abby's shyness disappeared and she was soon making Joe laugh with stories of the old biddies in chapel and imitations of Ernest Wheeler's hell and damnation sermons.

They put the last dish away and Joe grabbed Abby's wrist. 'Time for another kiss,' he said.

Abby was more than ready but just at that moment the door opened. 'Gonna give me a hand with the milking, son?' Dan said.

'Only if Abby can come too,' Joe said.

'Not scared of the cows any more, then?' Dan asked, a twinkle in his eye.

'Well, I'm all right if I don't get too close,' Abby said.

When they got to the milking shed, Abby watched the two men and their confident handling of the animals, amazed at how deft Joe's fingers were and how quickly the bucket filled with milk. He seemed a natural and she wondered why he'd chosen to leave all this and go to sea.

He looked up and smiled and her heart did a somersault. 'Want to have a go?' he asked.

'Not on your life,' Abby said, backing away.

'Come on, it's easy. They won't bite, you know.'

He and Dan were both laughing. She couldn't let them see how nervous she was. 'All right, then,' she said.

Joe gave her his stool and told her to get close against the cow's flank. 'Daisy's a gentle one. She won't shift around or kick the bucket over like some of 'em,' he said.

Abby started to laugh. 'Do they all have names?' For some reason it struck her as funny and she was giggling so much she only managed to get a couple of squirts into the bucket.

Joe was very patient but Dan had almost finished. 'Stop messing about, you two,' he said. 'We've got the churns to fill yet.'

'Sorry, Mr Leighton,' Abby said.

Dan laughed. 'Good job young Joe's in the navy — you'll never make a farmer's wife.'

It was the cue for Abby to blush again.

Joe seemed embarrassed too. 'Sorry, Uncle Dan — I've just realized how late it is. I'd better walk Abby home before it gets too dark.'

'Never mind, I'll finish off.'

The walk back to town passed far too quickly for Abby. When they got to Tanner's Court she wanted to ask him in but Dad might be there and he was sure to spoil everything. It had got much colder and, snuggled inside Joe's coat, Abby wished she didn't have to go indoors. But they couldn't stay out all night. After a last, lingering kiss, they pulled apart.

'You'll come and see me off, won't you?' Joe said.

'Try to stop me,' Abby said, smiling through her tears.

★   ★   ★

The next morning she reached the farm as Joe finished packing his kitbag. He hugged Hannah, shook hands with Wilf, and went into the yard to say goodbye to his uncle.

Dan was mucking out the byre. He dropped his broom and came over to shake Joe's hand. 'Guess we won't be seeing you for a while.'

Joe nodded. 'We'll be off any day now. Don't suppose I'll get away again, so it's goodbye.' He turned to Abby. 'We'd better go or I'll miss my train.'

As they set off down the lane towards Fishbourne Halt, Joe was silent. But as they neared the village, he spoke. 'What Dan said yesterday — about being my wife . . . '

'It's all right, Joe. I know he was teasing.' Abby wanted to reassure him. She knew how she felt about him and was sure he returned her love. But was he ready to commit himself, seeing as he'd be off to the other side of the world soon?

'Dan may have been teasing — but I'm serious. I want to ask you to wait for me, but it's not fair. I might get home for a bit in a few weeks but then I could be away as long as two years. You're sure to meet someone else . . . '

'I won't, Joe. You're the one . . . '

They stopped walking and put their arms round each other. His kiss told Abby that he felt the same as she did and she wondered how he could bear to go away for so long.

The train whistled as it went over the level crossing just outside Chichester and they ran the remaining few yards to the halt hand in hand. There was only time for one more kiss and Joe leapt aboard, slamming the door. Leaning out of the carriage window he held her hand until the train started to move.

'I'll write,' he called.

Tears streaming down her face, Abby nodded. 'I love you, Joe,' she said. But the train had rounded the bend and was out of sight. Wiping her eyes on her sleeve, she began the long walk back to Somerstown.

4

The New Year continued damp and dismal as Abby tramped the streets looking for work. She missed Joe dreadfully and wrote to him daily, trying to write neatly so as not to use up too much paper. She was running out of money and needed to save a little for stamps.

As she wrote she fingered the silver locket, reliving the moment Joe had put it round her neck and declared his love. He hoped to be back in a couple of weeks and she couldn't wait. Would he still feel the same way? She finished her latest letter with the usual row of crosses and put on her coat and the gloves Gran had knitted her for Christmas. There was still time to catch the post at the end of George Street.

A gust of wind nearly tore the envelope from her hand as she neared the corner and at first she didn't hear the voice calling her name. A hand on her arm stopped her and she turned round.

'I saw you out of the window,' Miss Thomasina said, panting slightly, her face red with exertion.

'What can I do for you?'

'It's what I can do for you, I hope. Mr Wheeler needs someone in his shop. Someone left to get married — in rather a hurry I'm afraid.'

'But I've never worked in a shop before.'

'That doesn't matter. He wants someone neat and tidy, polite and punctual — and you're all of those things, my dear.'

Abby felt herself blushing and stammered her thanks.

'Go along at nine o'clock tomorrow morning and say I sent you.' She smiled. 'I'm so glad I caught you.'

'Thank you, Miss Crocker. I won't let you down.'

Desperate as she was for work, Abby wasn't sure she'd like working for the Wheelers. His hell-fire sermons at chapel sent shivers through the younger members of the congregation. The wife was a bit of an ogre too and it was rumoured that she was the driving force behind The Emporium, the rambling department store in South Street. But she couldn't let Miss Thomasina down.

The next day, trying to quell the butterflies in her stomach she hurried down South Street and entered The Emporium, the largest store in Chichester. It had started out with one cramped bow-fronted room but over the years had gradually expanded as premises on each side became vacant. Connecting walls had been knocked down and a grand staircase installed to incorporate more departments.

Mr Wheeler, his wife and two daughters now lived in a big house in Summersdale on the outskirts of Chichester. But in the early days they had lived above the shop with the whole family helping in the business.

Now they employed more assistants than any other business in the town centre and the daughters lived a life of leisure, playing tennis and listening to jazz records — so Gran said with a sniff. Ethel, the elder, was a carbon copy of her mother, large, red-faced, with an overbearing manner. Cissie was pale and thin with a nervous smile.

At least she wasn't likely to come into contact with either them, Abby thought — that was if she got the job. She entered the shop, jumping as the bell over the door jangled. A pale young man hovered over the only customer, who was dithering over some fabric samples. He glanced at her as she came in, then returned his attention to the woman.

Abby patted her hair and smoothed down her skirt. Through an archway another young man on a stepladder was arranging items on a shelf. He didn't turn round as she approached and she coughed before saying,

'Excuse me, I have an appointment with Mr Wheeler.'

He gave an exaggerated start, pretending to fall off the ladder. 'Oh, my goodness, miss, I nearly had heart failure,' he said showing white teeth in a grin.

She smiled, her nervousness gone. 'Sorry. I'm here to see Mr Wheeler.' She hesitated. 'I wasn't sure where to go.'

He stepped off the ladder. 'I'll show you,' he said, leading her through a dark passage and up a narrow staircase. 'The main stairs are for customers only,' he explained. 'I presume you're here for a job.'

Abby nodded.

At the top of the stairs he pointed. 'That's the office — good luck.' He held out his hand. 'I'm Charlie by the way, but it's Mr Simmons on the shop floor.'

'Abby Cookson,' she replied. She knocked on the office door, her nervousness returning as the voice bade her enter.

Mr and Mrs Wheeler were seated on either side of a huge desk placed at right angles to the door. Mrs Wheeler looked up. 'Well?' she said.

'I've come about the job,' Abby said. The butterflies in her stomach were back in force.

'The new assistant, my dear,' Mr Wheeler said. 'This is the girl I mentioned, Abigail

Cookson — to help in the sewing room, remember?'

The plump face creased in a frown, the lips a thin line. 'Oh, yes, you're Mrs Thompson's granddaughter aren't you?'

Abby nodded, already resigned to failure. Mrs Wheeler knew whose granddaughter she was, but she was Wally Cookson's daughter too — Wally Cookson, the drunk and troublemaker, whose wife had run off with another man.

Mr Wheeler broke in before his wife could speak. 'Miss Crocker recommended her, my dear. She's polite and neat and tidy — and she attends chapel regularly . . . '

'But can she sew?' Mrs Wheeler interrupted.

Abby bit her lip. She hated sewing. She'd imagined herself serving customers. But she forced a smile. 'My grandmother taught me mending and darning. I'm no dressmaker though,' she said, honesty over-coming her desire for the job.

'If you can sew on a button or turn a hem that will be sufficient,' Mrs Wheeler snapped.

'I can do that, of course.' Abby was puzzled.

'Some of our customers require alterations,' Mr Wheeler explained. He turned to his wife. 'Well, my dear — it's your decision.

Shall we take Miss Cookson on?'

The dark currant eyes almost disappeared as Mrs Wheeler screwed up her face and appeared to hesitate. Abby crossed her fingers behind her back.

'We'll give her a week's trial,' the woman said at last.

'Thank you, Mrs Wheeler — and you too, sir. I won't let you down — '

'Punctuality, cleanliness, neat work, no shirking,' Mrs Wheeler interrupted. 'Those are the rules — see that you don't break them and we'll get on fine. Otherwise . . . '

'I'll do my best,' Abby said, wondering if she'd last the week out.

Mrs Wheeler pressed a bell on the desk and a few moments later a thin, harassed-looking woman appeared at the office door. 'Did you want me, ma'am?' she asked.

'This is Miss Cookson, your new assistant. On a week's trial. Make sure she understands the rules. You can give her Mrs Carter's frock to finish off. I'll come and inspect the work later.' Mrs Wheeler waved a hand. 'Well, off you go. Don't waste time.'

'Yes'm,' the little woman muttered.

Abby followed her up a narrow flight of stairs to an attic. Under a skylight, a bench ran the length of the wall with two stools in front of it. Piles of silks, satins and cottons, tangles of braids and ribbons, and boxes of multicoloured buttons littered the bench. In one corner was a treadle sewing machine with a length of blue material, half stitched.

The little woman, who hadn't said a word since leaving the Wheelers' office, scuttled over to the machine, sat down and immediately started to sew.

Abby watched for a moment then coughed nervously. 'Excuse me — Mrs Wheeler asked you to show me what to do.'

'I've got to get this finished this morning,' the woman said. 'Mrs Wheeler gets cross if things aren't ready for the customer. And I've had one interruption already this morning.'

'I'm sorry, Mrs — er — Miss . . . but I'm sure Mrs Wheeler won't mind if you stop and show me . . .'

'All right, just give me a minute.' She treadled furiously, bending over the machine so that her nose almost touched the material she was working on. She reached the end of the seam and cut the cotton neatly, pushed her chair back and turned to face Abby.

'I'm sorry, love. I get in such a state when there's a rush order to do. I can't afford to upset madam downstairs. She's forever popping up here, finding fault and looking for excuses to sack me.' She looked Abby up and down. 'And now you're here — young, fit, good eyesight too, I expect. I'll be out on my ear soon, you see.'

'Oh, no. I'm sure that's not right. Mr Wheeler said I was to help you. I'm sure that's what he meant.'

'Yes, but she has the last say.'

Abby was beginning to wonder what she'd let herself in for. She went over to the bench and picked up one of the ribbons, running it through her hands. She hated sewing but at least she'd be out of the rain. 'Well, what do I do?' she asked.

The woman took a dress off a hanger behind the door. 'This is one I've finished altering. See, I had to let it out over the bust, redo the darts. It just needs the buttons sewing on again. She's coming to collect it this afternoon, so look sharp.' She pulled out one of the stools. 'Sit here, under the skylight, so you can see properly. The buttons are in one of those boxes — the tiny pearl ones.' She scurried back to the sewing machine.

Abby cleared a space on the bench and spread the dress out. The work had been done so skilfully she wouldn't have known it had been altered. She found a box containing small pearl buttons. She pulled out the drawer under the bench to reveal needle cases, pincushions and reels of silk thread. Carefully lining up the buttonholes, she marked their position with pins. 'Are these the right buttons?' she asked, taking the box over to her new colleague.

'That's right. Better get started before madam comes up.'

'Thank you, Miss . . . ' Abby still did not know what to call the little woman.

'It's not Miss — it's Mrs Hill — but you can call me Daisy when Madam's not around.'

'I'm Abby.' She suppressed a grin at the thought of this funny little woman having the same name as one of Mr Leighton's cows. 'I didn't realize that Wheeler's did work like this,' she said.

'We wouldn't have to if they bought the right clothes to start with. Half the time they want it shorter, longer, wider, slimmer — I don't know.' Daisy treadled furiously, talking at the same time. 'It's the same with hats — oh, Mrs Wheeler I love the blue one, but could I possibly have a different feather?'

Her attempts to imitate their posh customers had Abby giggling. Maybe she'd like working here after all.

After half an hour she wasn't so sure. The material was slippery and it was hard to position the buttons, especially as her hands were so cold. The only heat in the attic was a smelly paraffin heater and before long her fingers were numb. Knowing Mrs Wheeler would come and inspect her work didn't help and when the door opened behind her she jumped, stabbing the needle into her thumb. She quickly fastened off and cut the thread, praying she wouldn't bleed all over the pale satin.

'Well, girl.' Her new boss examined the dress carefully, holding it up under the skylight. Her lips were pursed.

Abby put her hands behind her, trying to ignore the throbbing in her thumb. Daisy looked up from her sewing machine and gave an encouraging wink behind Mrs Wheeler's back, but she was too nervous to respond.

Eventually Mrs Wheeler gave a grunt of satisfaction. 'It'll do,' she said. 'But don't forget you're on a week's trial.'

'I'll do my best,' Abby said.

Mrs Wheeler stared at Abby. 'Dinner at twelve. Half an hour. No eating or drinking up here or in the shop. When it's fine you can sit in the yard, if it's raining in the stockroom. And no talking to the young men downstairs. I won't have my staff degrading themselves. Understood?'

'Yes'm,' Abby nodded.

Mrs Wheeler left the room and they listened to her heavy footsteps on the uncarpeted stairs.

When all was quiet again Daisy left her sewing machine and helped Abby sort out the tangle of ribbons and trimmings. Then Daisy showed her how to fold the dress in tissue paper to minimize creasing and packed it into a box which she labelled with the customer's name.

'When we go down for dinner I'll show you where we put the things for collection,' Daisy said. 'Have you brought some sandwiches?'

'No. I thought I'd have time to go home . . . '

'She doesn't like us going home in case we're late back. Never mind. You can share mine.'

Abby started to protest but the little woman stopped her. 'You can't go all day on an empty stomach. Besides, I've brought plenty.'

As they settled back to work, Daisy enlightened Abby about the shop and their employers. She didn't seem worried about Mrs Wheeler's injunction against chitchat. When she noticed Abby glancing nervously towards the door she laughed.

'Don't worry — there's plenty of warning when she's on the way. My eyes might be going but my ears are as good as ever. Besides, it's like a herd of elephants coming up those stairs.'

'What about Mr Wheeler?' Abby asked, smiling at the image.

'We hardly see him, thank goodness, except when the old girl's not around. Then he might pop up with an order. But usually he sends Charlie — have you met Charlie?'

Abby nodded. 'What about the other employees? How many are there?'

'Besides Charlie there's three men and a couple of lads, and Fred the van driver. The supervisor is Mr Lever — snooty bugger — calls himself the floor walker as if he's in one of them posh London stores. And Miss Davies. She's in lingerie, my dear — bloomers to you and me. Can't have men serving the ladies with their intimate apparel as old Wheeler calls it. Mr W does the ordering and bookwork and Mrs swans around as if she's in charge and bosses everyone around — including him.'

'I thought I'd be serving in the shop,' Abby said.

'Mr W's old-fashioned. He doesn't like employing women unless it's to cook and clean — and sew of course.'

'I don't see why women shouldn't work in the shop. After all, what do men know about ladies' fashions and hats?'

'Yes. And as for haberdashery — most of them don't know a pin from a needle,' Daisy said. She finished rolling up a length of blue satin ribbon and placed it in its box. 'There, that's all nice and tidy — until next time we have a rush on and haven't got time to put everything away. Now then, have you ever used a treadle machine before?'

5

The attic door closed and Abby stuck her tongue out as her employer clomped down the uncarpeted stairs. If only she could find another job. It was true she hated sewing but she was getting better at it. It didn't matter how hard she tried, though, she couldn't please Mrs Wheeler.

It was only her growing friendship with Daisy that made the job bearable. The days flew faster as they talked and worked together. Abby had told her about Joe — even read bits of his letters out to her. And Daisy had told her about Bert's suffering in the war and how much she missed Jimmy, her nephew who was in the army.

But Daisy wasn't here today. Bert was ill and she'd sent a message to say she couldn't leave him. And that was why Mrs Wheeler was in such a bad mood.

'It's not good enough. I shall have to dock her wages again. She should get a neighbour to sit with her husband,' she'd said.

Useless for Abby to say anything in her friend's defence. For so-called Christians the

Wheelers didn't seem to have much compassion. Their daughter Ethel was even worse. The only one Abby had any time for was the younger one, Cissie, who was quiet and shy, very firmly under the domination of her overbearing family.

As for Mr Wheeler, Abby had never liked him, and since coming to work at The Emporium she'd seen him for the mealy-mouthed hypocrite he was.

If she bumped into him in the stockroom downstairs he always smiled and asked how she was managing, patting her arm or brushing against her. His moist hands made her flesh creep and she avoided him whenever possible. Thank goodness he seldom came up to the attic, leaving that side of the business to his wife.

It was a chilly day in early spring and the bright sun, streaming through the attic skylight, made it easier to see her work. But it was still cold and Abby put down her needle and flexed her fingers, blowing on her hands. Thank goodness it would soon be dinner time. Half an hour wasn't really long enough to get warm. But she'd be able to read Joe's letter again. She bent over the sewing machine again, smiling as she felt the crackle of paper in her skirt pocket.

Joe was still in Malta but hoped to be back

soon. It depended on the international situation, whatever that might mean. Abby couldn't wait to see him again. Letters were no substitute for being together.

They'd only seen each other twice after the ship's sea trials were completed and before he'd set sail for the Mediterranean. They'd gone for a walk along Fishbourne Creek, Abby shivering in the cold wind until Joe put his arm around her. They talked for hours, exchanging life histories. Abby even confided the anger she felt at being deserted by her mother. Joe already knew the story from his uncle and he sympathized. He'd lost both his parents when he was young but he'd been fortunate to have a warm, loving relationship with Dan. And the Knowleses had been like a second family.

'I suppose Hannah needed someone to mother, having no kids of her own,' Joe said.

They arrived back at Applegate Farm, chilled to the bone yet warmed by their growing love.

A couple of weeks later Abby had gone on the train to Portsmouth on early-closing day, spending some of her precious wages on the fare. They'd snatched an hour together, snuggling in the back row of the cinema to get out of the cold. They were so engrossed in each other that they didn't see much of the film. When Joe noticed the time they ran through the streets hand in hand, laughing until they reached the dockyard gates and it was time to say goodbye again.

Although their meetings had been so few, Abby knew she loved him and there'd never be anyone else for her. Just a glimpse of his writing on an envelope was enough to get her heart racing.

Her thoughts were interrupted by the chiming of the clock on the City Cross just up the road. She grabbed her packet of sandwiches and ran down the narrow attic stairs to the stockroom, hoping Charlie wasn't there. Usually she enjoyed his company but today she wanted to sit and enjoy rereading her letter.

But he was already there, munching his way through a doorstep sandwich filled with corned beef and pickle.

'You look frozen,' he said, moving to make room for her by the stove.

She sat down and held her fingers out to the warmth, rubbing her hands together before opening her sandwiches.

'Not fish paste again?' Charlie grinned, knowing her dad worked at Shippams and got stuff cheap from the staff shop. 'Here, have a swap,' he said, offering her his corned beef.

'I'm all right, Charlie. I like fish paste,' Abby said.

'Well, if you won't have one of my sandwiches, will you come to the pictures with me?'

Abby couldn't help smiling at his cheeky grin, head on one side, a lock of dark hair falling over his forehead. 'Charlie, please don't keep asking. You know the answer.'

The grin disappeared, replaced by a scowl. 'Bloody Joe, I suppose' he muttered.

'Don't be like that,' Abby said, upset at his quick change of mood. She felt a bit guilty for hurting him. When they'd met she'd been pleased to see a friendly face and she'd responded to Charlie's banter, enjoying a laugh and joke during her brief breaks. It helped the boring day to pass more quickly.

But he'd misinterpreted her friendliness and begun to pester her to go out with him even after she told him she already had a boyfriend. When he discovered Joe was in the navy he'd made the usual comments about sailors. 'You might be true to him, but is he true to you?' he asked with a grin. Abby sensed he wasn't joking.

'Of course he is. We love each other,' she protested.

Charlie seemed to accept that and for a while he left her alone. But when she told him Joe was in the Mediterranean and she didn't know when he'd be home, he grinned and said. 'Never mind, I'll make sure you're not lonely.'

She was never sure whether he was joking. But today she wasn't going to let him get to her. She finished her sandwiches quickly and stood up, anxious to get back to the attic and read Joe's letter again without any comments from Charlie. He stood up too and grabbed her hand. 'I know you're staying true to Joe, but I meant it, Abby. If you get fed up waiting for him to come home, I'll still be here.'

Abby tried to pull her hand away. 'Please, Charlie, don't spoil things. You know I like you — but it's Joe I love.'

He still gripped her hand, his face red, breathing hard. 'Abby . . . '

The door opened and he let go quickly as their employer came in and gave each of them a long, hard look. Mr Wheeler pulled his watch out of his waistcoat pocket, glanced at it and spoke to Charlie. 'Time you were back at your counter, Simmons.'

Charlie scuttled out of the door and Mr Wheeler turned to Abby. 'As for you, Miss Cookson, I hear you're consorting with a sailor. And now, here you are, holding hands with young Simmons. It won't do. If there's no improvement in your behaviour, I shall have to reconsider your situation here.'

Abby burned with embarrassment. It wasn't fair. It wasn't her fault Charlie had grabbed her hand. And as for Joe, why did his being in the navy prejudice people against him? But she dared not protest.

Mr Wheeler put his hand under her chin and tilted her face upwards. 'I'm sure you're a good girl, in spite of . . . ' His voice trailed off and he smiled. 'I shall be keeping an eye on you, my dear.'

His hand dropped to his side and he turned abruptly. Abby was bewildered by his sudden change of mood. She wasn't sure what he meant. Her cheeks still burning, she ran up the stairs to the sanctuary of the attic. It was definitely time to look for another job. Things were getting too complicated at The Emporium.

★   ★   ★

Abby hadn't told Daisy that she was looking for another job but she couldn't wait to get away. She'd even written to a couple of the big stores in Portsmouth as there seemed to be nothing in Chichester. So far, there'd been no response.

Daisy would be upset if she left. But Abby couldn't stand the way Mr Wheeler looked at her, not to mention that Charlie was getting to be more of a nuisance, constantly pestering her to go out with him.

On top of everything else she hadn't heard from Joe for weeks. At first he'd written regularly, but lately there'd been long intervals between his letters. Abby wasn't sure whether he'd stopped loving her or if there was another reason.

Her heart lifted when she heard the postman's knock and she almost snatched the letter from him. It wasn't the one she'd been waiting for but she felt a thrill of anticipation as she opened it, until she read the short note.

'*We regret that we are unable to offer you employment at this time. Yours etc.*' She screwed the paper up and threw it in the fire. What was the use of trying? She was stuck at Wheeler's and might as well make the best of it. She couldn't afford to leave without another job to go to. Dad had started drinking again and had taken several days off work. It was only a matter of time before he got the sack. And there would be no more chances.

Now Abby sat at her work bench, wishing she could seek Daisy's advice, but the older woman seemed to have something on her mind too. Perhaps she was worried about

Jimmy. Despite Mr Chamberlain's assurances last year there were still fears of a war. When they'd let the siren off for a practice a couple of weeks ago it had scared her half to death.

Abby thought about Joe and the pictures she'd seen on the news-reels of German U-boats and their huge battleships.

'Do you think there'll really be a war, Daisy?'

'How do I know? You can't believe everything you hear on the wireless. Besides, I've got other things on my mind.' She started to cry.

Abby leapt up and put her arms round the little woman, feeling the sharp bones of her shoulders as they shook with sobs.

'It's my Bert,' she said. 'I'm so worried about him — but I've had too many days off lately. Now the old cow won't even let me go home at dinner time. She says she won't put up with me being late back any more or I'll lose my job.' Daisy sniffed and wiped her eyes. 'I hate leaving him alone all day when he's so poorly.'

'You mean worse than usual?' Abby asked. Bert Hill was always poorly. Like her father, he'd served in the Great War but he'd been gassed. For the past twenty years every breath he'd taken had been an effort, and each winter, when influenza was rife, Daisy thought she was going to lose him. Her whole life was taken up with drudging for the Wheelers and caring for Bert.

'He's usually better in summer but his cough's been awful — up all night. I didn't want to leave him this morning.' Daisy wiped her eyes and made a half-hearted attempt to resume sewing.

'Have you had the doctor?' Abby asked.

Daisy gave a short laugh. 'If I can't afford time off to look after my husband, I certainly can't afford a doctor,' she said. 'A neighbour's promised to look in but I don't like putting on other people.'

The door opened suddenly and they both jumped. For once Daisy hadn't heard Mrs Wheeler coming up the stairs.

'What's going on here?'

'I'm just helping Mrs Hill rethread the machine,' Abby said, thinking quickly. She hurried back to her bench and picked up the jacket she'd been working on. Daisy was already hunched over the machine again, treadling furiously as if her life depended on it.

Their employer looked from one to the other suspiciously. She placed the garment she was carrying on the bench. 'These darts need letting out,' she said. 'Get it done by closing time. Mrs Jones needs it for the

Mayor's concert tonight.'

At the door, she paused. 'By the way, Mrs Hill, some urchin came into the shop earlier on — said your husband's been taken to the infirmary.'

'Bert — in hospital? I've got to go . . . ' Daisy leapt up, her face ashen, hands trembling.

'You won't be allowed to see him so you might as well get on with your work,' Mrs Wheeler said. 'Keeping busy will take your mind off it. Finish this to my satisfaction and you can go early.'

When she'd gone, Abby threw her thimble down and stood up. 'The mean old cow. Calls herself a Christian? I don't know how she can hold her head up in chapel on a Sunday.'

'It's only what I expected. She's never once given me time off when Bert was ill,' Daisy said. 'I've a good mind to just go anyway.' Her shoulders slumped. 'I can't afford to lose this job, though.' She shrugged and resumed sewing.

By the time she'd finished it was almost time to go home anyway.

'I hope he's all right,' Abby said, as Daisy took her coat from the hook behind the door. 'Give him my love.'

Daisy managed a smile. 'Thanks, love,' she said and was gone.

Abby took the next dress from the pile and read the instructions Mrs Wheeler had pinned to it. It was hardly worth starting it so late but she was in no hurry to go home. Wally was back on the drink and although she tried to convince herself that a letter from Joe would be waiting, she was sure she'd be disappointed again.

She'd just finished and was inspecting her work when Mrs Wheeler came in. 'We're just locking up. You'd best be off.' She picked up the gown, examining it for faults. Abby knew it was perfect but her employer just pursed her lips and laid it back on the worktop. 'Get that packed up first thing tomorrow,' she said.

Once free from the constraints of The Emporium, Abby's spirits lifted. Dad didn't have any money so he wouldn't be drunk. She hurried under the archway into Orchard Street and crossed the road towards the warren of cottages that made up Somerstown.

Surely Joe would have written. It seemed ages since she'd heard from him. His last letter had been so short she'd wondered why he bothered. But he said he was busy and that things were 'hotting up' — she just hoped that didn't mean they were preparing for war.

Never mind, she'd write to him when she got home. Her letters, faithfully one a week, were filled with incidents and anecdotes which she hoped would bring her closer to him. She told him about Daisy and Bert and the Wheelers, how she'd been out to the farm and had tea with his Uncle Dan and the Knowleses, and about her visits to the pictures with Rhoda.

She hadn't mentioned going out with Charlie, though. Fed up with not hearing from Joe, she'd given in to his pleas to go to the pictures with him — and she'd regretted it ever since.

They'd gone to see *A Day at the Races*, but instead of laughing at the antics of the Marx Brothers, Abby had spent the entire evening slapping at Charlie's groping hands. In the end she'd stormed out of the cinema and run off through the back streets.

He caught up with her near the park and grabbed at her arm. 'What's wrong with you, Abby? It's just a bit of fun.'

'I told you, Charlie — I don't like that sort of fun.'

'Be different if it was Joe Leighton, I suppose,' he said, pulling her towards him.

'Yes, it would. I love Joe — but I don't love you. Why can't we just be friends?' She pulled away from him but he grabbed her again.

'I don't want to be friends. I thought you liked me. You don't know what it's like, seeing you every day . . . ' His hands dropped to his sides and he looked at the ground, scuffing his shoe against the pavement.

He looked so woebegone, so different from the happy-go-lucky lad who brightened her days at work, that Abby's soft heart was touched. 'I'm sorry, Charlie. I wouldn't hurt you for anything.'

He didn't answer and she walked away, leaving him staring after her.

Since then they'd hardly spoken to each other at work and she missed his clowning around every time she went down to the stockroom.

⋆   ⋆   ⋆

When Abby reached home there was no envelope propped up against the blue and white jug on the dresser. She even picked up the doormat and shook it, in case the longed-for letter had got pushed under it. Nothing. With a sigh, she heated up the soup she'd made the previous day and ate the remains of the loaf. From the dirty dishes in the sink she knew Dad had already eaten and probably gone out.

She cleared away and washed up, wiping down the table and shelves, leaving everything as tidy as possible. She sometimes wondered why she bothered. The cracked lino and flaking walls meant the gloomy little cottage never stayed clean. Since she'd been working for the Wheelers she'd done her best to make it more homelike, buying cheap remnants of material from the shop and using the sewing machine during her dinner break to run up new cushion covers and curtains.

She switched the wireless on and sang along to the dance band in a vain effort to cheer herself up. But they were playing *Smoke gets in your Eyes*, which always brought a lump to her throat. And then she couldn't stop thinking about Joe. Could a romance survive on a few meetings and a handful of letters? She'd thought so. But it was hard.

She didn't fancy an evening indoors brooding about Joe and Charlie. But she couldn't settle to writing another letter either.

As if in answer to her thoughts there was a knock on the door. It was her friend Rhoda. With her live-in job, they didn't see much of each other these days.

'I've got an evening off — how about the pictures?' Rhoda said. 'It's *Fire over England*, with Laurence Olivier.'

Abby didn't need asking twice. She took her coat off the hook behind the door and they left Tanner's Court arm in arm.

'Have you been out with Charlie again?' Rhoda asked.

'No. I like him, but he's just not Joe.' She hadn't told her friend what happened last time.

'Don't tell me you're still wasting time over that sailor. He's probably enjoying himself with some floozie while you're pining for him. What's wrong with Charlie?'

Abby shrugged. Rhoda would only laugh if she told her that Charlie only seemed interested in getting his hands inside her blouse and wouldn't take 'no' for an answer.

As Abby tried to lose herself in Laurence Olivier's romance with the beautiful Vivien Leigh, she was roused by a shuffling, accompanied by muttered curses as someone pushed their way along the row towards her. She didn't bother to look round until a voice whispered close to her ear. 'You can try to avoid me, but I'm not going to let you get away.'

It was Charlie. Why couldn't he accept she wasn't interested? 'Be quiet. I'm trying to watch the film,' she whispered.

To her relief he seemed to become engrossed in the film — until he put his arm round her. When she turned to protest he grabbed her and kissed her on the lips. This time he kept his hands on her shoulders, didn't try to paw her as he had before.

He let her go and whispered, 'There, that wasn't so bad was it?'

She had to admit it was quite nice but it didn't make her feel the way Joe's kisses did. Charlie was fine as a workmate, someone to laugh with, to relieve the tedium of the working day. But it was Joe she loved and always would, even if he hadn't written lately. She just had to make Charlie understand.

As the crowds streamed out of the Gaumont into Eastgate, Abby grabbed Rhoda's arm and pulled her down the narrow street between Shippam's factory and city wall.

Rhoda looked back. 'Where's Charlie? I thought he was going to walk you home.'

'I don't need anyone to walk me home,' Abby said.

'But Charlie's nice. And I saw him kissing you — lucky you.'

'I don't feel lucky,' Abby retorted. 'I wish he'd leave me alone.'

Rhoda laughed but Abby didn't join in. What was she going to do about Charlie?

★ ★ ★

Joe lay in his hammock, one leg swinging idly over the side, reading Abby's latest letter. The four pages of closely written news, the humorous descriptions of the people she worked with, brought his home town vividly to life. He smiled as he read:

Charlie was up the stepladder, getting down a box of collars, and Mrs Benson came in. Come down from there my man and attend to your customers she said in her loud posh voice. Charlie turned round so quick he fell off the ladder. Lucky he didn't hurt himself, but he bowed and said, your wish is my command, madam. Mrs W was furious, but she couldn't say anything cause Mrs B saw the funny side and started laughing herself. I hid behind the stock-room door so Mrs W wouldn't hear me laughing too.

Joe almost laughed too, until it occurred to him how often Charlie's name cropped up in Abby's letters. A stab of jealousy twisted his stomach. How could he expect her to be true to him when he was so far away? He closed his eyes, clutching the letter to his chest, and conjured up her dimpled smile, the unruly curls the colour of a newly fallen horse chestnut. He pictured her blue eyes which often held a depth of sadness but which could brighten to laughter in seconds. Abby, sweet

Abigail Cookson, who had stolen his heart the second he set eyes on her.

His heart lightened as he turned the page and read her closing words, the same words she ended all her letters with: '*I love you and miss you. Please write soon, your loving Abby.*'

Joe could never do a job like Charlie's, having to bow and scrape to snooty customers. He'd always dreamed of joining the navy, longed to get away from his home town. So far, the reality had lived up to his dreams. But now, as he read and reread Abby's letters, he wished he'd listened to his uncle and stayed in Chichester.

6

The day after the pictures Abby slipped through the back door of the shop and hurried up the back stairs. She wasn't ready to confront Charlie yet although she knew she shouldn't put it off. Daisy hadn't turned up again and in the quiet workroom she had time to rehearse what to say to him.

Lost in thought, her head bent industriously over the sewing machine, she jumped when the door opened.

'Miss Cookson, has my wife told you . . . ?' Mr Wheeler rarely ventured up to the attic workroom and Abby drew in her breath.

He coughed. 'Sad news, my dear. Mrs Hill's husband has passed away.'

'Poor Daisy.' Abby gave a little sob.

He assumed a pious expression. 'It was a merciful release. God has ended his suffering — now he's safe in the arms of Jesus.' His expression lightened. 'I've sent a message that she can have today to make arrangements — and a day off for the funeral.'

'That's very kind of you, Mr Wheeler.' Abby was quite proud that she managed to keep the sarcasm out of her voice. 'And don't worry about the orders. I can manage on my own today if I don't stop for dinner.'

'You're a good girl, Miss Cookson — Abby.' He leaned over her. 'No trouble with the machine?' he asked.

'It's fine,' she said.

'Perhaps it needs oiling.' He fiddled with it for a moment and she was conscious of his breath on her cheek. 'Excellent,' he murmured.

Why did he have to lean so close? Abby squirmed, her face and neck hot with embarrassment. Did he realize his hand had brushed against her breast?

The door opened and he leapt back as Mrs Wheeler came in, her eyes darting suspiciously around the room.

Mr Wheeler's face was red. 'Oh, there you are, my dear. I just came to tell Miss Cookson about Mrs Hill's husband.'

'I could have done that. I believe Mr Lever wants a word with you, Ernest.'

'I'll go right down.' He returned the material to the bench and scuttled out of the door.

Abby, diligently finishing off the seams, didn't turn round until he'd gone. For once she was pleased to see Mrs Wheeler. 'I'll stay late and finish Mrs Hill's work too if you like,' she offered. She wasn't being helpful to her boss, she just felt that in some way she was helping Daisy. She hesitated. 'Do you think I might have an hour off to go to the funeral?'

'But you didn't even know the man.'

'Mrs Hill is my friend and I know she doesn't have much family to support her.' A few tears spilled over at the thought of how her friend must be feeling.

'Nothing to cry about,' Mrs Wheeler snapped, opening the door. 'I'll think about it.'

When Abby went downstairs for her dinner her eyes were red from crying. The events of the morning had pushed her problem with Charlie to the back of her mind and she was pleased to see him.

'I heard,' he said. 'Poor old Daisy.'

'I asked if I could go to the funeral — Mrs W said she'll think about it,' Abby said.

'You'll be lucky. She wouldn't give you time for your own funeral.' Charlie gave a short laugh and opened his sandwiches. After a few moments he said, 'Abby, why did you rush off last night? I wanted to talk to you.'

'I didn't think you were interested in just talking.'

'I'm sorry. I got carried away. It's just . . . ' He shrugged. 'I know Joe's your boyfriend. But he's the other side of the world and I'm here. And I don't give up easily . . . '

Back in the attic she started to cry again. As she brushed the tears away she tried to tell herself she was crying for Daisy and Mr Hill. But her head was in such a turmoil. Joe had been gone so long now and it would be months before he came home. Would he still feel the same when they met once more? Would she? Would it hurt to go out with Charlie to cheer herself up?

The clock on the Cross struck six and Abby snipped her thread and put her work away. As promised, she'd worked through the dinner break and no one had been upstairs all afternoon. It had been a dreadful day, what with the news about Bert Hill, followed by Mr Wheeler's odd behaviour and then the talk with Charlie. She hoped she could slip out of the back door without encountering anyone.

But as she reached for her jacket Mr Wheeler appeared. 'My wife tells me you wish to attend Mr Hill's funeral. You may have an hour off — no longer. Let me know when.'

'Thank you, Mr Wheeler,' she said.

Before he could say anything else she hurried down the twitten at the side of the shop and into South Street. She didn't feel like going home. Dad had come in late last night, stumbling and swearing as he came up the stairs. And he was still in bed when she'd left for work. She couldn't face the inevitable argument on top of everything else. She decided not to go straight home but to call round at Daisy's.

★ ★ ★

On the day of Bert Hill's funeral Abby arrived at The Emporium just as Mr Lever was unlocking the front door. If it had been either of the Wheelers Abby would have ducked down the twitten and gone in the back way. They didn't like their lowly employees coming through the shop.

Mr Lever spotted her and gave a thin smile, holding the door open for her. 'Hurry up, girl,' he said, glancing up and down the street.

Abby ducked under the counter and pushed open the door to the stockroom where Charlie was already unpacking boxes of ties.

'Morning, Abby. Lovely day,' he said, his friendly open grin making her forget how annoyed she'd been. Maybe they could just be friends after all.

'Yes it is,' she agreed. 'Not so nice for Daisy though.'

Charlie nodded. 'You going to the funeral?'

'Mr Wheeler said I could have an hour off

117

but he hasn't mentioned it since. Mrs W has been in a bad mood all week because Daisy hasn't been here, so I haven't liked to say anything.'

'Mrs W won't be in today — taken the daughters shopping in Brighton can you believe?' Charlie rolled his eyes. 'As if they can't get all their fripperies and furbelows here.' He jumped as a voice called from the shop.

'Simmons, get in here with those ties.' Mr Lever put his head round the door. 'And you, Miss Cookson — isn't it time you started work too?'

'Yes, Mr Lever.' Abby's voice was meek, but as she climbed the stairs she was seething. How dare he order her about? He wasn't her boss. His attitude made her feel rebellious. She'd go to Mr Hill's funeral even if she did get into trouble. Mr Wheeler had given her permission. With any luck she'd be back before she was missed, although it was a long walk to the cemetery on the outskirts of town.

'I'd better finish these buttons before I sneak off,' she muttered.

She'd just sewn the last one when the door opened and Mr Wheeler came in. Why did he only come up here when no one else was around?

118

He picked up the jacket she'd just finished and seemed engrossed in examining her stitches.

'Excellent, my dear,' he said.

'Thank you, Mr Wheeler,' she managed to say. She pushed her chair back and scurried to the bench at the other side of the room. 'I've got the orders ready. Shall I take them down to the fitting room?' Anything to avoid being alone with him.

'Later,' he said, following her across the room. 'I believe I said you could have some time off today. Only an hour mind. We're getting behind without Mrs Hill.'

Abby picked up the garments and tried to pass him. But he took them away from her and returned them to the bench. 'I said, later. Now, my dear, I'm kind to you. Why aren't you kind to me in return?' He licked his lips and his eyes gleamed as he stared at her.

'I don't know what you mean,' she said. But she had a pretty good idea.

He reached out and twisted a lock of her hair round his finger. 'Such pretty curls, such soft skin.' His hand touched her cheek and she recoiled, but he didn't seem to notice. 'Just a little kiss — that's all.'

Abby put her hands on his chest and tried to push him away. 'Mr Wheeler, you're a married man. What's got into you?' She tried to laugh, as if she thought he was joking. But her voice trembled as his eyes hardened.

'Don't come the innocent with me, miss. I've seen you larking around with young Simmons. I don't suppose you begrudge him a kiss — and more?' He pulled her closer and fastened his wet lips on her neck. He was stronger than he looked and, despite her struggles, he pushed her back against the bench, tearing at the buttons of her blouse. His other hand fastened over her mouth. She gasped and tried to scream as his lips travelled down to her breasts. *Why doesn't someone come?*

Frantically, she kicked out. It seemed to make him more determined. 'Little vixen,' he muttered. 'That's the last time you torment me with your saucy looks.' He pulled her skirt up and thrust his hand between her legs.

She kicked out again, this time catching him on the shin. As he let go of her with a muttered curse, she pushed him away. Snatching up the dresses, she made for the door, dreading that he'd grab her and drag her back into the room.

She stumbled down the stairs, dumping the clothes on the table in the stockroom. Thank goodness there was no one around. She leaned on the table until her ragged breathing eased, alert for his footsteps on the stairs.

Several pins had fallen out of her hair and her hands trembled as she replaced them.

She took her handkerchief from her sleeve, scrubbing at the place where Mr Wheeler's wet lips had touched her skin, then tried to redo the buttons on her blouse. One of them had been torn off but there was no way she'd go upstairs for a needle and thread. Fortunately she'd worn her smart jacket for the funeral — that would hide the tear. She opened the door, cautiously. She'd go now. And she wouldn't come back — not after what had just happened.

Charlie looked up from dusting one of the mahogany counters. 'You all right, Abby? You look a bit upset.'

'Well, it *is* a funeral, Charlie,' she said, her voice unusually sharp. How could she tell him what had happened? It was too shameful.

He looked contrite. 'Sorry. So — he let you go, then?' He put his duster down and came towards her. 'Give Daisy my love. Tell her sorry, won't you.'

'Of course. I'll see you later. Don't want to be late.' She went out of the back door into the little lane that ran behind the shop.

She cut through the narrow streets to Eastgate Square and, as she began the long walk out of town to the cemetery, the events of the past hour replayed in her mind. What had she done to provoke her employer's outrageous behaviour? She wasn't what her grandmother called a 'flighty piece'. She didn't wear lots of make-up or low-cut necklines or go out with lots of different young men. But Mr Wheeler had implied just that, all because she was friendly with Charlie.

She couldn't believe it was her fault. She shuddered at the memory of his wet mouth, his hands invading her body, that *thing* pressing against her leg. Well, one thing's for sure, job or no job, I won't go back there, she thought.

She turned the corner into Church Lane, quickening her steps as she saw the cluster of black-clad figures gathered at the gates leading to the chapel and the cemetery beyond. This wasn't the time to think about such things.

★   ★   ★

The service was over at last and the mourners hung around in small groups. A young man in army uniform, who introduced himself as Daisy's nephew Jimmy, asked her to come back to the house for refreshments.

'I'm sorry, I must go back to work.' Despite her earlier decision never to set foot in The

Emporium again, she realized she'd have to go back. In her haste to get away she'd left her handbag on the work bench. 'I'll see Daisy at work tomorrow.'

'They've sacked her — sent a note, can you believe?' Jimmy said.

'Oh, how could they? Poor Daisy.'

Daisy was at the cemetery gates supported by neighbours and Abby hurried to catch up. 'I've just heard. What will you do?'

'I don't care at the moment.' Daisy dabbed her eyes with a sodden handkerchief. 'Pop round one evening. I can't talk now.'

Abby hugged her friend and promised to visit soon. As she walked back towards town she seethed with anger. Mr Wheeler regularly stood up in chapel to berate so-called sinners, yet behaved worse than any of the congregation. And his wife begged money for missionaries abroad, but was too mean-spirited to allow an employee a few days off for a bereavement. And these were the people her grandmother looked up to and respected.

Abby hoped Mr Wheeler wasn't around when she picked up her bag. But if he was, she'd tell him exactly what she thought of him. She didn't care if she couldn't find another job straight away. She couldn't stay there without Daisy. She'd be alone up there in the attic, worrying all the time that he'd come in and start pawing her. And next time she might not be able to fight him off.

She sidled down the alley and through the rear entrance, reaching the bottom of the back stairs before Mr Lever addressed her.

'Ah, there you are, Miss Cookson. Where have you been?'

'I wasn't gone long, Mr Lever . . . ' She began to stammer and felt herself flushing.

'Never mind, never mind. You're here now.'

His face was a bit pink and Abby realized that he thought she'd been out to the privy in the yard. She took a deep breath and said, 'Did Mr Wheeler want me for something?'

'No. He's been called away urgently.'

'I'll get on with my work then,' Abby said. She'd wait till he was busy and sneak upstairs to get her bag.

'Wait, Miss Cookson. I need your help. The Lady Mayoress is here for a fitting. Do you know if her gown's ready yet?'

'Yes. I'll attend to her if you like,' Abby said.

'Well, if you're sure.' Mr Lever led the way through to the main shop where the Lady Mayoress sat on a high-backed chair clutching a large handbag to her ample bosom.

Fixing a polite smile on her face Abby said, 'If you'd like to come through, madam . . . ?'

'Where is Mrs Wheeler? She always does

my fittings personally.'

'I'm afraid she's unavoidably detained,' Abby said, hoping the woman wouldn't ask what had detained her. She could hardly say that she'd gone on a shopping spree to Brighton. She showed the woman into the fitting room and took the dress from its hanger.

When the customer tried it on it was a perfect fit. She was delighted and Abby blushed at the compliment. It wasn't often she got the chance to see her work appreciated. She folded the gown in layers of tissue paper and put it in a box, promising that Charlie would deliver it on his way home.

When she'd gone, Abby realized that she'd almost forgotten how anxious she'd been to get away. She enjoyed dealing with the customers. If only she could work downstairs all the time. There were always people coming and going and there'd be less chance of her boss catching her alone. But Mrs Wheeler would never allow it, especially as Daisy would no longer be there to do the sewing. Besides, hadn't she already made up her mind to leave?

But when she got home another blow awaited her. The hearth was strewn with smashed china and, as she bent to clear it up, she saw the screwed up piece of paper. She smoothed it out and read the formal note. Dad had finally used up his last chance at Shippam's. He was not welcome at the factory, even to collect his wages. The tears she'd managed to suppress all day welled up at last. Now she'd have to stay at Wheeler's — at least till she managed to find another job.

'Dad, how could you?' she sobbed. But he wasn't there — gone to the pub to drown his sorrows, as usual.

★　★　★

Abby's steps slowed as she reached South Street. She wasn't looking forward to being stuck up in the attic on her own all day with no Daisy to chat to, her stomach churning every time she heard footsteps on the stairs. But with Dad out of work again she had no choice. Maybe Mrs Wheeler would let her work downstairs, dealing with the customers. But she didn't hold out much hope.

At the shop the blinds were still drawn and the employees were waiting outside.

'Hope he ain't too long,' Charlie muttered.

'What's happened?' Abby asked.

'Mr Lever's gone to fetch the keys. He locked up last night and took them round to

Wheeler's house. But neither of them has turned up this morning.'

It was unheard of for the shop to open late, and when Mr Lever returned alone the staff were agog. He urged them inside, unlocked the main door and adjusted the window blinds. When he saw there were no customers waiting he addressed the staff.

'I'm sorry to inform you that Mrs Wheeler was taken ill yesterday. She's in hospital in Brighton. Mr Wheeler spent the night there, but he hopes to bring her home this morning. It seems she had some sort of seizure. Mr Wheeler has put me in charge and has asked us to carry on as usual. He'll come in later if he feels he can leave his wife. Meanwhile, I hope you'll continue to carry on with your work as if your employers were here.' He waved a thin hand in dismissal.

As Abby turned away he called to her. 'I don't know when we'll get a replacement for Mrs Hill so I've taken it upon myself to refuse any more demands for alterations. I'll expect you to finish off the backlog, as well as to help with the fittings.'

'I'll do my best, sir,' Abby said with a broad smile. She hadn't had to ask after all. Despite her dislike of Mrs Wheeler, she was sorry the woman was ill. Still, it had given her the chance to prove herself. But she'd only stay till she was better, or until they took on another seamstress. Then she'd definitely look for another job.

★ ★ ★

Mrs Wheeler remained bedridden for weeks and Mr Wheeler hardly left her side. Even with the snooty Mr Lever in charge, the atmosphere in the shop was much lighter.

But when it became obvious that Mrs Wheeler wasn't going to get better, and a full time nurse was employed, Mr Wheeler returned to manage the shop.

By then the backlog of alterations had been cleared and Abby was working in the ladies' fashions department. It was always busy and with people around her she gradually started to relax. Sometimes she even managed to convince herself she'd exaggerated the incident on the day of Mr Hill's funeral.

But then she would catch Mr Wheeler staring at her with those glittering eyes and she knew it was only a matter of time before he attempted to molest her again.

At Sunday chapel, as he sat with his daughters, praying fervently for his wife's recovery, no one would believe he was anything but a devoted husband. But Abby knew how false his sentiments were and when his hand brushed hers as he passed the collection plate, she couldn't suppress a shiver of revulsion.

She'd tried to wriggle out of going to chapel but sometimes Gran insisted. One Sunday when Gran had stopped to speak to Mr Wheeler, he'd looked Abby up and down and smiled.

'I'm very fortunate in my staff, Mrs Thompson,' he'd said. 'And your granddaughter is a credit to you. I couldn't have managed without her during my poor wife's illness.'

Gran was pleased. 'You're lucky to have such a good employer, Abby,' she said. 'I'm glad you've settled down into a good job.'

If only she could tell Gran what he was really like. But she wouldn't believe her.

Then there was Charlie. He kept asking her to go out to go to the pictures with him. Sometimes she gave in. But she always asked Rhoda and her current boyfriend to go with them so he wouldn't think it was a proper date. She didn't want him getting ideas.

At least she'd heard from Joe at last — the ship would return to port early in the New Year and he might even get home for Christmas. It was a long way off but something to look forward to. Even better, he'd written, '*I can't wait to hold you in my arms again. It's the only thing that keeps me going out here.*'

It was all she wanted to hear and she made up her mind that she wouldn't go out with Charlie any more, even if he was keeping to their bargain of remaining 'just friends'.

★ ★ ★

On the first Sunday in September Abby didn't go to chapel but popped round to visit Daisy instead. Her friend had started her new job in the City Electric Laundry not far from her home and was making new friends. But she still grieved for her husband and said that the evenings were the worst time.

'How's Mrs Wheeler?' Daisy asked, ushering Abby into her cosy kitchen.

'No change. They say she'll always be like that now.'

'Well, I never liked the old witch and she treated me something dreadful but I wouldn't wish that on anybody,' Daisy said, filling the kettle and putting it on the range.

Abby shrugged. 'Never mind the Wheelers, what about you?'

'So-so. I can't get used to having no one to look after.' Daisy sighed and began to set out cups and saucers on the table. She filled the teapot and sat down. 'Mustn't grumble. I tell myself to be glad poor Bert's not suffering any more.'

'You must be lonely,' Abby said.

'The evening's are worst but Jimmy bought me a wireless for my birthday and that keeps me company.'

Abby smiled. 'And the new job — are you still enjoying it?'

'Enjoy's not the right word,' Daisy said, with a little laugh, spreading her red, chapped hands out on the table. 'It's not so bad. They don't mind us chatting so long as we get on with our work and we're always laughing. Not like at Wheelers.' She poured the tea and pushed a cup across the table.

Abby took a sip. 'I miss you.'

'You sound fed up.'

Abby couldn't tell Daisy what was troubling her. 'I like serving the customers in the shop — even the old biddies like Mrs Spencer and Mrs Benson.'

'What's the problem then? Has Charlie been playing up again?'

Abby pulled a face. How could she voice her growing fear of Mr Wheeler? 'It's not Charlie. I had a letter from Joe yesterday. He says things are getting worse and he might not get home — '

'That reminds me . . . ' Daisy leapt up and switched on the wireless. 'They said there's going to be an announcement this morning.'

Abby's stomach churned and she gripped

Daisy's hand as they listened to the Prime Minister's grave voice saying, 'this country is at war with Germany.' Ever since the sirens had gone off in April they'd been prepared, even as they went about their business trying to convince themselves nothing would happen. But it was still a shock when it was finally announced.

Daisy switched the wireless off and they gazed at each other in the silence.

'Jimmy,' Daisy said, her hand over her mouth. 'He'll have to go.'

Abby wondered how she could have been so thoughtless, so taken up with her own worries, never giving a thought to what war would mean. Young men like Jimmy would be sent abroad to fight, maybe to die. And Joe. She couldn't bear it if anything happened to Joe.

'What will happen now?' she asked.

'Haven't a clue where Jimmy will be sent. I hope he gets leave beforehand. And maybe Joe's ship will be recalled.'

Abby stood up. 'I'd better go. Dad'll be wanting a meal when he gets home, war or no war.'

'Still behaving himself, is he?'

'He got the sack from Shippam's but at least he's working — labouring on the new houses at Parklands. Don't know for how long, though.'

7

'Oh, Joe, why don't you write?' Abby murmured as once more the postman passed Tanner's Court without turning into the twitten. He hadn't got home for Christmas after all and she hadn't heard from him for ages. Despite the rationing and the blackout, it was hard to accept that the country was at war. Nothing seemed to be happening and Joe's infrequent letters didn't tell her much. In a way, that was even worse than knowing he was fighting in some battle somewhere, and she was worried sick.

Missing Joe wasn't the only reason for her misery. Dad wasn't working and this time it wasn't his fault. It was the worst winter for years and building on the new housing estate had stopped. Wally had been laid off and, with only her wages to live on, she was forced to stay at The Emporium. She didn't think she could stand it much longer.

It was all right while they were busy. But after the rush of customers wanting blackout curtaining, things slackened off. There was a shortage of goods and even rumours of clothes rationing. At this rate she wouldn't have a job either.

The bitterly cold weather dragged on but she was getting used to numb fingers and toes. She didn't dare go into the stockroom to warm up in case Mr Wheeler caught her alone in there. Since his assault all those months ago he hadn't put a foot wrong. But every time she looked round he seemed to be there, staring at her with that strange expression, half-smile, half-sneer.

One morning at the end of February she found it even harder to drag herself out of bed. It was so cold there were feathers of frost on the inside of her bedroom window and as she threw back the blankets, she shivered as her feet touched the lino. It was only the thought of a letter from Joe that got her moving. When she got downstairs the range had gone out and she cursed as she tried to get it going again. They'd almost run out of coal and goodness knows when there'd be another delivery. The fuel shortage only added to her misery. She'd come home from work yesterday to find Dad chopping up one of the chairs to burn.

She put the kettle on and glanced at the clock. She didn't want to be late and give Mr Wheeler an excuse to call her into his office.

Thoughts of her boss vanished when the

postman arrived. Her heart hammered and her mouth was dry as she tore the letter open. Was Joe back in port? She wasn't expecting him.

Good news — for us, if not for the ship. We've got engine trouble and are back for repairs. We could be here for a few weeks. I might be able to get a few hours shore leave in a day or two so will get the train to Chichester. Not sure what day or time so I will come to the shop. I can't wait to see you my dearest Abby — until then fondest love, Joe.

Abby crushed the flimsy sheet of paper to her breast and pirouetted round the room. 'Oh, Joe,' she whispered. She folded the letter carefully and tucked it into the pocket of her skirt. As she combed her hair and got ready for work she hummed a few bars of *'I've got my love to keep me warm'* which she'd heard on the wireless a few days ago.

As she opened the door, her father stumbled downstairs, yawning and scratching. He glared at the mound of bread, the pot of plum jam beside the plate. 'No butter? Is this all I get for me breakfast, girl? And what about a cup of tea, eh?'

'Sorry, Dad. The range was out. The kettle

will soon boil now I've got it going again.'

Her father didn't reply but gave her a sour look as he slumped into a chair. Abby wanted to tell him he was lucky to get anything at all since he wasn't working. Besides, he always managed to find a few coppers for a pint. It was her wages as well as her thriftiness that put food on the table. And *she* had to make do with just a couple of jam sandwiches for her dinner. But she was so happy at the prospect of seeing Joe she refused to let him upset her.

She made her escape, still humming as she stumbled over the mounds of frozen snow. It had been lovely earlier that morning, the sun catching the weathercock on the spire of the cathedral and glancing diamond-like sparkles off the frosty ground. But now the clouds had rolled in and she knew there was more snow on the way.

As she turned the corner she waved to Miss Crocker, who was taking her blackout curtain down. It was a reminder of the war and Abby's stomach churned. It had only just occurred to her why Joe's ship might have returned. Had it been damaged in a battle? And was Joe really all right?

Chiding herself for her foolish thoughts, she turned into South Street. But the sight of Mr Wheeler unlocking the shop door sent a shiver through her. What was it about her that made him think he could take liberties with her?

As she unwound the woollen scarf her grandmother had knitted her for Christmas and hung her hat and coat up before starting work, Abby knew she should be happy. Joe was coming home.

'Looks like more snow,' Charlie said as she went through the shop to the haberdashery department. 'How about going sledging up on the Downs on Sunday?'

'I don't think so, Charlie.' Abby glanced out of the window, hoping he was wrong. The bad weather had already played havoc with the trains. More snow could stop them altogether. She couldn't bear it if, after the excitement of getting his letter, Joe got stuck in Portsmouth. She fingered the letter in her pocket, reassured by the crackle of the paper. He'd make it, he had to.

★　★　★

The snow started in late morning and the number of customers dwindled as the day wore on. Abby was still determined to find another job, although she was happier since she been transferred to the haberdashery department. She loved the bright ribbons and trimmings and helping the customers to choose. But when things were slow, as they were today, she had too much time to think.

Charlie caught her eye through the archway separating their departments, trying to make her laugh, pulling faces behind Mr Lever's back. But today she wasn't in the mood for his antics. She was too excited about the coming reunion with Joe. She longed for another customer to come through the door to help the time pass more quickly.

Even the demanding Lady Mayoress, with her plummy voice and consciousness of her imagined importance, would have been a welcome break in the tedium. Not that Abby was idle. There were shelves to be tidied, the counter to be polished but these were mind-numbing jobs. Sometimes it was almost like being in service again. At least she'd been able to chat and laugh with the other servants, especially when the Grishams were away in London. How much happier and simpler life had been then. But then, she reflected, as she felt the letter in her pocket, if she'd stayed at the Manor she'd never have met Joe.

By mid-afternoon the snow had settled several inches deep, covering the icy mounds that had lain there for weeks. The lights had been on since midday, reflecting off the smooth whiteness, undisturbed by vehicle or pedestrian for the past half an hour. The fishmonger across the road had already rolled down his shutters when Mr Wheeler came in and addressed the staff. 'I'm going to close the shop now as it seems unlikely we'll do any more business today. However, I expect every one of you to be here on time in the morning — whatever the weather.'

Most of the staff had left by the time Abby had tidied her counter and got her coat and scarf from the back room. Miss Davies, who was in charge of the lingerie department, was still there and Mr Wheeler jiggled his keys impatiently as the older woman adjusted her hat and drew on a pair of kid gloves.

'Miss Davies, I believe the buses have stopped running and I can't expect you to walk to Fishbourne in this weather. I'll take you in the car — you too, Miss Cookson.'

'Oh, no, Mr Wheeler. The snow's not too deep yet,' Abby protested.

'Nonsense, you'll be frozen walking home through this.'

Miss Davies chipped in. 'Don't be silly, girl. Mr Wheeler's being kind. Get in.' She climbed into the back of the big black Humber waiting at the kerb.

Abby got in beside her although Mr Wheeler had opened the front passenger door. She wouldn't sit beside him. This was her first ever ride in a car and she should have been thrilled. Instead, she hunched in her seat, dreading the moment when Miss Davies got out and she'd be alone with her boss.

After several tries the car inched its way forward, Mr Wheeler leaning forward and peering through the fogged up windscreen. As they reached the main road out of town there was more traffic and the going was easier. It seemed no time before the car stopped outside the little cottage where Miss Davies lived with her elderly mother.

When she got out, Mr Wheeler turned round and smiled. 'Why don't you come and sit in the front? I've got the heater on.'

His smile sent a tremor through her and she shrank even further into her seat, shaking her head. 'I'm all right, thank you, sir. It's not far.'

Mr Wheeler shook his head and started the car again. He seemed to be concentrating on driving. But Abby felt trapped, as if they were the only two people in this quiet white world.

'There's no need to be nervous, my dear. I'll make sure you get home safely.' It was as if he'd read her thoughts. But he was referring to the driving conditions. 'The weather's not as bad as it seems. I've had the car out in far worse than this.' It was as if he'd forgotten their encounter a few months ago. Abby didn't answer.

He spoke again, his voice mild, kind even. 'I've been thinking, my dear. Since my wife's illness, you've done very well in dealing with the customers. It's time you were rewarded for your efforts. There'll be a little extra in your pay packet next week.'

'Thank you, sir,' she whispered. She should have been feeling elated but a rise in pay would never be enough to make her stay at The Emporium once she'd found another job.

The car was travelling slowly, but surely they were near home by now? She peered through the window but couldn't see anything through the blinding snow.

The car lurched and Mr Wheeler muttered a curse, wrenching on the steering wheel as it veered across the road. It skidded to a halt and Abby was thrown forward, her face hitting the seat in front of her. She tried to sit up but another jolt threw her back into the seat.

Dazed, she touched the bump on her forehead. A warm trickle touched her lip and she realized her nose was bleeding. The door beside her opened and Mr Wheeler leaned in.

'Are you all right?' He sounded genuinely concerned.

Abby nodded and the movement brought a wave of nausea.

He reached out and touched her knee, his fingers squeezing and kneading. 'Are you sure?' His hand moved up her thigh, pushing her skirt up. She scrambled back, squeezing herself into the far corner of the seat.

'What are you doing? I told you, I'm all right.' But her voice trembled.

He swore under his breath and climbed into the car. 'Come on, Abby, don't be shy.' His voice was hoarse as he loomed over her and fastened his wet mouth over hers, his hands tearing at her clothes. His strength belied his slight frame and she knew that this time she couldn't fight him off.

She screamed, hoping someone would hear. As he clamped his hand over her mouth, she tried to bite him. He gave a harsh laugh. 'Little vixen, aren't you?'

With one hand she fought him, while the other fumbled for the door handle behind her. If only she could get away. Darkness had fallen but there was a faint glow from a house nearby. Surely someone would help her?

She struggled harder but he was on top of her now, pressing her body into the seat. What was the use of fighting, she thought, closing her eyes and letting herself go limp. 'That's better, my dear. Just lie back and enjoy it,' he murmured. 'You know you want to really.'

His words fuelled her anger and she began to struggle again. But she was trapped, her hands now held behind her head with an iron grip.

She cried out as a searing pain tore through her, but he stifled her scream with a hand across her mouth. She resisted him to the end but it was no use. At last he pushed himself away and began to adjust his clothing. She slid off the seat and crouched on the floor, sobbing. The door was still open, swinging in the wind. But Abby was scarcely aware of the stinging snow on her bare legs as she tried to fasten her clothes.

He gazed down at her impassively. 'No need to make such a fuss. It's what girls like you expect.'

A voice called out of the darkness. 'Everyone all right there?'

Mr Wheeler hastily straightened, pulling his coat closed. He reached across and held out a hand. 'Are you hurt?' he said, his voice oozing concern.

A face peered over his shoulder, holding up a hurricane lamp. 'What happened?'

Relief flooded through her as she recognized Joe's Uncle Dan.

'Bit of a skid. I'm afraid Miss Cookson

took a tumble,' said Mr Wheeler.

She scrambled out of the car. 'Oh, Mr Leighton, I was so scared,' she sobbed.

'Abby, is that you? Sure you're all right? You look a bit shaken.'

Dan helped her out of the car. The Humber was on the wrong side of the road, half in the ditch. Her teeth began to chatter and Dan put his arm around her.

'Well, you won't get that going in a hurry,' he said. 'Good job I came along. You could have been stranded here all night. What were you doing out this way?'

Mr Wheeler retrieved his hat from the floor of the car and glanced round as if perplexed to find himself in a quiet country lane. 'I was taking my employees home. The buses had stopped and I couldn't expect them to walk in this weather. I dropped Miss Davies off in Fishbourne — must have taken a wrong turn.'

'I've got my cart and old Gertie here. We'll see you home all right.' Dan helped Abby up on to the seat at the front of the cart. 'You'll have to ride with the empty churns, Mr Wheeler.'

Abby was still shivering and Dan tucked a piece of sacking over her knees and put his arm round her. He clucked encouragingly and Gertie began to plod through the snow.

'Soon have you home in the warm,' Dan said.

Abby couldn't speak, she couldn't even cry, although huge sobs were lodged in her throat waiting to erupt. She clenched her teeth, trying to wipe out the memory of her boss's hands tearing at her clothes, his slobbering mouth, and — worst of all — his bare flesh against hers as he pulled up her skirt and undid his trousers. If only Dan had come along a bit sooner.

They reached the big house at the top of Broyle Road and Mr Wheeler climbed down from the cart. He hadn't spoken a word as the horse lumbered slowly up the hill. Now he muttered a brief word of thanks.

Dan touched his cap. 'Glad to oblige,' he said and jerked on the reins.

As the cart moved off, Wheeler called out. 'Miss Cookson — if the weather's as bad as this tomorrow, don't worry about coming in to work.'

Abby didn't reply. It was just like last time. He was acting as if nothing had happened. She had to tell someone, though. But if she told her father, he'd be straight round to The Emporium spoiling for a fight and causing yet more scandal. Abby couldn't bear the thought.

Maybe she could confide in Dan. He'd always been kind to her. But the thought filled her with shame. That was if he believed her. And suppose Joe got to hear of it? He wouldn't want to know her.

The trembling grew more violent and Dan tucked the sack more securely round her. 'Sure you're all right? Must have been frightening getting into a skid like that. Lucky the car didn't hit a tree,' he said. 'Still, it was good of your boss to give you a lift. And to give you the day off tomorrow. Most would insist on you turning up, even if there was six feet of snow.' He nodded. 'Yes, good man, Ernest Wheeler. Respected. Devoted to his poor wife too, I hear.'

Abby clasped her arms across her breasts, trembling again. She was right. No one would believe that a respected businessman, a pillar of the Chapel, would do such a thing.

★ ★ ★

The cottage was in darkness. Thank God her father wasn't home. Abby closed the door and leaned against it, breathing heavily. She lit the gas light and riddled the embers of the range, pulling the kettle over the flames. When the water was warm, she locked the door before taking off her torn blouse and skirt and washing herself all over. Careless of the bruises on her breasts and thighs, she scrubbed at the places where Ernest Wheeler's flesh had touched hers. Would she ever feel clean again?

Too late, she realized she should have confided in Mr Leighton. He'd seen her distress but had assumed she was shaken up by the car crash. Would he have believed her? Could she go round and tell Gran? No. She'd be even less likely to accept that the respected lay preacher was capable of such a thing. She would imply that Abby had encouraged him. As if she would, Abby thought with a shudder.

She crept upstairs to bed, shivering as she hugged the thin blankets around her shoulders. But it wasn't the cold that caused her to shudder. Her body was sore and aching and every time she closed her eyes she relived those moments in the car. If only Dan Leighton had come along earlier.

She should have been excited, anticipating Joe's homecoming. Tears of anger choked her. That man had spoiled her for Joe. Things would never be the same between them now.

What had she done to deserve this? She felt a momentary flicker of doubt. Had Wheeler's taunts been justified? Was she just like her mother? Was her flirting with Charlie as innocent as she liked to believe?

Well, she wouldn't be seeing Charlie again

and she wouldn't return to The Emporium, no matter how hard up they were. She'd have to try for a job at the laundry. It wasn't a pleasant prospect, Abby thought, picturing Daisy's chapped red hands. But anything would be better than risking another assault.

As she tossed and turned in bed and the sky grew light beyond the window, Abby wondered if she should confront Mr Wheeler, threaten to tell someone what he'd done if he ever attempted to molest her again. She'd have to go to the shop tomorrow if only to collect her pay. For despite her earlier defiant thought, she knew she couldn't afford not to, especially with Dad laid off indefinitely.

She turned over, trying to get warm, trying harder still to blot out the memory of her employer's groping hands, that *thing* pressing into her, tearing at her flesh.

She couldn't sleep and, with a sigh, she got out of bed and went across to the window, ignoring the icy linoleum under her feet. She knelt and looked out at the snow-covered scene, made magical by the glow of the full moon. The ugly tumbledown cottages and broken cobbled yard of Tanner's Court looked like something out of a child's picture book. She lifted the lid of the box where she kept her pitifully few treasures and took out the bundle of Joe's letters.

She couldn't make out the writing in the dim moonlight but she knew them all by heart anyway. She clutched the pages to her breast, sighing. She'd been so looking forward to seeing Joe, but how could she face him now?

As she put the letters away and got back into her cold bed, she told herself firmly that Joe loved her, he would understand.

★　★　★

The sound of scraping shovels clearing the frozen snow woke Abby next morning. It was still bitterly cold, despite the bright sunlight streaming through the thin curtains. Usually, she loved the snow which reminded her of childhood days before her mother disappeared, when they'd go to the park and play snowballs or slide down the Castle mound on makeshift toboggans. Today, she shivered and snuggled down in bed — and it wasn't just because of the weather.

Reluctant as she was to face Mr Wheeler, she had to collect her pay. Then she'd go and see Daisy and ask if they needed anyone at the laundry. She didn't know what she'd do if not. How would they eat or pay the rent if she was out of work too?

She sighed and dragged herself out of bed.

Downstairs she raked out the ashes from last night's fire, scattering them on the slippery path leading to the privy.

She prepared breakfast and called up the stairs to her father.

'Let a man sleep, can't you?' he grumbled.

Abby didn't reply. Let him stay in bed — she couldn't face him anyway. Later, she got Joe's letter out and read it again. Her spirits rose. He was coming home and she'd make the most of every moment with him. She wouldn't tell him what had happened. That pathetic, slimy old man couldn't be allowed to ruin her life.

She decided to wait till dinner time before going to the shop. Mr Wheeler usually gave out the wage packets then. She'd take her money and tell him she wasn't coming back.

It was the longest morning Abby could remember although she tried to keep busy, moving quietly so as not to disturb her father.

When she reached The Emporium there was no one about except Charlie, who came out of the stockroom when he heard the shop bell go. 'Where you been?' he asked.

'I didn't feel well,' Abby lied.

'Don't know why you bothered,' Charlie said. He told her that several of the staff who lived outside Chichester hadn't turned up and the weather had kept the customers away.

'I was hoping the boss would send us home,' he said. 'But he hasn't come in yet. Hope he turns up soon with our wages.'

'That's all I've come for,' Abby said and Charlie laughed.

'Cheeky thing,' he said.

Abby didn't feel like joining in the laughter and she got a duster from under the counter. 'Might as well do some work now I'm here.'

'What's up, Abby? Not your usual smiling self today,' he said.

She forced a smile. 'Nothing — just fed up with the weather, that's all.'

'Well, cheer up. It's starting to thaw already.' He leaned forward. 'How about coming to the pictures on Saturday?'

As she started to shake her head he grinned. 'Don't worry — no strings. Bring your friend if you like.'

'I'm sorry, Charlie. I've already made plans.'

His face fell. 'Another bloke, I s'pose?'

Abby felt herself colouring. 'Joe might be home. The ship's back in port — engine trouble.'

'And then he'll be gone again. Come to that, I might be gone myself. Expecting my call up any day now. Thought you might take pity on a bloke going off to war.' He spoke lightly but his expression was serious, not the usual happy-go-lucky Charlie she knew.

'I'll miss you,' she said. It was true.

'Really?' He grinned and grabbed her by the shoulders. 'One for luck,' he said, kissing her cheek.

Abby pulled away and came face to face with Mr Wheeler. He stared at her, a thoughtful expression in his narrowed eyes. But he only said, 'Your wages, Miss Cookson,' and handed her the small brown envelope.

She grabbed it and rushed through the shop to get her coat. There was no way she'd stay. Mr Wheeler had seen Charlie kiss her and he'd use that to justify his opinion of her. She was a slut who deserved everything she got and he'd seize the first chance he could to assault her again.

She peeped round the door, and, seeing him deep in conversation with Mr Lever, she crept through the shop. But as she reached the main entrance the bell jangled and someone came in.

'Finished work already?' he said.

Abby gasped. 'Joe,' she whispered. 'Is it really you?' She couldn't believe he was really there, slim and fit in his tight-fitting uniform, his face bronzed from the Mediterranean sun, his cap at a jaunty angle on his sun-bleached hair.

He laughed and grabbed her hands, pulling her towards him in a fierce embrace.

'Miss Cookson. I will not have this sort of behaviour in my establishment.'

Mr Wheeler had appeared, his face white, eyes burning as he faced Abby and shouted, 'Get on with your work, girl.'

Joe let go of her. 'Sorry, sir. Just got home. Our ship got banged up a bit and I had to let Abby — Miss Cookson — know I was all right.'

'Couldn't it wait till after closing time?' He turned to Abby, noticing she had her coat on. 'Did I say you could leave early?'

'I'm going anyway.' Her voice was defiant although her legs were trembling.

Mr Wheeler grabbed her wrist, pulling her close to him. His eyes blazed in his white face and he spoke in a low voice. 'Going out with sailors, flirting with my staff — not the little innocent you pretend to be are you, miss?' He pushed her away roughly.

Abby's stomach lurched. Had Joe heard him? She was so angry she didn't care. Drawing herself up, she looked him in the eye. 'I've done nothing wrong, Mr Wheeler. And I know you've nothing to complain about as far as my work's concerned. Besides, I don't work here any more.' She grabbed Joe's arm and almost dragged him out of the shop.

Outside, Joe put his arms round her. 'I'm sorry, Abby. I didn't mean to get you into trouble.' He gazed into her eyes, bent his head and kissed her lips. 'I've waited for this moment for so long,' he said as he released her.

She clung to him, tears threatening to overwhelm her. He was really here. But how could she let him kiss her, make love to her as if nothing had happened? She couldn't confide in him, nor could she pretend nothing had happened.

'Abby, you're shaking. Did you really mean to walk out?' Joe's face creased in concern.

She nodded. 'I've been meaning to leave for ages.'

'What will you do?'

'I'm going to try for the laundry — or I might join the forces.' She forced a laugh. 'Can you see me in WRNS uniform?'

Joe took her arm and they began to walk towards the Cross. 'If that's what you want. I suppose all the girls will be joining up now. There's posters all over Pompey.'

'Better than waiting to be called up and maybe sent to a munitions factory miles away.' She squeezed his hand. 'Let's not talk about me. I want to hear what you've been up to.'

'Can't tell you much — not allowed. But as

you see, I'm still in one piece.'

The words were spoken lightly but Abby could tell he had been through a lot since they'd last met.

He pulled her into the shelter of the Cross and kissed her again. The months since they'd last met faded away. His smile was the same, his firm yet gentle lips on hers were the same, and the feelings she'd had when they'd last been together were welling up all over again. For a moment she was able to put that dreadful experience out of her mind.

Joe gave an exaggerated shiver. 'Let's get out of the cold. Where shall we go, Abby?'

She couldn't think. Impossible to take him home. She didn't want Joe to meet her father yet. And if he was out, her grandmother was sure to find out they'd been alone in the house and she'd never hear the last of it.

'We could go to the pictures,' she said. 'It'll be warm in there.'

Joe laughed. 'I'd ask what's on but I don't think it matters. I have no intention of watching the film anyway.' He took her hand and they ran, splashing through icy puddles of slushy snow, arriving breathless with laughter at the old Corn Exchange in East Street which had been converted into a cinema a couple of years before.

The film was *The Prisoner of Zenda* which

Abby had already seen with Rhoda a few days earlier. The first time she'd seen it she'd cried when the lovers put duty before love in a bittersweet parting. This time she was hardly aware that the film had finished, snuggled down in the back row with Joe's arm round her, while they caught up with each other's news in a whispered conversation that had the people in front turning round to hush them from time to time. Between whispers, Joe stroked her hair and kissed her eyes, her neck, her lips until she thought she would drown in his love.

When the lights went up and the strains of *God Save the King* echoed round the auditorium, she stood to attention like everyone else. But it was as if she was waking from a dream as she followed the shuffling crowds out into the cold street. She was suddenly aware of her dishevelled hair, hoping no one she knew had been in the cinema and seen how she was carrying on. Her face burned as she recalled her boss's insinuating words. But this was different, she told herself. She loved Joe, and besides, they'd done nothing wrong.

'I suppose I ought to see you home now,' Joe said. 'Not that I want to leave you so soon.'

'When do you have to go back?' Abby

dreaded the answer.

'I have to report for duty first thing in the morning so I ought to get the last train back to Portsmouth. Let's get some fish and chips and I'll walk you home. There's plenty of time.'

'I'll walk to the station with you, see you on the train,' Abby said. 'I want to spend every minute with you.'

Joe wasn't too keen on her walking home alone in the blackout but Abby laughed and said she'd be quite safe.

'You sure?'

Abby nodded. She couldn't tell him she was in more danger at the shop than in the streets.

In the end he gave in and they bought fish and chips, then wandered down South Street to the railway station. The seats in the waiting room weren't very comfortable but it was cosy with the coke stove in the corner. They sat close together on the bench toasting their toes in front of it. There were more kisses but they tried not to get carried away, aware that a porter or the station master could come in to see what they were up to.

After one particularly breathless kiss, Joe pulled away with a wry laugh. 'God, Abby, you don't know what you're doing to me. You're such an innocent.'

She wasn't as innocent as he thought, especially after what had happened with Mr Wheeler. The thought made her shudder. It wasn't the same at all. She loved Joe — that made all the difference. She sat up straight and pulled her coat together, hoping he couldn't read her thoughts.

Joe glanced at his watch and she knew they didn't have much more time.

'I wish you didn't have to go,' she said.

'So do I.' He laughed. 'God knows when we'll be together again.'

'Do you know where you're going?'

'Not yet. I'll write as often as I can,' Joe said, putting his finger under her chin and looking into her eyes.

Abby responded to his kiss. 'While you're away I feel like I'm in a dream. I keep telling myself we've only met a few times. How could we possibly know . . . ?' Her voice trailed off.

Joe took her hand. 'But I do know, Abby. I think about you all the time. And I worry that you'll meet someone else.'

'There's no one else but you, Joe. And there never will be,' she whispered. It was true. But she wondered if he'd feel the same about her if he ever found out.

The noise of the level-crossing gates clanging shut and a distant bell warned them the train was approaching. Joe kissed her again and they hurried on to the platform. Smoke and steam engulfed them as the engine puffed into the station. Abby threw her arms round Joe. 'I love you. I don't want you to go,' she sobbed.

Joe kissed her and opened the carriage door, turning for another kiss before climbing aboard. The guard blew his whistle. Doors slammed and Abby stood with tears pouring down her face as the train pulled away. Joe leaned out of the window, waving until the train rounded the curve towards the Fishbourne junction.

The churned-up snow was turning to ice again but Abby didn't notice the cold as she trudged up South Street towards the Cross. Her feelings were in turmoil — sadness at Joe's leaving combined with joy in the knowledge that he returned her love, that she hadn't been deceiving herself all this time. But most of all she felt guilty.

Joe had pulled away before things went too far but she knew what he'd wanted. She'd wanted it too. She felt cold at the thought of Joe finding out that she wasn't as innocent as he thought. But surely it was different when you were in love. She refused to believe that her feelings for Joe were wrong.

8

Abby woke the next morning smiling at the memory of the magical evening she'd spent with Joe. Nothing could take that away from her. She scarcely noticed the cold as she swung her legs out of bed. But as she stood up her bruised and sore body brought back that other memory.

Well, she'd never see that man again if she could help it. Gran could say what she liked, she wouldn't be going to chapel again.

Daisy would be on her side. The little woman hated the Wheelers for their unfeeling treatment of her when her husband had died.

As she hurried across town to the little row of cottages backing on to the River Lavant, she realized that she should have taken Daisy's advice and left The Emporium long ago. And she should have told her about Mr Wheeler's behaviour too. But she'd been so afraid of not being believed. Everyone thought he was such a respectable family man, a pillar of the chapel.

Could she bring herself to tell Daisy what had happened? Abby cringed at the thought — she'd have to relive the whole sordid ordeal. She didn't think she could do it. Besides, what would be the point of telling her? She couldn't do anything about it.

She decided she'd just ask about the job.

Daisy was busy with housework but she seemed pleased to have an excuse to sit down for a chat. They talked about Charlie getting called up, and Joe's brief visit. But not about the thing that was uppermost in Abby's mind.

The conversation died and Daisy looked at her intently. 'I thought you'd be bubbling over, seeing Joe yesterday. I know you didn't have long together but it's better than nothing.'

This was the moment to speak up. But Abby couldn't find the words. 'I had a lovely time — but I wish he didn't have to go. It was bad enough before, him always being away. But now, I worry all the time. Not knowing where he is . . . ' She broke off with a sob. Talking about Joe was hard. Would he still want her after what had happened? Men were funny like that. Well, she'd make sure he never found out. She shook her head as Daisy laid a sympathetic hand on her arm. 'I just wish he was here.'

'It's hard, I know. I worry about Jimmy too.'

'Oh, Daisy. I'm so selfish, thinking of myself. Have you heard from him?'

'Not for a while.' Daisy patted her hand. 'We'll just have to do what women always do, love — wait and pray.'

Abby didn't think she'd be much good at the last two. She was about to say so but she caught a wistful expression on her friend's face and cursed herself for her thoughtlessness. Poor Daisy had gone through it all in the last war and, although Bert had come back, he hadn't been the same man. Her father, too . . .

She sighed and changed the subject. 'I've left Wheeler's,' she said. 'Do they still need people at the laundry?'

'Thought you weren't interested. What brought this on? Old Wheeler's not giving you trouble is he?'

Abby started. Had she guessed? She almost blurted it out but Daisy went on, 'He can be a bit of a stickler, I know, being chapel and all. So what is it, love? Just ready for a change, are you?'

The moment for confession was past and Abby convinced herself that Daisy wouldn't have believed her anyway. She shook her head. 'It's Charlie,' she said. 'He won't take no for an answer — and now he's trying to make me feel sorry for him 'cause he's going to be called up soon . . . ' It was true enough. She was getting fed up with Charlie's pestering, even if it was done in a light-hearted friendly way.

'You sure you want to work in the laundry, though? It's not everyone's cup of tea, although the money's not bad.'

Abby nodded. 'I thought about joining one of the women's forces. But I could be sent a long way away and I might not be able to see Joe when he's on leave.'

'All right,' Daisy said, 'I'll talk to Mr Peterson on Monday, then.'

★   ★   ★

Abby was waiting outside the double gates to the City Electric Laundry when Daisy finished work on Monday. It was a huge building on the outskirts of town, employing almost fifty people. Abby felt a bit nervous at the thought of working there; it was so different from her previous jobs. But it was work at least.

Her eyes lit up when Daisy said, 'You're in luck. One of the girls is leaving to have a baby and they need a replacement.'

'When can I start?'

'Come in tomorrow morning at nine.'

'I'll be there.'

Daisy held out her rough, reddened hands. 'You sure you want to end up like this?' she asked. 'You could get a better job — in another shop, maybe?'

'I'm quite sure.'

Daisy laid a hand on Abby's arm. 'Is there something you haven't told me?'

Abby shook her head, biting her lip.

'You didn't get the sack? Was it something to do with Charlie?'

'No, honestly, Daisy, I wasn't sacked.' At least she was telling the truth about that. 'I just had enough — and maybe Charlie will realize that I mean what I say if I keep out of his way.'

★   ★   ★

The snow had almost gone and spring was on the way. Abby was getting on quite well at the laundry although the work was hard and the hours long. But at least the other girls were friendly. They had the wireless on all the time, listening to 'Workers' Playtime' and 'Music While You Work' and sometimes she even found herself singing along with them.

Her hands were already red and chapped from constant immersion in hot water. She didn't care — at least she felt safe here. But she wondered what Joe would think when he came home on leave — if he ever did now that the phoney war seemed to be over at last.

Well, the sooner they got on with it, the sooner it would be over and Joe would be home again. Could she put that dreadful night in the snow behind her and carry on as if nothing had happened?

Although the memory was beginning to fade, there were times when it came back to her in a rush. When Norman Peterson, the manager, had leaned close to clear the rollers on the mangle, she'd recoiled, her breath coming in gasps.

Daisy noticed and called out, 'You OK, Abby?'

She pulled herself together and managed to nod. 'Just a bit hot in here,' she said.

Since then she'd stopped being nervous of Mr Peterson, who kept watch on the workers from his glass cubicle in the corner. He seldom interrupted the women unless one of the machines broke down. They all liked him and she soon learned she had nothing to fear. She shouldn't think everyone was like Mr Wheeler.

During her second week, Maggie, the supervisor, stopped beside her as she was filling the big boiler with sheets from the barracks and asked how she was getting on.

'All right I think, except for these.' Abby smiled and held out her hands.

'Goes with the job, I'm afraid,' Maggie

said. 'Try Vaseline — put it on before you start work, not after.'

It seemed to help and Abby began to think life wasn't so bad after all. The memory of Wheeler's assault was beginning to fade and, if it hadn't been for her worry about Joe, she'd have been happy despite the rationing and the constant wail of the air-raid siren.

★　★　★

One sunny Sunday in spring, Gran knocked on the door, Bible in hand. 'No excuses, miss. You haven't showed your face for weeks.'

Despite her resolution never to set foot in chapel again, Abby couldn't wriggle out of it. 'Is Mr Wheeler preaching today, Gran?' she asked, hoping she'd be spared his tirades about Jezebel and the 'whore of Babylon'.

'I don't think so.'

Her relief was short-lived and she cringed when he got up to speak. How she wished she was brave enough to stand up and denounce him in front of the congregation. His hell-fire sermons seemed the more hypocritical now that she knew what he was capable of.

She kept her head bent, trying to look devout, rereading Joe's latest letter which she'd secreted between the pages of her Bible. It was the only way to shut out the wicked thoughts of what she'd like to do to Mr Wheeler. She wasn't sure whether Gran was fooled by her piety but she didn't comment.

Outside, the black-hatted heads bobbed up and down as the chapel ladies discussed the sermon. 'He's right you know — plastered with make-up, showing their legs,' said one.

'Asking for trouble, if you ask me,' Gran said, pursing her lips and looking at Abby.

Abby couldn't help it. 'What about the men?' she burst out.

They turned as one, shock etched on their faces.

'What did you say?' Aggie Thompson's face flushed red.

'What about the men? Why don't they resist this temptation you're on about? It's not the girls' fault if the men try it on. But it's always their fault if they get into trouble.'

'Well, it's obvious you don't heed what the preacher says.' Mrs Spencer looked Abby up and down, taking in her short dress, bare legs and arms. She turned to Aggie. 'I think you should teach your granddaughter to have more respect.'

Abby realized she'd gone too far when her grandmother grabbed her arm and dragged her away.

'How could you humiliate me like that?' She dug her fingers into Abby's arm, berating her as they walked. 'Isn't it enough that I have to live down the scandal of your mother, without you carrying on as if you're going the same way.'

'But I haven't done anything wrong,' Abby protested.

They stopped outside the cottage in Cross Street and Aggie swung Abby round to face her. 'What about that sailor? And the lad at Wheeler's? I've heard all about your goings-on. You'll come to a bad end, my girl.' Aggie didn't have to add 'just like your mother'.

The words hovered in the air and Abby felt tears well up, as always when her mother's reputation was called into question. 'You think I'm like Mum. Well, she's your daughter, Gran. How can you think so badly of her? Haven't you ever thought she might have had a reason?'

'She broke her marriage vows. 'For better, for worse' should mean just that.' Aggie's mouth set in a thin line and she walked up her garden path, her shoulders rigid.

Abby sighed and turned away. In a way her grandmother was right. She too believed in the marriage vows, and she knew in her heart that if she and Joe ever got wed nothing on earth would make her leave him — whatever the provocation. But then, Joe would never carry on like her dad, getting drunk and smashing the place up.

★ ★ ★

Daisy had invited her for tea and by the time she reached the cottage she was feeling sorry she'd upset Gran. But it was so hard to bite her tongue sometimes, especially where Ernest Wheeler was concerned. Why couldn't anyone see what he was really like?

She felt better the minute her friend opened the door and said, 'I've got the kettle on, love.'

She couldn't help laughing. 'You've always got the kettle on.'

'Well, you never know who might pop in,' Daisy said, ushering her into the kitchen, which smelled of fresh baking.

Daisy pushed a plate of rock buns towards Abby. 'Go on, have one — fresh out of the oven.'

Abby bit into the cake, glad she hadn't gone back to Gran's house after chapel. Aggie Thompson didn't believe in working on the Lord's Day and that included any kind of cooking. Thinking about her grandmother recalled their conversation and her eyes clouded.

Daisy leaned forward and touched her arm.

'What is it, love? Dad upset you again?'

Abby shook her head. 'I had a bit of a set to with Gran — you know what she's like.'

Daisy nodded. 'She can be a bit sharp.'

'She was going on about my mother — saying I'd go the same way. She won't believe Joe and me haven't done anything wrong.'

'I'm sure you haven't, love. Your gran just worries about you, that's all.'

'Anyway, I don't know why she takes any notice of those chapel people — hypocrites they are.'

★   ★   ★

The weather had turned very warm and the girls at the laundry were suffering from the heat. Abby had felt unwell for several days, but she refused to give in, determined not to be thought a slacker. If little Daisy could put in the hours without complaint, then she could too.

But she felt even worse as time went on. Despite telling herself it was the heat and the damp cloying smell of the steam making her feel sick she couldn't wait for six o'clock to come so that she could escape.

She fed the sheets from the rinsing tub through the mangle, stopping to pass a hand over her damp forehead. Her eyes blurred and her stomach heaved. She grasped the edge of the tub. 'This blasted heat,' she murmured, unaware that her words were slurred.

Daisy, working alongside her, turned with a smile. 'Soon be hometime,' she said. The smile faded and she took a step towards Abby. 'You all right, my duck?'

Abby tried to nod but her legs felt like jelly. When she came to she was sitting on a box in the yard, a crowd of anxious faces peering down at her — Daisy, Maggie, and Mr Peterson, who was flapping his hands and telling the other girls to get back to their work at once. 'It's not knocking off time yet,' he said. 'Besides, give the girl some air.'

Daisy knelt beside Abby, patting her hand and saying, 'Come on, love. It's just the heat.'

'Mrs Hill, you'd better get her home,' Mr Peterson said. 'And you, miss, don't come in tomorrow unless you feel better. Can't have girls fainting at their machines — too dangerous.' His voice was gruff but there was kindness is his brown eyes.

Abby scarcely remembered the long hot walk through the city streets, Daisy telling her she'd feel better once she was home with a nice cup of tea inside her. All she could hear was the voice in her head, praying, 'Please don't let it be true.' And then the despairing wail which at times she was sure she must have uttered aloud, 'Oh, Joe, how can you ever forgive me?' The other voice, that told her it wasn't her fault, refused to make itself heard.

When they reached Tanner's Court, Abby protested that she was all right. But Daisy didn't want to leave her.

'I'm all right, really. You go on back to work,' Abby said.

So Daisy said a reluctant goodbye and hurried through the twitten, glancing around warily before emerging into George Street. She didn't fancy running into Wally Cookson or she'd feel bound to give him a piece of her mind for his treatment of his only daughter. And that wouldn't help Abby.

Like most people in the town, Daisy knew of Wally's reputation. It was an old scandal that his bouts of drunken rage had driven his wife into the arms of another man. Even after all these years, speculation was rife as to who the man was. Still more of a mystery was why Carrie Cookson hadn't taken her daughter with her, leaving her to suffer Wally's unpredictable temper. And the poor girl was still suffering. Not that Wally was to blame for what had happened this afternoon. But still . . .

Daisy wasn't fooled by Abby's cheerful pose, her willingness to have 'a bit of a laugh' with her friends. She was pleased the girl had found a sweetheart, a steady fellow who seemed to return her feelings. Pity he was so far away though. Daisy sensed that Abby needed him here. Something was troubling her, more so than usual. And, after this afternoon's little drama, Daisy thought she knew what it was.

It wasn't in her nature to interfere and she'd given Abby ample opportunity to confide in her. Still, something had to be done and the girl had no mother to help her. Biting her lip, Daisy turned the corner into Cross Street and marched up to Aggie Thompson's front door.

When Aggie opened the door, her eyes narrowed suspiciously. 'Daisy Hill — to what do I owe this honour, then?' she asked.

Daisy forced herself to speak civilly. She knew Aggie Thompson blamed her for enticing Abby away from a 'good job' into the 'low company' of the laundry girls. Her opinions didn't matter — Abby did.

'I just came to tell you that your granddaughter was taken ill at work. I've taken her home and put her to bed, but I thought you ought to know.'

'What's wrong with her? Was it an

173

accident? I knew she should never have left Wheeler's to go and work in that place.'

At least Ma Thompson seemed genuinely worried, Daisy thought. She hesitated. Should she tell the old woman what she thought ailed the girl? It wasn't her business really. Still, she could drop a hint. Abby needed a woman at a time like this. 'It wasn't an accident. She fainted — the heat, she said. Maybe you should ask her yourself. She might talk to you — '

'Say what you mean, woman. What's wrong with her?' Aggie snapped.

'It's not my business. Ask her yourself,' Daisy said, regretting that she'd said anything at all. She backed away as Aggie pushed past her and hurried down the short front path.

'I know what you're hinting, but I don't believe it,' she snapped.

Daisy watched her go, praying she was wrong. But all the signs were there. She slowly began the long walk home, her heart heavy, wondering what would happen to the girl she had come to love like a daughter.

Oh well, it wasn't unusual even for well-brought-up girls to anticipate their wedding night — especially those as much in love as Abby was with her sailor. Pity he was so far away. It had to be Joe, Daisy told herself. There wasn't anyone else, was there?

But then Daisy remembered how anxious Abby had been to leave The Emporium. Surely she and Charlie hadn't . . . ?

★ ★ ★

The slamming of the front door woke Abby from an uneasy doze and she pulled the sheet over her head. She couldn't cope with her father's temper today. Maybe he'd think she was still at work.

She sat up when she heard her grandmother calling, followed by footsteps on the stairs. The bedroom door flew open and she shrank back as Aggie strode towards her. 'What've you been up to, girl?' She wagged an accusing finger in Abby's face. 'And don't lie to me. Young healthy girls don't faint just because of a bit of a heatwave.'

Abby knew it was no use protesting — her face had given her away. 'You don't understand, Gran. It wasn't my fault . . . ' Her voice trailed away and tears rained down her face.

'No use crying now the damage is done,' Aggie snapped. 'Who was it? That sailor, I suppose. I told you no good would come of it. Well, he'll have to marry you, like it or not. When's he due back?'

'It wasn't Joe,' Abby whispered.

'Well, who then? That Charlie Simmons, I suppose.' When Abby shook her head, still crying, she said, 'Don't tell me you don't know — oh, I just knew you'd go the same way as your mother. How many men have you been messing about with?'

Anger stopped the flow of tears and Abby sat up, swinging her legs out of bed and facing her grandmother defiantly. 'Don't talk about my mother like that — or me. You don't know a thing about it. It wasn't Joe or Charlie — and I haven't been messing about, as you call it.'

Aggie gave a coarse laugh. 'You don't get in that state by holding hands, my girl,' she said. 'So what are you going to do about it? You'll have to marry the lad, whoever he is.'

'I can't.'

'Can't? Won't, you mean.' Aggie's voice rose. 'What's got into you, girl? I made sure you went to chapel, taught you to be a respectable God-fearing — '

At that, Abby began to laugh hysterically. 'Oh yes, I went to chapel, listened to that *God-fearing* preacher. Why don't you ask him . . . ?'

Aggie grabbed the girl's shoulders and shook her. 'What do you mean — ask who?'

'Mr Ernest Wheeler, of course — that fine upstanding pillar of the chapel, respectable married man . . . ' Abby's laughter turned to deep, racking sobs.

Aggie made no move to comfort her. 'You wicked girl, to accuse him . . . You're just trying to cover up your own badness — '

'He's the wicked one. And I'm going to make sure everyone knows it.' Abby glared at her grandmother. 'The minister won't be asking him to preach by the time I've finished.'

'No, Abby, I don't believe it. And even if he did . . . ' Her voice faltered, regained strength. 'You must have led him on . . . '

'Oh, yes. It has to be my fault, doesn't it? I'm the bad girl — just like my mother.' Abby shoved her feet into her shoes and pushed past her grandmother. She grabbed her bag off the chest of drawers and ran downstairs. With no clear idea of where she was going, she ran out of Tanner's Court and through the maze of streets towards the park.

As she ran the fierce anger that had propelled her out of the house eased and she began to cry again. She sat on a bench in the corner of the park, hoping no one she knew would see her. Not that it mattered. Soon everyone would know of her disgrace — there were few secrets in this small town.

What was she to do, where could she go? Not home. Once her father knew, his anger would be even worse than Gran's. Aggie had hurt her with words — Dad would use his fists, his belt and even his boots — on her, not Mr Wheeler.

She shuddered and stood up. Crying wouldn't help. She wiped her tears away and found herself walking towards Daisy's cottage. She couldn't tell her friend what was wrong — she'd say she'd had a row with her dad. Daisy would let her stay. It would give her time to think and plan what to do. One thing was sure — she must leave Chichester before Joe returned. She couldn't bear to face him.

9

Daisy listened quietly without comment as Abby poured it all out, the story punctuated with shuddering sobs. At last she drew a shaky breath, accepted the hankie Daisy offered, blew her nose.

'Oh, Abby, why didn't you tell me before?'

'I was trying to pretend it hadn't happened,' Abby said. 'But then, when I realized . . . ' She gestured towards her waist and tears welled up again.

Daisy stood up and paced across the kitchen, sat down again. 'When you fainted I guessed what was wrong but I thought it was Joe — or maybe Charlie.'

Abby almost laughed until she realized Gran had jumped to the same conclusion. 'I would never be untrue to Joe — you know that.'

'Sorry, love. 'Course not. But who'd have dreamt . . . ?' She clenched her fists. 'He should be locked up — the evil swine.'

'I was ashamed. I couldn't help wondering if it was my fault . . . '

'Oh, love.' Daisy's arms came round her, patting her back. 'I wonder how many other girls he's ruined,' she said. 'I've a good mind to give him a piece of my mind.'

'No — I couldn't bear . . . ' Tears threatened once more. 'What am I going to do?'

'I'll think of something but first you need a good night's sleep. Go on, love — I keep the spare bed made up for Jimmy.'

She ushered Abby into the back bedroom and clucked around while Abby took off her skirt and blouse and slipped between the cool sheets in her underwear.

'Thank goodness that heat's let up a bit. Maybe we'll have some rain. I'll leave the window open, though. That's right, my duck, you settle down. I'll fetch you a nice cup of cocoa and one of my rock cakes — don't suppose you had any tea?' Without waiting for a reply she tucked the counterpane in and smoothed Abby's hair.

Abby tried to thank her, but her lips trembled. She turned to face the window, listening as Daisy left the room. Her throat felt tight but she had no more tears left.

★ ★ ★

She woke to pale sunshine. The curtains stirred and there was a fresh, earthy smell in the air. As she sat up, yesterday's events flooded back. But the weight of despair had lifted. Daisy was a true friend, listening without judgement and, best of all, willing to help — though what she could actually do, Abby hadn't a clue. Still, it was comforting to know that she was willing to try.

She started to get out of bed, hesitating as a knock came on the front door. Her heart started to pound as she recognized the voice. How did Joe's uncle know she was here? But her breathing returned to normal when the door closed and she heard the familiar sound of Gertie's hoofs, Dan's voice echoing down the street, 'Milko, milko'.

How could she be so foolish? Dan Leighton wouldn't be looking for her any more than her father or grandmother would.

The door opened and Daisy came in. She picked up the mug from the night before, a scum of cold milk congealing on top of the cocoa. Abby hadn't even heard her bring it in. 'Looks as if a night's sleep has done you good,' she said.

'I feel much better, thanks. I'd better get ready for work.'

'You sure? It won't hurt to have a day off.'

'I don't want the other girls talking behind my back.'

'They won't. I'll put them straight. Say you had a tummy upset. You're worn out with all this worry. Have a rest and when I get home we'll talk about — you know, your situation.'

Abby quickly dressed and followed Daisy downstairs. 'Did I hear Mr Leighton just now?' she asked. 'I didn't realize he was your milkman.'

'I've known him for years — he was in the war with my Bert.' Daisy smiled. 'He's a good man — I'm sure his nephew takes after him.'

Abby smiled. 'He's always been a good friend to me,' she said, remembering the left-over jugs of milk and his concern on that dreadful night in the snow.

'Don't worry, love, I didn't tell him anything. I know you'll tell Joe when the time's right.' Daisy patted her arm. 'Now, I really must get off to work — thank goodness it's half-day today.'

When she'd gone, Abby sat at the kitchen table thinking about what Daisy had said. When would the time ever be right to tell Joe? She'd had her chance last time he was home. She'd carried on writing to him as if nothing had happened. Now . . .

She ran her hand over her stomach and a lump came to her throat. She couldn't pretend now — soon there would be visible evidence of what that swine had done to her. She remembered exchanging giggly girly confidences at school when Rhoda had assured her it couldn't happen the first time. Rhoda was wrong.

With a sigh she wondered how she'd fill the hours till Daisy came home. The kitchen was clean and tidy, a cup, saucer and plate upended on the draining board. Daisy had told her to help herself but she didn't feel like eating.

At least she didn't feel sick today. For days she'd tried to convince herself it was just the heat. But what should have happened several weeks ago hadn't — and she knew why. Still, she refused to give in to despair. She was sure it wasn't the first time a girl had 'got into trouble' through no fault of her own and at least she now had someone on her side.

The thoughts churned in her head, always coming back to Joe and she prayed he'd never find out how she had let him down. For, despite Daisy's assurance that she wasn't to blame for Ernest Wheeler's assault, she couldn't help thinking it was partly her fault. If she hadn't been larking about with Charlie, he would never have thought she was 'that sort of girl'. If only she'd left The Emporium the first time he'd molested her.

Too late now, she thought, pushing her chair back. Pain squeezed her heart at the thought of the letter she must write. She was convinced Joe wouldn't want her if he knew the truth — not that she'd tell him. She'd find some way of breaking it off with him.

As she was hunting in the dresser for pen and paper Daisy came in, bringing with her the comforting aroma of hot meat pies from Shippam's shop in South Street.

'Now, about your little problem,' Daisy said, unwrapping the pies and sitting at the table. She paused and bit her lip. 'This is for your own good, Abby, love. You need to get away from Chichester so I'm going to ask my cousin Ivy in Southsea if you can stay there for a bit. She'll look after you and, when the time comes — '

'It'll have to be adopted, won't it?' Abby interrupted, crumbling the pastry in her hand. She couldn't eat.

'Yes, love, but it's for the best. There's nothing else you can do except — well, we won't even consider *that*.'

Abby only had a vague idea what she meant but she nodded anyway. 'Why can't I stay here?' she asked, momentarily forgetting that only last night she'd been desperate to get away. The thought of going through the coming ordeal among strangers was terrifying.

Daisy put a hand on her arm. 'Oh, Abby duck, you know I'd love you to stay but it's impossible — everyone would know. You'd

184

never live it down, get a decent job, find a husband . . . '

'I don't want a husband.' She had made up her mind to forget Joe and try to make a new life alone.

Daisy spoke between bites of her pie. 'And if you want to come back afterwards we can tell people you weren't happy with your new job. You'll have to tell Joe of course, but I'm sure he'll understand. By the time he's home again it'll all be over.'

'No, Daisy, I can't tell him . . . ' Abby burst into tears, despite her vow not to cry any more.

'That's up to you, love. But you love him, and surely if he loves you . . . ?'

But Abby just shook her head as the tears flowed unchecked.

★ ★ ★

She didn't know how she got through the following week. She avoided the other girls during the dinner-break, sure they'd guessed and were whispering behind her back.

Dad wasn't home when she went back to pack her clothes and retrieve Joe's precious letters. Neither he nor Gran had been in touch with her. They knew where she worked so there was no excuse. But Dad didn't care and Gran would never forgive her for 'getting into trouble' as she put it. No one apart from Daisy cared about her, and when not at work she stayed indoors, helping Daisy with the housework or writing long letters to Joe that ended up on the fire. She couldn't tell him the truth, neither could she pretend that everything was all right.

★   ★   ★

Daisy had gone to the market and Abby was washing the kitchen floor when Charlie knocked at the door, grinning cheekily. 'Aren't you going to ask me in then?' he said.

'What for?' Abby didn't want to talk to him.

'Just a friendly visit.'

'How did you know where I was?'

'I saw Daisy in the market. She said you'd had a row with your dad.'

Abby nodded. 'I had to get away.'

'I just came round to say goodbye. Got me call-up papers and I'm off next week.'

Abby gasped. The war was the last thing on her mind. 'Where are they sending you?'

'Training first — Royal Sussex Regiment. Might even get home for a bit before they send us over there.' Charlie grinned. 'Can't wait to go, really. I'm fed up with Wheelers.

It's not the same without your smiling face.
They're all so strait-laced. And now Miss
Ethel's practically taken over . . . '

Abby couldn't help smiling. 'I'm glad I'm
not there any more,' she said.

'What about the laundry? Any good-looking
fellers like me there?'

'It's mostly women,' Abby said, taking a
deep breath. 'Anyway, I might not be there
long. I'm going for a job in Portsmouth
— well, Southsea, actually. A seaside
boarding house, live in.'

Charlie's face fell. 'Bloody Joe — I suppose
you want to be near him when he's in port.'

It was easy to let him believe that. 'Do you
blame me?'

Charlie kicked at the doorstep, not looking
at her. 'So, there really is no chance for me?'

'No, Charlie. Maybe, if I'd never met
Joe . . . '

'Bloody Joe,' he said again.

Abby wished Daisy hadn't sent him round.
If it was Rhoda she'd be crowing with delight
at the thought of two men in love with her.
But Abby had enough complications in her
life. Daisy was right. The sooner she got away
from Chichester the better.

★   ★   ★

Every morning she watched for the postman as expectantly as she'd once waited for letters from Joe. But Ivy Henson hadn't replied to Daisy's letter — and who could blame her, Abby thought. Why would she agree to take in a total stranger, one who'd committed the unforgivable sin of becoming pregnant by a married man?

Suppose Ivy refused to have her? Would she end up in one of those dreadful homes for unmarried mothers that she'd heard about?

Abby shifted her feet, trying to concentrate on feeding the sheet into the pressing machine without dropping the end on the floor. Daisy gave an encouraging smile. 'Nearly break-time,' she said.

When at last the hooter went Abby grabbed her bag, rushed outside and found a secluded corner in the yard. Near by, two of the van drivers were talking about the war.

'It's true, I tell you. My mate's got a boat down at the harbour and he's taken it over to France. There's hundreds of 'em, all trying to get our blokes home.'

'What's up with the Royal Navy then? Ain't that their job?'

'There's ships waiting to pick them up but they can't get right inshore. And they're being bombed day and night. Bloody Luftwaffe . . . '

'Joe,' Abby whispered as their voices faded and she willed herself not to faint.

One of the van drivers came over. 'You all right, love?'

She brushed aside his outstretched hand and stumbled inside, making for the women's cloakroom. Behind her, she heard him say, 'Shouldn't eat fish paste sandwiches in this hot weather. Bound to upset . . . '

Behind the bolted lavatory door, Abby groaned. The fish paste wasn't to blame. She was sick with terror for Joe. She couldn't let him suffer — she must write and pretend that all was well.

* * *

The next day she came downstairs and saw the letter on the mat. Her heart leapt, although she knew it couldn't be from Joe. How could he know where she was if she didn't write to him?

'Is it from your cousin?' she asked, handing it to Daisy.

Her friend scanned the single sheet and nodded. 'She says you can go whenever it suits you. How about next Sunday?'

Abby couldn't wait to get away but common sense told her she should give a week's notice. Then nobody would wonder why she'd left suddenly and she'd have a little money to tide her over. Even if she managed to get a job in Southsea, she wouldn't be able to carry on working once her condition became obvious.

Daisy agreed. 'But only if you feel well enough. Can't have you fainting again,' she said.

'I'll be all right. It was just the heat,' Abby said, valiantly attempting a smile. She got up and started to clear the table. At the sink she turned. 'Daisy, why should your cousin help me?'

'I told Ivy that in spite of what other people may think, you're a good girl.' Daisy paused. 'Besides, she knows how hard it is. She went through it all herself — years ago. Like you, it wasn't her fault. But everyone blamed her and the man got off scot free.'

'What happened to the baby?'

'Jimmy — me and my Bert brought him up as our own. Couldn't have any of our own see, so it all worked out in the end. But poor Ivy had to go through life having her son call her auntie and never able to tell him the truth.' Daisy's voice broke and Abby laid a hand on her friend's arm.

She nodded towards the photograph of the handsome young soldier on the mantelpiece. 'Does he know?'

'We never got round to telling him — he thinks he's an orphan. He calls me auntie too. We thought it best as everyone knew we were too old to adopt officially.'

I'm not the only one with a secret, Abby thought, touching her stomach, as Daisy sighed and briskly set about the washing-up.

Later that evening they listened to the wireless, holding their breath as the newsreader spoke of the evacuation from Dunkirk and the terrible toll of lives lost. Daisy choked back tears, gazing at the photo of Jimmy and praying he was among those rescued. And Abby tried not to think about Joe's ship being shelled night and day.

As she got ready for bed Mr Churchill's words echoed in her head — 'the battle of Britain is about to begin.' The reality that she might never see Joe again came home to her. She shouldn't put off writing to him any longer. Hadn't he said it was only her letters that kept him going? Would it really hurt to pretend everything was all right, to tell him she was moving to Southsea to work? Ivy was going to arrange for the baby to be adopted and maybe he'd never need to know. It went against everything she believed in, but she told herself it was for Joe's sake too.

* * *

Joe hefted his kitbag on to his shoulder and began walking the mile and a half from the station to Applegate Farm. He couldn't wait to see Abby but she was probably still at work so he'd go home first. Maybe Dan would know what was going on. He was friendly with Daisy Hill and she'd know what Abby was up to if anyone did.

Thank God they'd returned to Portsmouth instead of one of the other ports. And he'd been lucky enough to get a day's leave. At last he could confront her, find out why she hadn't written. He climbed over a stile and cut across the fields. He didn't want to believe she'd found someone else. But he'd been away for months now. It wasn't as if they were engaged, and hadn't he told her he'd understand if she didn't want to wait for him? But surely she wouldn't just drop him without an explanation.

At the farm Mollie, the old sheepdog, managed to drag her arthritic body away from the warmth of the range to lick his hand and give a feeble wag of her tail. Joe threw his kitbag in a corner and bent down to fondle her ears. 'Didn't think I'd get to see you again, old girl,' he said.

Hannah's voice choked. 'I think she were waiting on you coming home. I don't think she'll be with us much longer.' She coughed and flapped her hands at him. 'Now you stop making a fuss of that old dog and get your hands washed. We've been waiting tea for you.'

Dan stood up and pumped his hand. 'Thank God you're still in one piece, lad. We were that worried when we heard on the wireless — '

Joe clapped him on the shoulder. 'Well, I'm here now as you can see — large as life and twice as ugly.'

Laughter covered their emotion as they sat down at the table. Joe complimented Hannah on her cooking as always. But he didn't eat with his usual enjoyment. He didn't want to talk about his experiences during the Dunkirk evacuation, covering the awkwardness by asking about the farm. Really, there was only one thing on his mind. Had Dan seen Abby lately and what was she up to? But he couldn't bring himself to mention her name.

At last the meal was over and, while Hannah cleared away and Wilf went out to check the animals, Dan sat by the range, gesturing to Joe to join him.

'It's good to see you, son,' he said. 'We never expected you to get leave.'

'We'll be off again soon.'

'This war's put the kibosh on your plans, hasn't it?' Dan paused to light his pipe. 'My plans too — me retiring, you taking over the farm when you got your discharge.'

'Got to do my bit,' Joe said.

'So what about you and young Abby? Will you get engaged this leave?'

Joe sighed. Obviously Dan was no wiser than he was. He didn't know what to make of it. He gazed into the fire, lost in thought.

'What's up, son — has she given you the elbow, then?'

'Not exactly. It's just I've had no letters for ages. Have you heard anything — is she seeing someone else?'

'Not that I know of. Haven't seen her since she left home.' At Joe's exclamation, Dan leaned forward. 'Sorry, lad. I thought you knew. She fell out with her dad and her gran — moved in with Daisy Hill for a bit. Then she got a job away.'

That still didn't explain why she hadn't written to tell him herself. Maybe her letter had gone astray — they did sometimes. And, knowing Wally Cookson, he wouldn't have sent any letters on to his daughter. They were probably gathering dust on the mantelpiece at Tanner's Court — or thrown in the fire, more likely.

'I didn't know — as I said, I haven't heard from her.' Joe stood up. 'I think I'll go and give Wilf a hand with the animals.' He

194

couldn't bear talking about it any more.

'Hold on, son. There must be a reason. She's mad about you. Daisy said she was always reading your letters, almost wore them out.'

'So why hasn't she written, then?'

Dan drew on his pipe. 'I expect she sent her new address and you didn't get the letter. I mean with everything that's going on out there . . . ' He waved his pipe to indicate the war and Joe's part in it. 'I'm sure you're worrying about nothing. Go and see Daisy in the morning, she'll give you the address.'

'You're right, Uncle Dan. I'm probably getting het up over nothing. It's just — I was so looking forward to seeing her . . . I nearly stayed on the train to call in at her house. And now you say she's left Chichester . . . '

'Don't fret, son. I'm sure it'll all work out.' Dan sucked on his pipe again, staring into the fire, his face sombre.

'You're thinking about Carrie, aren't you, Abby's mother?'

'I don't want history repeating itself, that's all. I let her go and then, when we had a chance of putting things right . . . '

'What happened? I know she left her husband. But why didn't you get together after that?'

'We had it all planned. She was supposed

195

to meet me — with little Abby — but she never turned up. I thought she'd got cold feet, frightened of what Wally would do to her . . . ' Dan covered his face with his hands. 'I'd have protected her, done anything for her.'

Joe waited for the rest of the story, a story hinted at but never fully explained.

When Dan recovered his composure he looked at Joe. 'That's the worst thing — not knowing. She just went and no one ever heard from her again. I guess she wasn't brave enough to defy her husband. But it wasn't herself she was afraid for — it was me, and Abby too. At least that's what I've told myself all these years.'

'Why leave Abby behind though?'

'She probably meant to come back for her when she was settled.' Dan sighed. 'Oh, well, it's all a long time ago. But the thing is, Joe. I don't want you to suffer like I did. If you really love her, don't give up just because of a few letters going astray. We're at war now and, well, you never know . . . ' Dan stopped, looking embarrassed.

Joe knew what he meant. He couldn't go back to his ship without knowing where he stood. 'I'll go and give Wilf a hand now,' he said. 'And I'll go and see Daisy tomorrow.'

10

Abby got up at six o'clock and crept down the attic stairs, past the first-floor bedrooms and into the bathroom. After a quick wash she cleaned the bath and washbasin and put disinfectant down the toilet. She stretched and massaged the small of her back, glancing down at the bulge of her stomach which the loose smock overall did nothing to hide. Thank goodness she'd escaped from Chichester before it started to show.

Did the guests at Sea Haven accept Ivy's story that Abby was her niece, married to a sailor serving in His Majesty's Navy? She fingered the cheap ring that Ivy had given her, trying to convince herself she didn't care. She just wanted to get through the next few months, though what would happen after the baby was born she still wasn't sure. She couldn't imagine going back to her old life.

Would Ivy let her stay, working for her keep as she was now? She didn't dare to hope, although they'd taken to each other straight away, quickly dispelling Abby's nervousness. She'd had time to wonder if she was doing the right thing as she made her way from

Portsmouth station through the narrow streets of the old town towards Sea Haven, a tall Victorian house which, despite its name, was in a side street a few minutes' walk from the beach at Southsea.

Ivy, a larger, plumper version of Daisy, with her cousin's warm smile, had bustled her up to the attic that would be her room.

'Come down when you like. I've got the kettle on, my duck,' she'd said, sounding so like Daisy that Abby was ready to burst into tears.

Now she was determined to repay the older woman's kindness by working hard and relieving some of the burden of running the guest house, not that there'd been many guests since the air-raids started.

She went along the landing and got clean towels out of the airing cupboard, arranged them on the rail. Satisfied that their only guest would find nothing to complain about, she went down to help with breakfast.

Ivy was already in the kitchen, clasping an earthenware bowl to her ample bosom and vigorously beating eggs. Scrambling them made them go a bit further.

'Morning, love, would you get the bacon out?' she said. 'Only one rasher each today.'

'I'll go down to the Co-op later on, see what they've got in,' Abby said.

'You sure you don't mind?' Ivy said. 'It's

198

not much fun queuing in your condition.'

'I'm all right — the fresh air will do me good.' Abby had been living in Southsea for nearly three months now and, for the first few weeks she'd avoided going out. Portsmouth was always full of sailors and she'd found the sight of their uniforms unbearable. Besides, she couldn't risk bumping into Joe if his ship happened to be in port. But she couldn't stay cooped up indoors all summer.

Since the bombing had started a couple of weeks ago the guests, a couple of commercial travellers, had gone home. And the usual summer guests hadn't turned up, which was not surprising with the promenade cordoned off with barbed wire and the anti-aircraft guns on the common, not to mention the all too frequent daylight raids.

Abby wondered how Ivy would manage with hardly any money coming in. Thank goodness for Sid Jenkins, a jolly red-faced man from Norfolk, who looked more like a farmer than a kitchenware salesman. He'd turned up a few days ago in a little Bullnose Morris and Ivy had greeted him enthusiastically. He was clearly a regular — and a favourite of Ivy's.

Abby could see why. She'd taken to him as well, his bluff kindliness reminding her of Joe's Uncle Dan. She wondered how the war would affect his business — and Ivy's. She gave herself a mental shake. Why was she worrying? She'd soon be gone, free of the burden of an illegitimate child, free to make a new life for herself.

With the thought, her hands started to shake and she could hardly light the gas under the heavy skillet. The baby wasn't a burden to be got rid of as soon as possible. Despite the circumstances of its conception, she wanted the best for it. But suddenly, the thought of giving it away to strangers seemed almost unbearable. She'd seen the heartbreak and loneliness Ivy was still suffering all these years later. Would that be her lot too?

She'd been enjoying the luxury of life at Sea Haven — luxury compared to the tumbledown cottage that had been her home, day-dreaming the days away and deliberately shutting out thoughts for the future. But she couldn't go on like this. She must face up to things and decide what she was going to do after the baby was born.

She turned the bacon over in the pan as a gurgle from the bathroom pipes signalled that Mr Jenkins was almost ready for his breakfast. She reached for a slice of bread as Ivy came in from the hall carrying the daily paper and a bundle of letters.

'There's one for you, Abby,' she said.

Heart thumping, she gasped as she recognized the writing, saw the postmark. It had taken three weeks to get to her. Dismay warred with joy as she tore it open. How did he know where she was, who had told him? It must have been Daisy. How could she? But Daisy had told her time and again that she shouldn't keep Joe dangling. It was only fair to break it off completely — that was if she was sure she was doing the right thing.

Her hands trembled as she unfolded the single sheet of paper and she could scarcely focus on Joe's small neat writing.

Abby, my love, it's been so long since I heard from you. I've been worried at not getting any letters. Please write and say you still love me and will wait for me. I can't help worrying since I heard from Mrs Hill that you are now working in Southsea and I know the bombing in that area has been bad and will probably get worse. Normally I would be pleased to have you so near when my ship docks in Portsmouth but it's not likely I'll be home any time soon. I would feel easier in my mind if you were safe back in Chichester. I can understand you wanted to get away from your dad but you need friends and family at times like this.

Abby gasped and her hand went automatically to her swelling abdomen.

'Is everything all right, Abby?' Ivy asked looking up from her own letter.

'I don't know really,' Abby said, sitting down at the kitchen table and turning the page over. She sighed with relief, realizing from Joe's next words that he'd been referring to the war, not her pregnancy.

The letter ended with the usual endearments and the hope that he would soon have a letter from her. She kissed the place where he'd signed his name with its row of crosses underneath, holding the paper close to her face and inhaling its scent as if that would bring him closer. How could she bear never seeing him again? Despite her resolve to shed no more tears, she couldn't stop a sniffle escaping.

Ivy put her own letter down and took off her reading glasses. 'Not bad news, I hope?'

'No, it's from Joe. I haven't heard from him for ages.' Abby rubbed her eyes and tried to smile.

'He's your young man, isn't he — the sailor?'

Abby nodded.

'Thank God he's all right. I suppose there's no chance of him coming home before the baby's born? What a pity.' Ivy shook her head.

'I wonder how many other girls there are in your position — waiting for their men to come home and sort out the mess they've left behind.' Her normally placid voice held a note of bitterness.

Abby blew her nose. 'It's not like that. It wasn't Joe . . . ' Her voice trailed away. She could see what Ivy was thinking as her lips tightened.

'Didn't Daisy tell you what happened?'

'She said you were in the same position as me all those years ago and that you needed my help. But then she said you had a boyfriend overseas and I thought . . . ' She sat down abruptly. 'Does he know about the baby? Surely he'll marry you when he gets leave.'

'He doesn't know and I don't want to tell him — it's not his, you see. But it wasn't my fault. My boss attacked me and I couldn't tell anyone . . . ' Abby was crying in earnest now as the memory of that awful day when she'd been silly enough to accept Ernest Wheeler's offer of a lift home came flooding back to her with all its pain and humiliation.

Ivy put her arms round her, patting her back. 'Look, you don't have to tell me . . . ' she began, then gave a little shriek and leapt towards the cooker. 'Oh, goodness, the toast,' she cried, grabbing the grill pan and waving her other hand to disperse the smoke. She opened the back door, letting in a blast of damp air.

Abby rubbed her face with her overall and rescued the bacon. 'Ivy, I'm sorry. You don't want to hear my troubles. I thought Daisy had told you everything.'

Ivy threw the burnt toast in the bin and put two more slices under the grill. 'I promised Daisy I'd look after you and I'll gladly listen to your troubles. But not while I'm trying to get Mr Jenkins's breakfast.' She put a saucepan on a low gas and poured the beaten eggs into it. 'Now, you keep an eye on that while I finish setting the table. When he's gone off to work we can sit down and you can tell me the whole story.'

Abby didn't want Ivy thinking the worst of her — not after she'd been so kind. But to her amazement she actually felt better after she'd poured it all out, including the way her grandmother had accused her of being just like her mother. As the last words spilled out she bit her lip, wishing she had kept quiet.

'What about your mother, love? I thought she'd died. Daisy said you only had your dad and he wasn't exactly a good father to you . . . ' her voice trailed away.

'My mum left my dad when I was little — ran off with another man, they say. My gran's never forgiven her.' Abby rubbed her eyes on the corner of her overall and stood up abruptly. 'My dad's not the easiest person to live with, always getting drunk and losing his job, so I can understand her leaving him. But why didn't she take me with her?'

'Maybe the man — whoever he was — didn't want another man's child.' Ivy put her arm round Abby's shoulder, giving a comforting squeeze. 'Maybe she meant to come back for you when she was settled.'

'But she didn't — and it still hurts even after all these years.' She was silent for a few moments, not crying now, just rubbing her stomach and looking at the bulge under her overall. 'I try to tell myself I hate this baby because of — you know . . . '

Ivy nodded sympathetically.

Abby went on, 'But I don't want it growing up feeling like I do, that he wasn't wanted. After all, poor little thing, it wasn't his fault was it?'

Ivy pushed her back into the chair and sat down herself. 'Look, love, I know how you feel. Believe me, I went through all the same thoughts and feelings. But if your young man won't accept it as his, then you don't have any choice. Surely it's better for it to have a loving home — which I'll make sure of, I promise.'

'At least you knew where your baby was and could see him grow up.'

'How do you know that wasn't even harder — him thinking his mother was dead and I was his auntie?' It was Ivy's turn to cry now and Abby felt ashamed.

But when she tried to apologize, Ivy brushed her away. 'It's all right, love. I've had years to get used to it. Trouble is, once you start lying, you have to keep it up. I can see why you don't want Joe to know what happened to you . . . ' She hesitated a moment and sighed. 'Maybe it would be better if you told him the truth.'

Abby shook her head. 'I couldn't.' She reached for the letter in her overall pocket and smoothed the paper out on the table. Whatever she decided to tell him, she had to write something.

★　★　★

The letter from Joe was crumpled and stained from constant rereading, but still Abby hadn't replied. She knew she should, but what could she say? She'd long since forgiven Daisy for giving Joe her address. As she'd explained in her last letter, he'd looked so miserable and she felt sorry for him. She just hoped he wouldn't get leave and turn up at Sea Haven, now he knew where she was.

She told herself she didn't have time to write but with only one guest they weren't busy. Most evenings, she, Ivy and Sid settled at the kitchen table to listen to the nine o'clock news, although more often than not the siren would wail and they'd spend most of the night in the shelter at the bottom of the garden.

The worst raid had been at the end of August. Bombs rained down on Portsmouth in a daylight raid that seemed to go on for hours and over a hundred people were killed. Since then there'd been a little lull but tonight the siren went before the news had finished.

Sid gathered up the playing-cards and Ivy collected the Thermos, together with her handbag containing the precious ration books.

They passed the time playing crib by the light of a hurricane lamp, while Abby tried to concentrate on her knitting. She wasn't very good at it at the best of times but each time an explosion shook the shelter, sending shadows dancing on the corrugated iron walls, she dropped another stitch.

At last the all-clear went and Abby stood up, rubbing her back. 'Do you think there'll be another one tonight? I'd rather go up to my own bed.'

'Who knows? But you rest while you can, love,' said Ivy.

'You need to take care of yourself,' Sid said with a kind smile.

Abby felt awful — he was so kind and here she was, living a life of deceit and lies. What would he think if he knew the truth?

As she undressed she wished with all her heart that the life she was living was the real one — that Ivy really was her aunt and that she had a husband in the navy. Sid's kindness reminded her of Joe's Uncle Dan and with the thought came memories of her life in Chichester. In spite of what had happened she missed the familiarity of the little streets, the Cross and cathedral.

Even the thought of her grandmother's sharp tongue and stern unforgiving nature brought a lump to her throat. But she couldn't get away from the truth. She was the daughter of the town drunk, her mother had run off with another man and she herself would soon be the mother of an illegitimate child. Would she ever be able to go back and face them all?

★ ★ ★

Over the next few weeks there was a lull in the air raids but it didn't last long. Threats of invasion had receded since the Battle of Britain began, but the Luftwaffe continued its assaults on Portsmouth dockyard and Abby was now used to spending nights in the air-raid shelter.

The tension seemed to be taking its toll on Ivy too. She hadn't been her usual self for ages.

One chilly morning in late October Abby found her sitting at the kitchen table, a cup of tea going cold in her hand. She was usually so busy and cheerful, that Abby feared something dreadful had happened. Was it Daisy, or Jimmy? Fear clutched at her chest.

'Not bad news?' She sat down and reached across to touch Ivy's hand.

Ivy managed a smile. 'It's nothing really. I'm just being silly.' She stood up and picked up the teapot. 'Must get on, lots to do.'

In minutes she was her usual self, trying to make two eggs do the work of four for their breakfast. But Abby could see that, despite her efforts at normality, there was something on her mind.

She was reluctant to pry and, after clearing up the kitchen, she took a duster and a tin of polish, deciding to keep out of Ivy's way. She went into the parlour at the front of the house, and was startled as she realized that someone was in the room.

Sid Jenkins, after returning to Norwich for a while, had turned up again a week ago. He looked up from his newspaper.

'Sorry to disturb you, Mr Jenkins. I thought you'd gone out,' Abby said.

'Nothing to go out for,' he said. 'I've tramped round everywhere but no orders coming in.'

'What will you do?'

'Find another job, I suppose.' He folded the newspaper and stood up. 'I've picked out a couple of likely ones so I'd best be off.' He paused at the door and winked at her. 'Wish me luck, love. I need an excuse to stay in Southsea.'

Abby grinned as she polished the sideboard. Now she knew why Ivy was in such a bad mood. She wanted Sid to stay and he didn't want to leave. She liked having him around as well. When he wasn't working he made himself useful in many ways — not like a paying guest at all. If it hadn't been for him the Anderson shelter at the bottom of the garden would still be a pile of corrugated iron sheets. What would Ivy do without him?

Ivy's face lit up that evening when Sid announced he'd been taken on in the dockyard as a storeman. 'With all the young blokes gone they need us older men.' He fidgeted, looking down at his feet. 'There's only one thing, Ivy. I'll have to find permanent lodgings. I can't stay here for ever.'

'Whyever not? Something wrong with my cooking?' She laughed nervously.

''Course not.' His face relaxed into his usual crumpled grin. 'Can I stay, then?'

'As long as you like,' Ivy said.

Abby, busy at the stove, smiled, sensing romance in the air. She was happy for them but she couldn't help a twinge of envy. Thanks to evil Wheeler, she'd lost her own chance of happiness. Hatred welled up and she prayed that one day he'd get his come-uppance.

She hadn't answered Joe's letter and for the hundredth time she told herself it was for the best. He'd find someone else. But what would happen to her?

★　★　★

The bombing continued day and night and Ivy was worried that Abby would go into labour during a raid. Sid had offered to take her to the mother and baby home in his little car. When petrol rationing came in he'd stopped using it. But there was enough for the short distance to the home.

'There's plenty of time yet,' Abby said

when Ivy confessed her fears. 'It's not due till November.' She didn't want to think about it, not that she could avoid it with the baby's movement keeping her awake at night.

'Suppose it comes early? You'll let me know the minute you feel a twinge won't you, love?' Ivy still looked worried.

★   ★   ★

Abby rubbed her back. Another restless night in the shelter. Surely it couldn't go on for ever — then Joe would be home for good. Perhaps she should have confessed everything and hoped he'd understand. Was it too late? But she didn't think she could bear it if he rejected her.

She was feeding sheets through the mangle when she felt a sharp pain and a groan escaped her lips.

Ivy turned from emptying the water down the drain. 'You all right, my duck?'

'Just a twinge,' she said, straightening up. It couldn't be the baby, she thought. There was another three weeks to go yet. She carried the basket of washing down the garden and began to peg it out, shivering in the chill wind off the sea. Her back was aching and she longed to sit down. But then, she always felt tired on washday.

She pegged the last sheet and followed Ivy indoors. The ache grew stronger as the day went on but Abby didn't want to believe the baby was coming. She convinced herself that the backache had been caused by lifting the heavy laundry basket.

When Sid came in from work he gave his usual cheery greeting. 'How's my two best girls, then?' But as he sat down at the table he looked keenly at Abby. 'You look a bit pale, girl. You all right?'

'Just a backache,' she said, gasping as another pain, stronger this time, swept over her. She gripped the back of a chair.

'Ivy, I think the baby's coming. We'd better get the girl to the home — quick.'

Ivy turned from the stove, a ladle in her hand. 'You silly girl, why didn't you say something?'

'I thought it was just backache — it's too early.'

Sid grabbed his hat and jacket. 'I'll go and get the car,' he said.

But as he opened the front door, the air-raid siren went. 'Get down the shelter, both of you. I'll be back in a tick.'

Abby was still gripping the back of the chair, gasping as the pains came faster. Ivy put her arm round her. 'Come on, love. Let's get to the shelter and get you comfortable.'

The ack-ack guns on the common had started up and there was the steady drone of aircraft overhead. Clutching Ivy's arm, Abby stumbled down the path to the shelter and collapsed on the bottom bunk.

Ivy lit the lamp and turned to Abby. 'Even if Sid gets the car, I don't think we'll have time to take you to the home — it's right over Hilsea way.'

Abby was past caring. An explosion nearby shook the shelter and dust rained down. She bit her knuckles, gazing up at Ivy with frightened eyes. But it wasn't the bombs that had scared her. This was worse than she'd imagined. 'Please, let it be over soon,' she wailed.

After that it was a blur of pain which seemed to go on for hours. She was hardly aware that the all-clear had gone and that the pain had receded until she heard Ivy's voice, thick with emotion.

'It's a boy.'

Abby struggled to sit up as a thin cry reached her ears, holding out her arms for the baby. 'Give him to me,' she said.

But Ivy clung on to the little bundle, tears rolling down her cheeks. For a moment she wondered if the baby was all right, until she realized that Ivy was reliving the moment when Jimmy was born.

'Let me hold him,' she said.

Ivy dragged her eyes away from the baby. 'You'll have to feed him, love. But take care you don't get too attached.'

It was too late, Abby thought, as she gazed down at the little red face with its shock of dark hair. How could she give him up, this precious bundle? It wasn't his fault he'd been conceived in violence.

⋆ ⋆ ⋆

By the time Sid came back Abby was asleep, the baby tucked into a drawer taken from the dresser.

'Best leave her here in case the siren goes again,' Ivy said, closing the door and following Sid into the house.

'Sorry I didn't get back in time. The warden saw me running and made me go to the shelter — officious little bugger. Wouldn't let me explain.'

'It's all right — we managed.' She sat down at the kitchen table, twisting her hands together. 'Poor girl, what's going to happen to her?'

'Let's hope her young man gets leave soon. He ought to do the right thing by her — she's a lovely girl.'

'It's not like that, Sid. He doesn't know

— it's going to be adopted.' She poured the tea and sat down.

'But surely once her sailor knows he's a father . . . '

Ivy interrupted. 'He's not the father, though.' She told him the whole story, relieved to share her concern for the girl with somebody else. She still thought Joe ought to be told. Daisy seemed to think he was man enough to accept the baby as his own and everything would turn out all right. Suddenly she found herself confiding in Sid, confessing her own story as well.

He reached out a hand and took hers, giving a comforting squeeze. 'Sounds like you've both had a rough time.'

She smiled, grateful that he wasn't shocked by her confession. 'I often wish I'd defied convention and brought Jimmy up myself but it would have been impossible. At least I was able to watch him grow up. But poor Abby might never see her child again and the loss will be with her all her life.' Ivy wiped away a tear. 'I wouldn't wish that on anyone.'

'Seems that poor girl hasn't had many chances in life. But she has to make her own decisions. All you can do is be a friend — support her, whatever she decides to do,' Sid said.

'You're not shocked?' Ivy said.

'About you, or Abby?' he said with his crooked grin. He shook his head. 'No, these things happen. You were young — taken advantage of — just like young Abby. I've always thought it's a pity the woman gets all the blame, while the men get away with it.'

'I'm glad you understand, Sid. I'll have to get that baby into the orphanage before she becomes too attached to it.'

'Poor kid, it's going to be hard for her. She'll need our support.'

Ivy stood up abruptly. 'I'll go down tomorrow and make arrangements.'

But when she reached the mother and baby home she found it boarded up, a notice on the door saying they'd been evacuated to somewhere in Wiltshire. Anyone needing help could see the vicar of the church which ran the home or go to the town hall.

The vicar wasn't there and, at the town hall, by the time she'd found someone willing to listen to her problem, Ivy was almost in tears. The prim officious woman behind the desk looked down her long nose. 'You should have made arrangements for your niece before the baby was born.'

'I did, but the baby came early — and the home that was arranging the adoption isn't there any more.'

'All the children in the city have been

evacuated — with their mothers, if appropriate.'

'But she wasn't a mother when the evacuation started. So, what do we do now?' Ivy asked.

'I'll make some enquiries. Come back in a few days.' The woman turned away to answer a ringing telephone and Ivy, biting back an angry retort, walked away.

When she got back to Sea Haven, Sid greeted her at the door. 'Problems, love?' he asked.

While he made her a welcome cup of tea, she told him what had happened. 'You could see she thought dealing with illegitimate children was beneath her. She said a few days — but Abby's getting attached to the baby already. The longer she keeps him the harder it'll be.' Ivy sighed. 'She's decided to join up as soon as it's settled so I won't tell her about the home. I can cope with the little mite for a week or two if necessary.'

★ ★ ★

'You must persevere,' Ivy said. 'He'll have to have a bottle when his new parents take him on.'

Abby looked up sharply and a spasm of grief crossed her face. It hurt to have it spelled out in such a matter-of-fact manner. In a day or two, Ivy had told her, the adoption people would come to take him away.

Ivy patted her arm. 'Sorry, love, but you must face it. You know you can't keep him. You're young and one day, who knows, you'll meet someone else, have more children.'

Abby looked down at the tiny bundle in her arms. He'd accepted the bottle teat and was sucking contentedly. Love welled up and her eyes filled with tears. How could she part with him? But Ivy was right. Not about getting on with her life or finding a new love. That would never happen. But she had to do the best for little Joe. And a loving adoptive couple was the best — the only — option.

She looked up at Ivy. 'I wish I could stay here,' she said. 'But I can't put it off. I'll go in to the recruiting office when he's asleep.'

'Good idea,' Ivy said. 'They'll probably send you somewhere far away — give you a chance to start a new life.'

When little Joe, as she thought of him, was asleep, she left him with Ivy and got the bus into Portsmouth town centre. Sandbags surrounded the entrance to the guildhall and as usual there were sailors everywhere. The sight of the uniforms brought a lump to Abby's throat. She'd never be able to see the striped collar or jaunty cap without thinking of Joe. Maybe it was as well she was leaving Portsmouth where there was always a chance she'd bump into him. As Ivy said, she must get on with her life.

A group of girls in WRNS uniform walked past as she got off the bus. How smart they looked. But it wouldn't do for her — she'd always be reminded of Joe. When she reached the recruiting office she still couldn't decide between the WAAFs and the ATS or some other war work. They needed people in the factories up north but that would be too much like the laundry — noisy machines and chattering women. She couldn't decide. Maybe she should wait to be called up and go wherever they sent her.

Another poster caught her eye — a girl wielding a pitchfork. '*For a healthy, happy life, join the Women's Land Army*' it said. She'd never be happy again, she thought, remembering the visits to Dan's farm and her walks over the fields with Joe. But working on the land appealed to her. Before she could change her mind, she went inside.

The woman stared at her, eyes flicking over her slight figure, then back to the application form. 'Are you sure you want farm work?' she asked. 'You don't look very strong.'

Little Joe's birth and the following sleepless

nights had left her pale and exhausted. But Abby had made up her mind. 'I'm very fit,' she said. 'I've been working in a boarding house, and before that I was in a laundry, that's hard heavy work.'

'Well, you *might* do, then. But the hours are long and believe me, it's very heavy work indeed.' She scanned the form again and said, 'Have you any experience of farm work at all?'

'A little. I — '

'Well, why didn't you mention it on the form?' She made a note then looked up. 'There are several places which desperately need people. If you've had experience we can send you straight to a farm — no need to go for training. You'll learn on the job.'

Abby tried to explain that she'd only done potato picking and that she was still nervous of cows, but the woman gave her no chance.

'Here's one — West Chilton Farm — over near Chichester. Their cowman's just joined up so they're desperate.'

Abby registered the local place name and the word 'cows' and began to wish she'd gone for the forces instead. She'd imagined being sent far away, to Norfolk perhaps, which she had a vague idea was all cornfields, or the Lake District where they kept sheep.

The recruiting officer was still speaking.

'It's a mixed farm — small dairy herd, a few sheep and some arable, just over the Downs from Chichester.'

It was too late. She'd signed the form. Instructions concerning uniform, rules and regulations and a time and date for reporting for duty were rattled off and Abby found herself outside clutching a piece of paper. She was now a member of the Women's Land Army '*for the duration of the war*', or as long as her country had need of her.

★ ★ ★

Abby packed her belongings, trying not to think of the parting from little Joe.

The door opened and Ivy came in. 'Best say goodbye now.'

She nodded, swallowed hard and tucked little Joe up in the drawer. He was sleeping soundly as she bent and kissed the soft cheek for the last time. She was determined not to cry but she couldn't suppress a sob as she turned away. When Ivy gathered her into her arms, the tears flowed freely.

'There, love, let it all out,' she said, patting her back.

At last she wiped her eyes and Ivy nodded. 'Now — you've had a good cry. It's time to put it behind you like I said. Easier said than done, I know, but you're doing the right thing.'

'I know,' Abby whispered.

'All right then,' Ivy said, trying to sound brisk. 'You'd better be off before the adoption people get here — it'll be easier that way.' She hugged her again.

Abby attempted a smile and kissed her cheek. 'I don't know how to thank you,' she said.

Ivy just patted her shoulder.

Abby went to the front porch where Sid was waiting with the car. At the station he offered to accompany her on to the platform.

'I'd rather say goodbye here,' she said, trying not to start crying again. 'Take care of Ivy, won't you?'

'You can count on it.' He handed the case to her and gave a little wave as she trudged away.

As the train neared Chichester the sight of the cathedral spire gleaming in the sun caused Abby to question her acceptance of the posting so near home. She should have insisted on being sent to another part of the country. As the train rattled over the Fishbourne level crossing and she saw Dan's farm in the distance bringing memories of more carefree days she didn't think she could bear it.

And there were new memories now — a little rosy-cheeked face with a tuft of dark hair, a warm body snuggled up to hers, tiny pink hands and feet. She stifled a sob. How could she have left him to strangers? It took great determination to keep the tears at bay as she asked herself what else she could have done.

The sooner she got the bus to West Chilton and started her new life on the farm, the sooner she could put it all behind her, she told herself. But she had to see Daisy first. Goodness knows when she'd get another chance.

As she jumped off the train and began walking up Southgate, she thought of her mother for the first time for ages. The familiar anger bubbled up. If I'd had someone to turn to, surely these bad things wouldn't have happened to me, she thought. How could she have left me? However unhappy she was she shouldn't have abandoned me.

It was a sobering thought that she'd done exactly the same thing.

But when she reached Daisy's house the warmth of her greeting drove such thoughts away. Daisy knew the truth and didn't blame her.

Her friend drew her into the kitchen, leaving her case in the passage. 'I managed to get some sausages from Elphick's — thank goodness they're not rationed,' she said. 'Oh, you must be exhausted lugging that case all the way from the station. I wasn't sure what train you'd be on, otherwise I'd have got Dan to fetch you in the cart. I'm glad you came on Saturday so I was at home. Couldn't have you arriving at an empty house, although you know where the key is.'

Abby let the chatter roll over her, relieved that she didn't mention the baby.

When Daisy paused for breath, she said. 'You didn't tell Dan I was coming back — or anyone else?'

'I did mention it. Well, I had to — everyone keeps asking how you are. So I said that the job in Southsea didn't work out and you were hoping to get your old job at the laundry back.' She poured the tea and pushed a plate of biscuits towards her. 'That was all right, wasn't it?'

'Of course. But Dan's sure to tell Joe. And I don't want him to find out . . . ' Her voice broke.

'He won't. Dan has no idea why you went away. He thinks you wanted to get away from your father.'

Abby didn't want to think about her father — someone else she'd have to face sooner or later. Had he guessed why she'd left

Chichester? And then there was Gran. She knew the truth but at least no one would find out from her. She'd refused to believe that Ernest Wheeler was responsible but she'd keep her granddaughter's disgrace a secret.

Daisy chattered on, saying she hadn't heard from Jimmy for ages and moaning about the rationing. Abby only half-listened until Daisy said, 'Your friend Rhoda's joined up — the ATS.'

'That's what I've done,' Abby said abruptly.

'What? But I thought you were coming back to the laundry. I was looking forward to working with you again.'

Abby sighed. 'Sorry, but I'm bound to be called up before long anyway. I've joined the land army.'

Daisy looked upset and Abby hastened to reassure her that she wouldn't be far away and would visit on her days off. 'Besides, I can't stay here — '

They were interrupted by a knock on the door. Daisy had started peeling some potatoes and asked Abby to answer it. 'Probably one of the neighbours asking for the loan of a bit of sugar or flour,' she said.

Abby grasped the edge of the door as she took in the uniformed figure standing there, his cap in his hands. Joe's surprise was as great as hers and they stared at each other wordlessly for a few moments.

'Abby — is it really you? I didn't expect ... I came to ask Daisy ... ' He was stuttering. 'Aren't you going to ask me in?'

She couldn't face him. He'd ask her why she hadn't written. And how could she stop herself telling him the whole sordid story? How could she bear the shock, the horror, the disgust she would see in his face? But she calmly stepped back and walked slowly into the kitchen, leaving him to follow.

'It's Joe,' she said, amazed at how calm she sounded.

Daisy turned round, flustered. 'Oh, Joe, nice to see you.' She dried her hands on her apron. 'I've just remembered — got to pop next door for a minute.'

Before Abby could protest, she was gone.

She turned to Joe, her heart hammering but she couldn't let him see how he affected her. 'Sit down, I'll make you a cup of tea,' she said.

'I don't want to sit down and I don't want any tea.' Joe seized her shoulders and turned her to face him. 'I just want an explanation. Why didn't you answer my letters? I've just come from Southsea but they said you didn't work there any more.' He gripped her shoulders harder and shook his head. 'Oh, Abby, how could you do this to me? I thought you loved me . . . '

She almost gave in then. But she managed to push him away. 'If you sit down and drink your tea, I'll try to explain,' she said, still keeping a tight rein on her feelings.

The kettle whistled and she filled the teapot. Leaning against the sink, she took a deep breath and said, 'I hoped you'd understand. I did try to write, but I couldn't find the words.' She bit her lip to stop it trembling, then forced herself to tell the lie. 'I hoped you'd forget me.'

Joe took a step towards her, a protest on his lips, but Abby stopped him with a gesture. She sighed. 'A few meetings, a few kisses, how do I know you aren't saying the same thing to every other girl you meet when you're away in foreign parts?'

It was easier to attack him than to defend herself but she knew she'd hurt him. His face blanched. 'How can you say that? You know it's not true.'

She softened. 'I'm sorry, Joe. That wasn't very nice of me. But I hardly know you really . . . '

'What about your letters? We didn't see each other for ages but you let me think you loved me. And last time I was on leave . . . '

'It's hard, Joe, with you away so much.' If only it didn't sound so feeble. 'And now, the war . . . ' She twisted a tea-towel between her fingers.

'The war doesn't influence how I feel, Abby. I could be away for months, years even . . . ' His voice broke. 'I might not even come back at all. But, don't you see, that's why I need to know you're here, waiting for me. Knowing I've got you to come home to . . . ' He crossed the small room, grasping her shoulders again. 'I don't understand — you keep changing jobs, moving away from Chichester, now you're back. What happened?'

Abby went cold. Had he guessed? But he was shaking her. 'Is there someone else? Tell me.'

'Of course there's not, truly. It's like I said. I fell for you after only one meeting but I was barely eighteen, Joe. I need to — I don't know — stretch my wings a bit. I don't want to be tied down.'

'I don't want to tie you down — I just want to know you're here and that there's a chance for us. Please, Abby, at least say you'll keep writing. It would mean so much to me.'

Abby couldn't resist the appeal in his eyes. All the love she'd tried so hard to stifle welled up in her. 'Oh, Joe,' she murmured, leaning against him. His arms came round her and she raised her face for his kiss, surrendering to the feelings she couldn't suppress.

His tenderness, swiftly turning to passion, was hard to resist. His lips on hers, his hands moving over her body. The edge of the sink cut into her back, bringing a sharp memory of other hands tearing and groping at her, careless of the pain they caused. With a gasp, she tore herself free, flailing at him, her nails catching his cheek. 'Leave me alone. Don't you understand, I don't want you,' she sobbed.

Joe let go of her and stepped back, breathing raggedly. He raised a hand to his face, then looked at the blood on his fingers. 'I wasn't going to hurt you, Abby. I thought you wanted . . . '

'Well, I didn't,' she snapped.

His shoulders slumped. 'I'm sorry. I think I'd better go,' he said.

She didn't try to stop him and at the door he paused. 'I must get back to my ship but I won't give up, Abby,' he said.

She didn't answer and he turned away. When she heard the door close, she flung herself into a chair and the sobs she'd been holding in burst out like a dam breaking. He'd said he wouldn't give up, but she knew she'd forfeited any chance of future happiness. She was still crying, mopping her eyes with the sodden tea-towel, when Daisy came back.

PART TWO

1942–1944

11

Abby leaned on the gate and watched the herd ambling towards her, remembering Farmer Phillips's scorn at her nervousness when she'd arrived at West Chilton and realized she'd be responsible for the care and milking of the small dairy herd.

It wasn't so much fear of the animals, more anxiety as to how she'd cope with these daily reminders of the happiest time in her life when Joe had showed her how to milk, with Dan and Wilf looking on and laughing.

But she was coping, and often to her surprise she sometimes even felt happy despite the constant fear for Joe's safety. She couldn't forget little Joe either. He'd be coming up to two years old now, walking, probably trying to talk. She thought of him every day, but despite the constant ache in her heart, she didn't think anyone here guessed her secret.

Here on the farm she was outwardly content, although, as the land army recruiting officer had said, it was hard and heavy work. This was a rare moment of relaxation, of escape from the war, and Abby savoured the feeling.

After three years she wondered how much longer it could go on. On such a day it was hard to believe they were at war. The air was warm as if summer was reluctant to break its hold on the countryside just yet. She watched a yellow leaf parachute to the ground, reminding her of the planes which constantly droned overhead.

Even here, deep in the Sussex countryside, it was impossible really to forget the war. At the thought, the thin veneer of content dropped away and she began to wonder where Joe was now. She prayed he was safe. When Farmer Phillips turned on the wireless for the nine o'clock news she would tense at any mention of naval battles, even though she had no idea where he was. Sometimes she regretted making Daisy promise to burn his letters and not to tell anyone where she was.

When Daisy had come home that dreadful day and found her in tears, she'd tried to persuade Abby to write to Joe. 'Tell him everything,' she said. 'It's easier to pour it all out in a letter. It'll be up to him then.'

But Abby could only imagine the look of disgust on his face at the thought of her with another man. Useless to tell herself she wasn't to blame — the woman always paid. 'I can't do it, Daisy. Best to make a clean break.'

Would it do any harm to write — just to reassure herself that he was all right? But it was almost two years now — surely he'd have forgotten her by now. Besides, how could she put it into words, expect Joe to understand? The alternative was to write, pretending everything was all right, but she couldn't lie any more.

No use dwelling on it. Maybe she could have handled things better but, although she'd gone over it time and again, she still couldn't see how things could have turned out differently.

The leading cow reached the gate and nudged against it, breaking Abby's train of thought. There was work to be done and, besides, brooding did no good. She opened the gate and followed the cows as they ambled down the track towards the milking parlour. She'd have plenty to keep her busy this evening.

The last of the farm hands had joined up a couple of weeks ago and Farmer Phillips had applied for more land girls. But, despite the WLA representative's assurances, they hadn't arrived. By the time Abby finished milking and washing down the machines and the floor, she'd hardly have the energy to eat her supper before falling into bed. Thank goodness Mr Phillips didn't expect her to lug the ten-gallon churns down to the gate as well.

'Come on, my beauties,' she called, ushering the cows into the shed. From long habit they went to their appointed places and started munching from the baskets of turnips which Tommy Phillips, the farmer's seventeen-year-old son, had put there. As they ate, she began the laborious process of washing their udders before attaching the metal suckers to their teats. At least she didn't have to milk them by hand as Dan and Wilf did.

'Tommy, where are you?' she called, as she switched off the machine and began filling the churns from the huge vat into which the milk was collected. He was supposed to help with the stripping, squeezing out by hand the last remaining drops of milk which the machines weren't able to extract.

There was no answer and Abby shrugged. Tommy was a good lad who willingly helped around the farm in the holidays and when he got home from school, especially now they were so short-handed. But he couldn't wait to join up.

As he helped stack the churns Mr Phillips grumbled. 'That lad of mine should be doing this.'

Abby grabbed another churn, rolling it on its edge towards the cart. 'Be all right when the other girls arrive,' she said.

'I'll believe it when I see it,' the farmer said.

★ ★ ★

Abby shivered as she threw back the blankets and got out of bed. Yesterday's illusion of a lingering summer was gone and there was an autumn chill in the air. She dressed quickly, pushing her feet into her boots and winding a scarf round her neck. When she stepped out into the farmyard the sky above the Downs was streaked pale pink and yellow. By the time she'd rounded up the herd and pointed them towards the milking parlour the sun had struggled through and promised another fine day.

Mr Phillips came in as she was finishing off. 'Fancy coming into market with me after breakfast?' he asked.

'I don't know. There's a lot to do. I was going to restack those hay bales in the barn and set some traps. I'm sure there's rats in there.'

'You can do that when we get back. The missus says you're to come with me. You ain't had a day off for weeks — '

'I don't mind,' Abby interrupted.

Mr Phillips laughed. 'Well, I shall need a

hand unloading so it ain't exactly a day off, is it?'

Abby was running out of excuses to avoid going into town. Besides, she felt guilty for not keeping in touch with Daisy. Maybe she'd pop round to the laundry and have a chat.

As they drove down the hill past the barracks, Abby turned her head away from the narrow streets of Somerstown where she'd grown up. The memories were too painful. Besides, she dreaded catching a glimpse of her father or grandmother.

Despite petrol rationing the town was busy, as it always was on market day. Apart from the varied uniforms the only sign of war seemed to be the sandbags piled against the council offices in North Street. The nearby airfields had been bombed several times, but so far there had only been one bad raid on Chichester when several houses near the railway had been damaged.

At the market Abby helped Mr Phillips unload the pigs and herd them into a pen. 'That's it, then,' he said. 'You can be off now — why don't you go and see your gran. Meet me back here in a couple of hours.'

Abby had no intention of visiting her grandmother. She walked towards the Cross, keeping a wary eye out for anyone she knew. Surely they'd guess why she'd gone away for those few months in 1940.

It was too early to meet Daisy and she'd decided to return to the market when a voice hailed her. It was Charlie, striding along in his army uniform. Despite the sling holding his left arm in place, he seemed all right.

'What've you been up to?' she asked.

'Nothing to worry about. Got me a spot of leave, though.' He grabbed her hand. 'It's good to see you. Last I heard you'd gone to work in Southsea.' He looked her up and down. 'Uniform suits you,' he said.

'You too. You're looking well — apart from . . . ' she gestured towards the sling.

'I won't be needing it much longer, then we'll be off again — God knows where.'

'Well, good luck. It was nice to see you, Charlie.' She made to turn away.

'Don't go yet, Abby. Come and have a drink or something. I don't want to lose you again.'

'Don't be silly, Charlie.'

'I suppose it's still sailor boy, is it?' Charlie looked disappointed.

'I finished with Joe,' Abby said, before she could stop herself.

Charlie grinned. 'So there is hope for me then?' He grabbed her hand again and grew serious. 'Abby, please let me write to you — it would mean such a lot.'

'I can't stop you writing — but don't go reading anything into it mind,' Abby said, snatching her hand away. 'You can write care of Daisy — you know her address?'

'And you'll write back — promise?'

'All right. But I must go.' She walked away, conscious that he was staring after her. What had possessed her? She liked Charlie, he'd been fun to work with but he just wasn't Joe. And, like everyone else, if he ever found out her secret he wouldn't want to know her. She was just storing up yet more heartbreak for herself.

12

It was dusk by the time Abby and Tommy had finished milking and cleaning out the milking parlour. Thank goodness the new girls were expected soon. Since Abby had come to West Chilton two and a half years ago the work force had dwindled as the younger men joined up and the older ones grew more infirm. Abby did her best with Tommy's help but it would be even harder when he was gone. Despite his parents' pleas, Tommy had joined the RAF and would be off to training camp soon.

Abby was permanently tired, but at least falling into bed each night in a state of exhaustion stopped her dwelling on the loss of her child. It was always there, though, at the back of her mind, wondering how he was, what stage he was at — first tooth, walking, probably chattering away by now, calling another woman 'Mummy'. And Joe — where was he? Was he thinking of her? Or had he given up? Despite telling Daisy not to send on any letters, she couldn't help feeling a little rush of excitement when Bill, the postman arrived. But the unreasoning hope swiftly turned to disappointment when it turned out to be another letter from Charlie.

'Come on, Ab, stop day-dreaming. Mum will be dishing up.' Tommy punched her arm playfully.

They hurried indoors, stopping short at the sight of a young woman wearing the smart green jersey of the Women's Land Army seated at the kitchen table. She stood up and held out her hand. 'I'm Cynthia Harwood.' She was a tall strikingly pretty blonde, with a posh voice which reminded Abby of Lady Grisham's daughter and the friends who used to come to the manor for weekend house parties.

'And these two are the Wheeler sisters,' Cynthia continued as the kitchen door opened again.

Abby drew in her breath, but before she could say anything Ethel glared at her. 'We're already acquainted with Miss Cookson,' she said. 'She used to work for our father.'

'Good evening, Miss Wheeler, Miss Cissie.' Abby found the formal way of addressing them hard after all this time. As she sat at the table, her heart was pounding. Why did they have to end up here of all places? And how long would it be before Ethel was raking up the old scandal of Abby's mother, just to be spiteful?

'Eat up,' Mrs Phillips said, ladling stew and passing plates round the table as if she hadn't noticed the frosty atmosphere. 'We won't wait for Mr Phillips. He's gone to a meeting in the village hall — more war regulations. Percy thinks we should be left alone — they're always coming up with new schemes. But as he says, his family's farmed here for generations, so he should know best.'

'We heard similar sentiments at the training farm, didn't we?' Cynthia said, turning to the Wheeler sisters.

Ethel took a mouthful of stew and nodded, while Cissie just smiled and agreed. She'd always been the quieter one, meekly accepting her bossy sister's lead, Abby remembered.

Anxious to avoid any questions about her connections with the Wheelers, Abby broke the awkward silence by asking Tommy about one of the cows. But he was more interested in the newcomers, especially the beautiful Cynthia.

At last the meal was over and Abby excused herself, saying she was tired and had to be up early next morning.

'You'll be up early too, girls,' Mrs Phillips said, 'so off you go. I've put Miss Harwood in with you, Abby. The other two are in Tommy's old room.'

'I'm in the attic now,' Tommy said. He

243

grinned proudly. 'Won't be for long. I'm off to join my unit in a week or two — RAF.'

Cissie and Ethel had already gone upstairs and, after helping to clear away the dishes, Cynthia followed Abby up to their room.

As soon as the door closed, Cynthia said, 'What's with you and the sisters?'

'I worked in their shop — they think I'm beneath them.' Abby was reluctant to go into details.

'What nonsense. We're all the same now,' Cynthia said, climbing into bed.

Tired as she was Abby couldn't stop thinking about the sisters. I'll have to ask for a transfer, she thought, as sleep claimed her at last. Still, Cynthia seemed all right — for a posh girl.

★　★　★

The milking parlour door opened and Cissie Wheeler came in, rubbing her eyes.

'Mr Phillips says you're to show me the ropes,' she said.

'Good, I could do with some help,' said Abby. 'Did you learn milking at the training farm?'

'Yes. I'm not keen though.'

'You're not frightened of cows, are you?'

Cissie bit her lip and nodded. 'I've tried to

get over it, but . . . '

Although Abby didn't like her, she couldn't help feeling sorry for the girl. Why on earth had she decided to join the land army? 'I was scared at first,' she said. 'They're so big, aren't they? But they're gentle animals really. The secret is to not let them see you're afraid.'

'Were you really scared?' Cissie asked. 'You seem so confident.'

'It just takes practice. Here, I'll show you.' Abby proceeded to remove the suckers from the cows' udders, then showed Cissie how to squeeze out the remaining milk. 'Surely you did this at training?' she said.

'Yes, but Ethel always helped me.'

Abby tried to hide her impatience. With a bossy mother and sister like hers, it was no wonder Cissie lacked confidence. She just stood, twisting her hands together, while Abby began stripping the cows' udders. 'See, it's easy,' she said. 'Now, you finish off while I wash down the machine. There's lots more to do before we can go in and have breakfast.'

When Cissie still hesitated, Abby's patience snapped. 'You'll never learn if you don't try.' She pushed Cissie down on to the milking stool and turned away to get on with her own job.

As she worked Abby surreptitiously glanced at the other girl, suppressing a smile when she saw that Cissie seemed to have got the hang of it. Of course Abby had started her off with Buttercup, the most gentle and amenable of the herd.

She finished cleaning the machine and came over to the stalls. 'I'll do this last one, then we can fill the churns together.' She didn't tell Cissie that Bluebell, the cow in the end stall, was the most cantankerous of the lot and liable to kick the bucket over if she was in a bad mood.

'There, that wasn't so bad, was it?' Abby said as she and Cissie crossed the yard to the farmhouse a bit later.

'Thanks,' Cissie said. 'I didn't expect you to be so nice to me. Ethel said — '

'I can guess what she said.'

'Well, when your grandmother disowned you . . . ' Her voice trailed away.

Abby almost flared up. 'You shouldn't listen to gossip,' she said.

'Is it going to be awkward working with us?' Cissie asked timidly.

They were washing their hands at the pump and before Abby could reply, Ethel and Cynthia came out of the nearby barn. Ethel strode up and grabbed Cissie by the arm. 'I told you not to talk to that trollop,' she said, dragging her away.

'I say, that was a bit uncalled for,' Cynthia

said, raising an eyebrow.

Abby shrugged but she knew she was blushing. Had her secret got out somehow? And what would Cynthia think if she discovered she'd had an illegitimate child?

Cynthia touched her arm gently. 'I know what small towns are for gossip. And Miss Ethel Wheeler strikes me as a narrow-minded bigot. I got to know the sisters quite well at the training farm and you can imagine how I felt when we were sent here together.'

Abby managed a small laugh. 'The same as I felt when they walked in last night. I think I might ask for a transfer.'

'Oh, you can't do that,' Cynthia said. 'I know we only met last night but I hoped we'd be friends. Besides, if you leave, I'll have to ask for a transfer too.' She laughed and Abby had to smile.

'All right, I'll stay. But if Ethel starts on me, she might get more than she bargained for.' Abby sounded more confident than she felt. She knew she wouldn't say anything, but she couldn't help thinking that Ethel Wheeler might not be quite so outspoken if she knew what her father had done.

As they ate breakfast, Abby scarcely listened as Farmer Phillips expounded his views on the meeting he'd attended, together with the contents of the buff envelope that had arrived that morning. 'More regulations,' he said, banging his knife down. 'And they say we've to plough the top field. Bloody ridiculous if you ask me. I've already put every possible inch under the plough. But will they listen? Nothing will grow up there — it's all bloody chalk.'

'Language, Percy. There's ladies present,' Mrs Phillips said.

'Can't you lodge an appeal, Mr Phillips?' Cynthia asked.

'Waste of bloody time. Anyway what do you know about it?' His chair scraped noisily on the tiled floor as he stood up, drowning out his wife's further remonstrations. He put his cap on, grabbed a jacket off the back door and went, banging the door behind him.

'More tea, anyone?' Mrs Phillips asked. When the girls hesitated she laughed. 'Take no notice of him. He'll be right as rain come dinner-time. Just needs to let off steam.'

'But he hasn't told us what to do,' Cissie said.

'Abby knows the routine, she'll take you round.'

Ethel looked daggers and Abby suppressed a smile. She drained her cup and stood up. 'Come on then, lots to do.' She turned to Cynthia. 'Miss Harwood, the rest of the turnips need digging out of the clamps. They're stored near the byres for winter feed but they're nearly all used up now. We need to make room for the fresh ones when they're harvested. Then, as it's a fine day, the cows can be turned out down by the stream. You and your sister can do that, Miss Wheeler, then you can come and help us.'

Mrs Phillips started clearing the table. 'That's settled then. By the time you've done, Percy will have simmered down and you can ask him about the other jobs.'

'Best get started then,' Abby said, tucking her dungarees into her socks and pulling on her boots.

'Before we start, can I suggest we dispense with all this 'Miss this and that'? I notice Mrs Phillips calls Abby by her Christian name,' Cynthia said.

'I don't mind,' Cissie said quietly, ignoring her sister's spiteful look.

'Well? What do you say, Miss Wheeler?'

'My parents didn't like us getting too familiar with the staff,' Ethel said.

'Oh, for goodness' sake,' Cynthia snapped. 'Miss Cookson — Abby — is not working for your parents now.'

Ethel gave a reluctant nod. 'Very well, as my sister agrees.' Her sour look let them know how she felt about it.

The sisters disappeared down the track

towards the meadow and Abby started shovelling the turnips into a barrow. Cynthia went into the barn and turned on the chopping machine.

When they'd finished they hitched the horse up and shovelled piles of straw and manure from the yard on to the cart, working in companionable silence.

At mid-morning Abby stopped and rubbed her back. 'Time for a tea-break.'

They perched on the edge of the cart and drank from the flask Mrs Phillips had prepared for them.

'Foul stuff, this,' Cynthia said, pulling a face. She shook the remaining drops from the metal cup and screwed it back on the flask. As Abby jumped down from the cart and retrieved her spade, Cynthia put a hand on her arm. 'You didn't tell me what the problem is with you and the sisters.'

'I worked for Wheeler's Emporium — the big store in Chichester. They sacked my friend through no fault of hers. I was going to leave too but when Mrs Wheeler was ill they persuaded me to stay. But I couldn't stand it. I left without giving notice.' Abby was shaking as she finished.

'I get the feeling there's more to it than that,' Cynthia said quietly. 'Still, it explains their animosity.'

'Ethel's the nasty one. Cissie just follows her lead.'

They began work again and when the last shovelful went on the cart, Abby took hold of the pony's bridle. 'We'll take this up to the top field then go back to the house for dinner,' she said.

As they walked towards the farmyard Cynthia said, 'I had to laugh this morning when you were giving them their orders. I thought Ethel would explode.' She giggled. 'You do know Cissie's scared of cows, don't you?'

'I didn't do it to be horrible,' Abby protested. 'I could see how nervous she was in the milking parlour this morning. I was just as bad when I first came. But the more she works with the herd, the sooner she'll get over it.'

⋆   ⋆   ⋆

Cissie did get over it. Within a few weeks she was handling the milking as if she'd been doing it all her life. She was no longer a timid, withdrawn girl, but a confident young woman. She'd even learned to stand up to her older sister. The change in her was remarkable and Abby put it down to Cynthia and her forthright common sense. She had a way of jollying them all along, turning the work into fun. Even Ethel managed a smile occasionally, although her attitude to Abby didn't change.

Fortunately, the farm was quite large so they managed to keep out of each other's way most of the time. It was only during the evenings that sometimes a strained atmosphere crept in.

Thank goodness for Cynthia, Abby thought, as once more the older girl managed to deflect one of Ethel's barbed comments with a joke. Abby would have flared up and caused a row.

'Market day tomorrow,' Percy Phillips announced, folding his newspaper and preparing for bed. 'Which of you's coming this time?'

'Why don't you take all of them, Perce?' said Mrs Phillips. 'They haven't had a day off for weeks and they've been working hard with the spring planting.'

The farmer nodded. 'Don't see why not.'

'There's lots to do. I don't mind staying behind,' Abby said. Since the Wheeler sisters had arrived she'd managed to avoid going in to Chichester. She didn't want to run into anyone she knew, sure that Ethel would have told everyone she was working at West Chilton. Once the chapel ladies found out, they'd soon let her grandmother know. Abby still wasn't ready to face her.

'Don't be silly,' Cynthia said. 'If Mr Phillips says we can all go, you should jump at the chance. Go and see Daisy — you said you hadn't heard from her lately.'

When they were in their room with the door shut Cynthia turned to Abby, hairbrush in hand. 'Why are you so reluctant to go into town? Is there someone you want to avoid?'

Abby almost laughed. Where to begin? Dad, Gran, Mr Wheeler, Joe's Uncle Dan . . . The laugh turned into a sob. Gran had disowned her but if she bumped into her, she'd have something to say. And though she'd written to Dad giving him her new address, he'd never tried to get in touch with her — no doubt Gran had informed him of his daughter's disgrace. She couldn't face any of them.

Cynthia, brushing her long blonde hair, interrupted her thoughts. 'It's all right, Abby. I won't pry. But there's something on your mind. It might help to talk about it. You know it would be just between the two of us.'

Abby believed her. In the weeks they'd worked together they'd become firm friends. She didn't want to risk losing that friendship. 'I can't tell you,' she said, her voice choking on a sob. 'But thanks anyway. Goodnight.'

'You are coming into town tomorrow. I

won't take no for an answer,' Cynthia said firmly.

Abby didn't reply. But as she lay down, she thought about the daylight raid on Chichester last week. They'd heard from Bill, the postman, that there'd been considerable damage in the town centre. Although it was nowhere near her home or Daisy's, she'd been worried, especially as she hadn't heard from her friend for a while. Maybe she should go.

Next morning she'd almost decided to stay behind, until Ethel called out, 'Mr Philips is waiting.'

She hesitated and Ethel's lips twisted in a sneer. 'Scared of who you might bump into in town? I thought you'd want to see your grandmother.' She saw Cynthia coming towards them and raised her voice. 'Oh, I forgot — your grandmother's disowned you, hasn't she? I heard her say you were just like your slut of a mother.'

Abby clenched her fists to stop herself hitting the other girl. She took a step forward. 'I don't care what you say about me, but leave my mother out of it.'

Cynthia grabbed her arm. 'Take no notice,' she said, glaring at Ethel.

Abby reluctantly followed her towards the lorry and they all climbed in. As they set off down the bumpy track, the calves set up a mournful lowing as if they sensed their destination. Abby knew how they felt.

Instead of driving through the town centre the lorry turned off into the narrow lane past the college. 'North Street's cordoned off,' Mr Phillips said. 'That last raid did a lot of damage.'

Abby was relieved they weren't going through Somerstown. She was still nervous of seeing anyone she knew.

At the market they herded the calves into the pen and followed Farmer Phillips into the auction ring. The auctioneer's shouts and the bellowing of the bull being led round the ring vied with the cacophony of bleating, lowing and baaing from the pens outside.

During a lull the farmer said, 'I've seen a couple of nice heifers I want to bid for. You girls needn't hang around.'

'I'll stay,' Cynthia said. 'I love all this — the noise, even the smell. It's quite exciting, isn't it?' She laughed when Ethel wrinkled her nose.

'Suit yourself,' Mr Phillips said. He turned to the others. 'Don't be late back. If I'm not here, you'll find me over the way.' He gestured towards the Cattle Market Inn on the other side of the road.

The sisters hurried away, leaving Abby wondering how she'd fill in the time. Daisy would be at work, Rhoda and Charlie were both away in the forces, and she couldn't face anyone else.

At the refreshment stall in the corner of the market she handed over some coppers to the stall holder, and took her tea over to the calf-pens. She leaned on the railing, bending to stroke the soft muzzles of the animals which gazed up at her with large trusting eyes.

Poor little things, taken away from their mothers like that, she thought, trying not to think of their eventual fate. That was the drawback to farming. It didn't do to get too fond of the animals — like people, she thought. You gave them your love and affection and then you lost them. A sob rose in her throat as a picture of little Joe, round and rosy with his tuft of dark hair and those big eyes gazing at her above the shawl. Of course he wasn't a tiny baby now. She gave the calf a last stroke and drained her tea. At least little Joe was with a family who loved him, she told herself, willing it to be true. She sighed and turned to take the mug back to the stall.

Almost blinded by the tears, she bumped into someone. Muttering an apology she hurried away, stopping as the man called her name.

'It's Abby, isn't it?'

She dashed her hand across her eyes, recognizing Wilf Knowles from Applegate Farm.

'Hello, Mr Knowles, how are you?' she said.

'I'm fine. But what about you?' He took in her uniform and his eyes twinkled. 'Don't tell me you're working with cows.'

She nodded and managed a smile. 'Yes. Sorry, can't stop.'

'Hey, wait up. Dan's around somewhere — he'll want to say hello.'

'I'm late,' she said, hurrying away. Dan Leighton was the last person she wanted to see.

★ ★ ★

Daisy yawned and shuffled along the narrow passage to pick up the letters from the mat — three today. She examined them eagerly — one from Jimmy, another with a Norwich postmark. It was ages since she'd heard from Ivy. And one addressed to Miss A Cookson, care of Mrs Hill.

What should she do? She'd sent on the one from Charlie Simmons. But this one was from Joe. The others were still there, tucked behind the clock on the mantelpiece over the range — quite a bundle now. She couldn't quite bring herself to burn them as Abby had requested.

With a sigh, she put today's letter with them and sat down to read the one from

Jimmy. He didn't have much to say, just that he was safe and well and getting fed up with the flies and sand in his food. So, he was still in the desert, Daisy concluded. She knew from the wireless that the allies were winning out there but there was still a lot of fighting going on.

She turned to Ivy's letter, wondering how things were working out for her and Sid. She'd told Abby they'd closed up the boarding house and gone back to Sid's place in Norfolk. She wasn't prepared for the bombshell that followed.

I wasn't sure whether to tell you, Ivy had written, but little Joe is still with us. The baby home was evacuated and we had problems contacting the adoption people. We didn't mean to keep him but what else could we do? I had to get him registered so we could put him on my ration book, so I said I was his auntie and his parents were away in the forces. I only meant to keep him until we found someone to take him in, but when we decided to move it seemed right to take him with us away from the bombs. Sid thinks I should tell Abby in case she's changed her mind about having him adopted. I just don't know what to do, Daisy. I wouldn't do anything to hurt Abby but at least her baby is being brought up by people who want him and really love him. Still, I'll leave it up to you what you tell her.

'Oh, Ivy, what have you done?' Daisy murmured, glancing back at the clock with its bundle of letters. She stared out of the window, her tea growing cold on the table beside her. She understood her cousin's actions all too well. But Ivy had no legal rights and, besides what would she tell the boy when he grew up and started asking questions? She just prayed he'd never discover how he'd been conceived. And suppose Abby found out?

Daisy decided to put off answering her cousin's letter and walk to the market. As she was about to leave, she snatched the letters from behind the clock and put them in her handbag. Whether Abby would read them or not was another matter. But at least the decision would be out of her hands once she'd sent them on.

As she hurried towards Eastgate Square her heart started to beat faster. Foolish old woman, she told herself, getting into a state just on the chance that she might bump into Dan Leighton.

Last time she'd seen him he'd treated her

to a shandy and a meat pie in the saloon bar of the Cattle Market Inn. Of course, he'd only wanted news of Abby, she thought now.

It wasn't until a land girl turned up with the milk one day that Daisy realized how much she'd come to look forward to hearing the clop of Gertie's hoofs on the road outside her cottage and Dan's voice calling 'milko'. From sharing news of Abby — or rather the lack of it — and exchanging the usual concerns about the progress of the war they'd become firm friends. He'd often stop for a cup of tea and they'd talk about their nephews, Jimmy in the army and Joe in the navy. They even talked about Bert sometimes.

With a pang Daisy realized that she thought about Dan more than she did her late husband these days. But Bert had been gone for four years and, although she still missed him, she was fed up with being on her own. It was time to move on. If only Dan felt the same way — but she was sure he still carried a torch for Abby's mother. Still, friendship was better than nothing.

The market stalls were already packing up — nothing for them to sell, Daisy thought. But, from the noise over by the animal pens, the auction was still going on. She pushed through the crowd of farmers gathered round the auctioneer, but Dan wasn't there. Time she was getting to work anyway if she wanted to get a bite in the canteen before her shift started.

She turned away and bumped straight into Dan.

'Whoa, what's the hurry?' he said, his face breaking into a grin.

Daisy felt herself blushing. 'I've got to get to work,' she said.

'Plenty of time. I happen to know your shift doesn't start till two. Come and have a drink.' He took her arm and crossed the road towards the Cattle Market Inn. It was packed and the noise was deafening. Dan led Daisy to the snug and found her a seat before going up to the bar to order.

As they settled down with their drinks and meat pies Dan asked the usual question. 'Any news of Abby?'

'Not for months. Last time I saw her she said they were short-handed and I know she works hard but you'd think she'd drop me a line now and then.' Daisy's eyes clouded. 'It's as if she wants to cut everybody out of her life . . . ' She stopped, afraid she'd said too much.

'I don't understand the girl,' Dan said, taking a sip of his stout. 'I know she and Joe fell out but that's no reason to drop all her old friends, especially you, Daisy. I know you've been like a mother to that girl.'

'Have you heard from Joe lately?'

'Just last week. He's a good lad, writes regular. But he don't say much — not allowed to, I daresay. I do know he thinks the world of Abby and he doesn't understand what went wrong. Has she got another feller, do you think?'

'No, I'm sure that's not it.' Daisy paused uncertainly. She'd love to confide in Dan. But it wasn't her secret to share. 'I don't think she wanted to be tied down — with the war, the uncertainty of things . . . '

Dan nodded. 'I made that mistake during the last war,' he said. 'And I lost the girl I loved. I wouldn't want the same thing to happen again.'

Daisy knew about Carrie, Abby's mother. Dan, thinking he was unlikely to return from the trenches, had thought it unfair to ask her to wait. She'd married on the rebound and by the time he got home Carrie had realized her mistake. But it was too late — she was expecting Abby.

Before Daisy could think what to say, Wilf came into the bar.

'There you are, boss. I've just seen young Abby.'

'When?'

'Where?'

Dan and Daisy spoke in unison.

'About half an hour ago. She was by the calves.'

'I'll go and find her,' Daisy said. She'd pass Joe's letters on instead of posting them. Whether Abby read them or not would be up to her.

'Too late — she was just leaving,' Wilf said.

Dan drained his pint. 'Want a drink, Wilf? What about you, Daisy?'

'No thanks.' Daisy picked at her pie. How could Abby come into town and not see her? She really did seem determined to cut herself off from the past.

'Sorry,' said Wilf. 'If I'd known you were here I'd have brought her over.'

'I'm worried about her. How did she look?'

'Well enough, healthwise. Blooming actually. Farm life seems to agree with her. But she didn't seem happy. Shame about her and Joe. I wonder what went wrong?'

'Some silly tiff, I expect,' Dan said, coming back and putting the glasses down on the table. 'I wish I'd seen her — I'd have put her straight. It's not fair, throwing a chap over when he's away fighting a war.' His voice was bitter.

Daisy longed to comfort him but he shook her hand off. She picked up her handbag. 'Time I was getting to work,' she said.

Dan grimaced. 'Sorry to get so het up, love. Poor old Joe says he's written umpteen times but she doesn't answer. He's really worried.'

'She hasn't had the letters,' Daisy said abruptly. 'I've still got them.'

'Well, why haven't you sent them on?'

'She told me not to.'

'Never mind what she said — maybe if she reads them she'll change her mind.'

'Dan's right,' Wilf said.

'I agree — in fact I've already decided to do just that. Now I really must go.'

'Let me know if you hear from her,' Dan said. 'I'll probably be in town next market day.'

Daisy's heart lifted. It was the nearest he'd ever come to arranging to see her again. But it wasn't thoughts of Dan that occupied her as she hurried to work. Why hadn't Abby come to see her while she was here? The hurt faded a bit when one of her colleagues told her a land girl had been asking for her.

She'd post Joe's letters on tomorrow. But she wouldn't tell Abby that little Joe was still with Ivy. It might give her the false hope of seeing her child again. What she didn't know couldn't hurt her, Daisy reasoned.

13

Daisy wasn't at work and there wasn't time to go to her cottage. Abby dawdled back to the market, hoping she wouldn't bump into Dan. She couldn't bear to talk about Joe.

The other land girls were already waiting by the lorry and she saw that Cissie had been crying. 'What's wrong?' she asked.

Ethel didn't give her the chance to reply. 'Mother needs us at home and Father said we should stay . . . '

'But you can't take leave just like that,' Cynthia protested. 'We're in the land *army*, which is just like being in the real army. How would it be if all the soldiers and sailors just upped and went home if someone in their family was ill?'

'I told Father we'd have to get permission,' Ethel said, tossing her head.

Mr Phillips caught the tail-end of the conversation. 'I thought your mother had a nurse,' he said. 'Besides, I need you girls, so let's hear no more about it.' He climbed into the lorry and Cynthia swung the starting handle. Ethel got into the cab while the others scrambled into the back and tried to

265

make themselves comfortable on the bales of hay he'd bought.

'Mr Phillips seems a bit grumpy today,' Cynthia said.

'He's probably fed up at having to buy hay after ploughing the top field instead of leaving it for grazing,' Abby said, clutching the side of the lorry as it went over a pothole. Her own troubles receded as the problems of farming in wartime occupied her mind. She wondered how Dan was managing. At least he still had Wilf, who was too old to be called up. And there was a land girl at Applegate Farm now. Thank goodness she hadn't been sent there, she thought.

Now that she'd got over the shock of bumping into Wilf she realized how pleased she had been to see him. She should have asked for news of Joe, despite her resolve to put him out of her heart and mind.

She turned to Cissie. 'Would you go home if you got permission?' she asked.

Cissie shook her head. 'I only joined because Ethel wanted to but I've grown to like it.' She gave a faint smile. 'I don't even mind the cows now.'

'Do you always do what your sister wants?' Cynthia said, raising an eyebrow.

Cissie nodded. 'I know it's feeble, but she's the elder . . . '

'She's a bully, you mean,' Cynthia said.

Abby was surprised that Cissie didn't leap to Ethel's defence. 'Maybe — anyway, I had my own reasons for wanting to leave home,' she said quietly.

'It can't be much fun having a bedridden parent,' Cynthia replied with a sympathetic smile.

The lorry began to bump over the rutted farm track and they were too busy hanging on for further conversation.

Cissie was the first to jump down. 'I'll go and fetch the cows in,' she said.

Ethel followed Mr Phillips into the house and Abby said, 'I'll give Cissie a hand.'

Cynthia touched her arm. 'Let her be. She's obviously upset about something.'

As she helped Cynthia to stack the bales she found herself saying, 'I don't like their parents — they were awful to work for. I knew them before that of course — through the chapel. He's a lay preacher, one of those fire-and-brimstone types.'

Cynthia rolled her eyes. 'I can imagine. Those poor girls — no wonder Cissie wanted to get away.'

Abby nodded agreement. 'I'll go and help with the cows,' she said, wondering if she could get Cissie to confide in her.

But when she got to the milking-shed Ethel

was already there. 'Mr Phillips is going to speak to the WLA representative and ask if we can take turns going home to help with Mother — on compassionate grounds, he said.'

Cissie pressed her face into the cow's flank and didn't answer.

Abby began to roll the churns towards the door. Maybe she'd get a chance to talk to Cissie later.

★ ★ ★

A few days after her visit to the market Abby was stamping the mud off her boots before going in to breakfast when Bill, the postman, wobbled up the farm track on his ancient bicycle. He leaned it against the porch and paused to catch his breath.

'That old wind'll be the death of me,' he panted, handing the pile of letters to Mr Phillips.

'More rubbish,' he said, throwing them on to the dresser and sitting down at the table where Ethel and Cynthia were already tucking into bowls of thick porridge.

Mrs Phillips turned from the stove. 'Sit down, Bill. Any news from town?' She put a mug in front of him.

He took a long slurp of tea, wiped his moustache and stood up. 'Best be off, a few miles to bike yet.' He nodded towards the letters on the dresser. 'Worth coming all this way for that lot. One of you girls is popular.' He laughed.

Cynthia pushed her chair back and leapt up, snatching the letters and whisking through them. Abby concentrated on her porridge. There might be one from Charlie but she wasn't bothered. She looked up when Cynthia giggled. 'Oh, Abby, you're a dark horse. Didn't know you had more than one beau.'

'I haven't,' she said. But she could feel the tell-tale blush creeping up her neck.

'Well, these aren't from your soldier.' Cynthia handed a bundle of letters to her. The rest she gave to Mr Phillips, who gave them a cursory glance then turned to the girls. 'No time for that now. Finish your meal and get back to work.'

Abby was glad of the interruption. She shoved the bundle of letters into the pocket of her dungarees and went to the porch to retrieve her boots, hoping for a quiet moment later. She didn't want anyone around when she discovered what Joe had to say.

Although the wind up on the Downs was fresh, the sun was shining. Maybe spring had arrived at last. Abby hitched up the harrow to the tractor, pleased that she could now manage on her own. Tommy had taught her to drive when she first came and it had taken her some time to learn the quirks and foibles of the old machine.

She liked working alone and was especially pleased this morning to be spared Cynthia's knowing looks and the Wheeler sisters' disapproval. From her brief glance at the envelopes she'd realized that Joe's letters had arrived at Daisy's address ages ago. Why hadn't she destroyed them and what had prompted her to send them on now?

Up in the top field she started on the harrowing, trying not to think about the letters. A moment's inattention on these slopes could overturn the tractor — with fatal results. But as she manoeuvred around the steeply sloping field she could feel them burning a hole in her pocket.

When she reached the end of the row she switched the engine off and climbed down. She couldn't wait. Resting her back against the tractor wheel, she took the letters from her pocket. Daisy had put a note in with them and she opened it first, putting off the moment when she'd have to face what Joe had to say.

Sorry I missed you on market day. Dan tells me you were in town. He said Joe's been asking about you so, although I know you asked me not to, I'm sending his letters on. I think you should write to him if only to tell him it's all over between you. Don't let the poor chap go on hoping. Well, you know how I feel about it — you should tell him what happened. If he really loves you as I think he does he will understand.

Abby sighed as she reached the end. Daisy had her interests at heart but did she really understand how soiled she felt, how hard it was to forget that dreadful day? It was more than three years now and still she had nightmares of that man's hands on her, his hot breath whispering those foul words in her ear. But how could she expect Joe to believe that Mr Wheeler's assault had not been her fault after the wanton way she'd behaved with him in Daisy's kitchen?

She put the letters in date order and opened the first one, written more than two years ago, just after he'd come to Daisy's house. A sob rose in her throat as she read his apology — no mention of her behaviour. He blamed himself entirely saying he'd missed her so much he got carried away.

She gazed round at the seemingly tranquil scene, the sweep of the hill with the cluster of farm buildings nestling in the hollow. But all she could see was Joe's anguished face as she pushed him away and told him she didn't want him. Maybe he would have understood if she'd tried to explain.

I know you're not that sort of girl and I shouldn't have pushed myself on you like that. Please write and say you forgive me. I will always love you — your loving Joe.

Biting back a sob, Abby turned to the next letter, dated a couple of months later. It was very short.

I don't know when you'll get this as we're at sea — can't tell you where. All I can say is that it is bitterly cold. I haven't heard from you and I hope that is because of the problems with the post and not because you have decided not to write. I will keep hoping — love Joe.

By the time she finished the last letter, tears were rolling down Abby's cheeks. As well as saying once more that he would always love her, he had poured his heart out about the long lonely night watches on board ship when all he could do was pray that he would survive to get home and tell her how he felt. *It's only the thought of you that keeps me going*, he wrote. *I can't say much as you know but you must hear the news.* The next bit had been blanked out by the censor. He ended with the hope that she would write back.

She clutched the sheet of paper, heart racing as she realized the significance of those blanked-out words. For the first time she faced the fact that he might never come back. How selfish she'd been. Surely it wouldn't hurt to give him a little hope, something to live for in the dark days ahead?

Dark clouds had built up while she'd been reading. She should finish the field before the rain started. She smoothed the letters out, folded them carefully and put them in her pocket. As she swung the starting handle, a voice hailed her.

'Having trouble?' It was Cissie.

'It's all right now,' Abby said, glad the other girl hadn't come along earlier.

'Mr Phillips wants you to bring the tractor back as soon as you're done. He needs it for another job.'

Abby looked across the field, measuring with her eye. 'It shouldn't take long.' She glanced behind her, making sure the tines of the harrow were in line. When she reached the end of the row and looked back, Cissie was still there, staring after her. By the time she'd turned the tractor round, the younger girl had gone. She could sense that Cissie had something on her mind but Joe's letters still occupied her thoughts and she soon forgot about her.

When she entered the farmhouse kitchen an hour later Mrs Phillips was tending to a newborn lamb. 'Am I glad to see you,' she said. 'Can you give me a hand? I'm trying to get dinner ready and this one needs feeding.'

Abby was glad of the chance to sit by the welcoming warmth of the range. Looking after the lambs was one of her favourite jobs. It was so rewarding when they built up their strength and she was able to put them outside with the rest of the flock.

When the others came in for their midday meal, Ethel gave her a dirty look. 'Some people get all the best jobs,' she muttered. Her nose was red and her hair was plastered to her neck with the rain.

Abby decided to ignore her.

After supper, as the others gathered round the wireless for the nightly news, Abby excused herself and went up to her room. She had no idea what she was going to say to Joe but she had to write now. She wouldn't make any promises about the future but it wouldn't hurt to give him a little hope. Who knew what would happen as the long months of war dragged on? If he came through safely it would be easier to let him down gently afterwards.

She promised herself it would just be a brief friendly note. But soon she found herself filling page after page, telling him about the farm, about meeting Wilf in the market, her suspicion that Dan and Daisy were becoming more than just friends. She didn't tell him why she hadn't written for so long. She hoped he'd think her letters had gone astray. It was the sort of chatty friendly letter she normally sent to Charlie.

14

The weight of the secret Abby carried still felt like a stone in her stomach, but once she'd written to Joe it didn't seem quite so heavy. Surely it wasn't wrong to try and cheer him up when he was facing such danger? She hadn't confessed, of course — she'd face up to that when he came home. But just knowing she'd done a little towards making him feel better had helped — that and having his reply to look forward to, although it was now several weeks since she'd written. Perhaps he'd given up on her after all.

She resolved to let the future take care of itself, to do what so many were doing during this long painful war, and live for the moment. She wouldn't let the burden of the past weigh her down so that she turned into a miserable, spiteful old maid like Ethel Wheeler. Neither could she be carefree and fun-loving like Cynthia. But at last she was beginning to regain her zest for life, to join in the laughter at the evening gatherings in the farmhouse kitchen.

Despite the permanent feeling of weariness, she enjoyed her work. As spring turned to summer the days grew longer with hay-making and harvesting in addition to caring for the animals. Work in the fields continued till dusk and sometimes the girls stumbled from exhaustion as they plodded back to the house and a late supper.

Abby seemed to thrive. Her slight figure had filled out, her face and arms tanned a golden honey colour. In contrast, the hard life had taken its toll on Cissie. She'd always been a pale version of her sturdy elder sister but now she was thin and drawn. When Abby tried to draw her out, Cissie shrugged her off.

She mentioned it to Cynthia one night as they were preparing for bed.

'She's worried about her mother,' Cynthia said. 'And her father's making her feel guilty — telling her she should come home.'

'Mrs Wheeler's been bedridden for years. I don't think it's just that,' Abby said, with an inward shudder at the thought of Cissie's father. Who could blame her for wanting to leave home?

'Well, there's nothing we can do about it,' Cynthia said, sweeping a hairbrush through her blonde waves. 'Besides, you don't even like the sisters.'

'I don't like Ethel but I feel sorry for Cissie.' As Abby turned out the lamp and settled down to sleep, she realized it was true.

For a long time she'd hated the whole Wheeler family. Now she realized only one person was to blame.

★ ★ ★

Life on the farm was hectic and time passed quickly. It was only when she fell into bed at night that Abby allowed herself to think about Joe and wonder why he hadn't answered her letter. Had she left it too late?

Autumn came round again and, despite Mr Phillips's dire predictions, the harvest was a good one. It was time to celebrate.

'It'll be nothing like the harvest suppers before the war,' Mrs Phillips said. 'But there'll be a social in the church hall after the harvest festival service. I'll need your help, girls.'

Abby and Cynthia joined in the preparations willingly, scouring the hedgerows for branches laden with berries to decorate the church and hall.

As they loaded the cart Mr Phillips appeared with a basket of fruit. 'Take these as well,' he said. 'And don't be late for milking.'

'Cissie and me can do that,' Ethel offered.

'It's up to you,' said Mr Phillips.

Ethel seized the advantage. 'Our parents don't approve of dancing, so can we go home instead? We can attend chapel too.'

Mr Phillips thought for a moment before agreeing, saying they could stay overnight. 'I know how worried you are about your mum,' he said.

'I'll stay,' Cissie said, ignoring her sister's frown. 'Someone has to be up early to see to the cows and I don't mind. Cynthia and Abby can have a lie in for a change — especially if they've been out dancing the night before.'

A lie-in meant getting up at 6.30 instead of 4.30 but those two hours made all the difference. Abby was about to thank Cissie for her consideration when Ethel snapped, 'Don't you care about our mother?'

Cissie's eyes filled but she stood her ground. 'You know I care. But there's nothing we can do. You go on your own.'

'Are you sure?' Cynthia asked. 'We don't mind getting up, do we, Abby?'

'Of course not. You go while you can.'

'I don't like seeing my mother like that,' Cissie said. She picked up an armful of greenery, changing the subject. 'Come on, I'll help you load the cart.'

Ethel walked off in a huff but Cissie for once ignored her. 'I'm fed up with her bossing me about,' she said.

'About time you stood up for yourself. Why don't you come to the social with us?' Cynthia said.

'All right.' Before Abby or Cynthia could say anything, Cissie took the carthorse's bridle and started down the lane.

The three of them spread the berried branches along the window sills, piling autumn leaves among them. The apples and pears from the orchard were heaped on a table at the other end of the hall with more contributions from local farmers. They'd be distributed to the village children and evacuees after the social. The rest of the produce would be donated to the cottage hospital. Nothing would be wasted.

As they walked back to the farm, Cissie said, 'Promise you won't tell Ethel I'm coming with you.'

'Cross my heart,' said Cynthia, rolling her eyes, and Abby laughed.

★ ★ ★

Ethel had caught the bus into town and Cissie offered to finish off the dairy work while Abby and Cynthia went to the church service with the farmer and his wife.

'I hope the vicar doesn't drone on too long,' Cynthia whispered, as they walked up the path between the gravestones. 'I want to get on with the dancing — not that there'll be many worth dancing with. I can just picture it

— a few old men and boys up one end of the hall, all the women at the other and the kids fighting to get at the buffet table.'

Abby nudged her in the ribs as they entered the church. 'Behave yourself,' she whispered, trying not to giggle.

She settled in her seat, taking in the elaborately carved roof beams and stained glass — such a contrast with the austere chapel she was used to. It was beautiful, she thought, especially now it was decorated for the harvest festival. Despite wartime restrictions, the villagers had put on a good show.

Cynthia's elbow in her ribs focused her attention on the vicar's welcoming speech. 'Our Canadian friends are here to help in the immense battle we are waging against an evil force,' he said. 'I've invited them to join us in the village hall after the service and I know you will give them a very warm welcome.'

'Hear, hear,' Cynthia whispered.

Abby looked round at the group of young men in unfamiliar uniforms occupying the rear pews. One or two gave sheepish grins when they saw Cynthia and Abby staring.

After the service Cynthia hurried across to the hall, dragging Abby behind her. 'Thank God we're not wearing our uniforms,' she said. 'I look such a sight in that hat.'

Abby couldn't help laughing. Cynthia couldn't look a sight if she tried. 'What's the rush?' she said.

'I want first pick,' Cynthia replied.

The music had already started, played on an old wind-up gramophone. The few young men present were bunched at the end of the hall near the buffet table.

'Where's Cissie?' Abby said.

'Never mind her, I want to dance.' Cynthia made a beeline for the Canadian servicemen who'd followed them in and now stood hesitantly near the door.

Abby hung back as her friend introduced herself and, picking on the tallest and best-looking in the group, said, 'I hope you know how to dance.'

'Sure do,' he said. 'Lead the way.'

One of his friends grabbed Abby and whisked her away and before long everyone was dancing. To her surprise she found that, as the evening wore on, she began to enjoy herself. In more carefree days she'd loved dancing and had often braved Gran's disapproval to accompany Rhoda to Kimball's dance hall in North Street. This wasn't quite the same but it was a chance to have fun and forget the war for a few hours — not to mention the other troubles that constantly weighed her down.

Halfway through the evening there was a stampede for the buffet and she spotted Cissie who had donned an apron and was helping with the teas. When Abby held out her cup to be filled she gave a wry smile. 'I don't think Ethel could object to this, do you?' she asked.

'I suppose not. But it's supposed to be an evening off,' Abby said.

'I don't mind. I'm happier doing this.'

Before Abby could reply, Cynthia appeared, the tall Canadian in tow. 'I never dreamed a boring old church social could be so much fun,' she said. 'What do you think of Larry, then — gorgeous, isn't he?' She smiled up at him. As he whisked her away on to the dance floor once more, she whispered, 'Don't wait up for me.'

'She certainly knows how to enjoy herself,' Cissie said and to Abby's surprise there was no hint of censure in her voice. If anything she sounded slightly envious. Once again Abby found herself sympathizing and thought how different she was away from her older sister's influence.

The Canadians were friendly and polite and Abby was happy to dance with them. But when at the end of the evening one of them asked if he could walk her home she said, 'I promised to help with the clearing up.'

'I'll give you a hand too,' he said. 'Come on, lads.'

Several of them stayed behind to stack the chairs and trestle-tables and one of them followed Abby into the kitchen.

'I'm Jim,' he said, grabbing the tea towel from Cissie. Soon the three of them were working side by side. Jim was friendly but not so loud as his friends and Abby noticed that Cissie blushed whenever he spoke to her.

When they'd finished and all the crockery was put away Larry and Cynthia reappeared, Cynthia looking rather flushed.

Outside, Larry offered to give them a lift back to the farm. Cynthia accepted, getting into the cab with Larry. Jim helped the others into the back where they were crammed with the other Canadians.

Larry dropped them at the end of the lane, promising Cynthia she hadn't seen the last of him. 'Now I know where you live,' he said.

The girls stumbled up the uneven lane, giggling like schoolgirls, even Cissie joining in. Inside Mrs Phillips had left a lamp alight and a jug of cocoa.

Abby only wanted her bed and she took her mug upstairs. She'd just settled down when Cynthia crept in. When her friend whispered, 'Are you awake, Ab?' she pretended to be asleep. She couldn't bear to listen to a blow-by-blow description of Cynthia's conquest.

★ ★ ★

Despite their late night Abby was awake before the alarm went off. She'd hardly slept, alternately racked with guilt for allowing herself to have fun when so many were suffering and then telling herself not to be silly. Her grandmother would only say she was living up to her reputation for being 'flighty' but surely there was no harm in it. Those young servicemen deserved cheering up when everyone knew that soon they'd be going off to fight.

Cynthia had done her share of 'cheering up' she confessed to Abby. 'I think this is it — Larry thinks so too,' she said. She stopped in the middle of fixing the suckers to the cows' teats and pirouetted across the floor, humming one of the dance tunes from the night before. She turned a dreamy face to her friend. 'Oh, Abby, do you believe in love at first sight?'

Abby nodded, remembering how she'd felt that night so long ago — Joe's first kiss and the realization that he was the one for her. No matter what happened, he always would be.

'Thinking about your sailor boy?' Cynthia

asked. 'He's not just a pen friend, is he?' For once her voice lacked its usual teasing note.

They worked in silence for a while, only looking up when Cissie joined them.

'Glad you came, then?' Cynthia asked.

'It was fun,' she said, her cheeks a little pinker than usual.

How different she was without Ethel's glowering presence. But Ethel would soon be back, showering them all with sharp comments and disapproving looks.

Cissie herded the cows down to the meadow, leaving the others to clean up. Mr Phillips helped load the churns on to the cart and, as they crossed the yard for their breakfast, Abby spotted a bicycle leaning against the fence. She hurried indoors. Surely there'd be a letter from Joe today.

Her welcoming smile dropped away as she realized it wasn't Bill sitting at the scrubbed kitchen table.

Dan looked up and attempted a smile. 'Hello, my duck.' His face was grey, his hands trembling on the sheet of paper he held and there was a hint of tears in the warm brown eyes.

Abby rushed across and grasped his hand. 'Joe?' she whispered. 'Tell me it's not Joe — please.'

Dan nodded and held out the crumpled

telegram. 'Missing in action, it says. We heard something on the news but couldn't be sure it was his ship. But then this came. I could've phoned the village shop — got them to bring a message. But I couldn't leave it to a stranger — I thought it best to tell you in person.'

Abby could only hold on to one thought — missing — not killed. 'He's not dead. I know he's not,' she said. And then the floor came up and hit her.

15

Abby woke to find herself on the sofa in the front parlour. Someone had covered her with a blanket and pushed a cushion under her head. She sat up, stiff and cold, momentarily unsure of why she was there.

Then it came flooding back in a nauseous rush — Dan's grief-stricken face, the telegram crumpled in his hand. Her own voice — 'It's not true, he can't be dead.'

Dan had tried to comfort her, patting her hand and saying, 'It says missing — there's still hope.'

But Abby wouldn't believe it. She was being punished — for flirting with Charlie, for giving her baby away, for daring to enjoy herself at the dance, and most of all, for the way she'd treated Joe. And now she'd never have the chance to put things right. She shook her head. 'Oh, why was I so horrible to him?' she wailed.

It was getting light. How could she have slept? She could hear sounds from the kitchen, subdued voices, a chair scraping on the flag-stones. She must get up. There was work to be done. She struggled to stand but fell back as dizziness swept over her.

It was quiet when she woke again. Everyone must have started work. She went along the stone-flagged passage to the kitchen and, as she opened the door, the warm smell of newly baked bread filled her nostrils.

Mrs Phillips turned from the range and smiled. 'Come and sit down. You missed breakfast so you must be starving.'

'I'm not hungry.'

'But you must eat.' Mrs Phillips cut the end off one of the new loaves and put it on a plate. She pushed the butter dish towards Abby. 'I'm sorry about your young man. I didn't realize you were serious about him.'

Abby realized she was getting confused with Charlie, but she didn't correct her. She couldn't stop thinking about Joe, thankful that she'd written at last and managed to open her heart. She just prayed he'd received it and forgiven her before . . .

Images of the stricken ship, so familiar from the newsreels, threatened to overwhelm her and she pushed her chair back. She couldn't eat.

Outside, in the frosty air, Abby stood in the farmyard and looked about her. She could hear the tractor chugging in the distance, and from the barn, Cynthia's voice singing '*Don't fence me in*'. The band had been playing it at the social — was it only two nights ago? It all seemed so normal and unchanging. How could that be when her world had turned upside down?

Cynthia came out of the barn with a forkful of mingled straw and cow dung. 'You OK?' she asked.

Abby shrugged. 'I think so.' She grabbed a fork and attacked the heap of muck in the barn, scarcely pausing for breath.

After a while Cynthia grabbed her arm. 'Hey, slow down. You'll wear yourself out.'

'That's the idea,' Abby said, grabbing a bucket and yard broom.

★   ★   ★

During the weeks after Dan's visit to the farm, Abby worked from dawn till dusk, scarcely stopping to eat, falling into bed at night to lie sleepless until exhaustion claimed her. Next day she would wake and start all over again. When the Phillipses and Cynthia expressed their concern she brushed them aside.

Although she told herself she'd accepted that Joe was dead, she still nurtured a tiny flicker of hope. But the weeks passed and gradually hope died. Even if he'd been taken prisoner, word usually got through. After a while she stopped looking for Bill each morning.

She immersed herself in the routine of the farm, refusing to go to market or to the pictures with Cynthia on their evenings off. As for dancing — she would never dance again. She'd been out enjoying herself, albeit innocently, while Joe was . . .

At this point Abby would shake her head and once more give all her attention to whatever job she was doing at the time. She refused to picture Joe maybe fighting to get on deck, or for a place in a life raft, struggling in the freezing ocean.

At first Cynthia was kind and supportive, listening while Abby berated herself, offering comforting platitudes. In the end she shrugged her shoulders and left her alone.

In her grief, Abby pushed everyone away although she knew they were trying to help. She couldn't help herself. It was easier to withdraw and get on with things.

★   ★   ★

Two weeks before Christmas Daisy wrote that Dan was ill.

I think it's the worry about Joe. He's not been himself for ages. The girl that brings

291

the milk told me he had a fall. I'm going to see him on my next day off. A visit from you would cheer him up too. He always asks about you — but of course I can't tell him anything since I haven't heard from you.

Abby felt a twinge of guilt for neglecting her friend. And the news of Dan was a reproach too. She wasn't the only one who loved Joe. Hannah and Wilf, too, who'd known him since he was a child, would be grieving. It was enough to shake her out of her own depression.

On impulse she asked Mrs Phillips if she could borrow her bicycle the next day.

''Course you can. And I'll say you're due a day off.'

Despite the cold wind it was warm work pedalling uphill and Abby paused for breath when she got to the top. The cathedral spire was shrouded in mist and she couldn't see the creeks and inlets of the harbour. She turned off the main road and freewheeled down the winding hill to where Dan's farm nestled in its hollow.

The wind tugged at her hat and she revelled in the freedom of sailing along the country lane. For the first time for weeks she felt alive. A brief flash of guilt, then she told herself she had to cheer up — for Dan's sake. He wouldn't want to see the state she'd been in these last couple of months.

Hannah came out of the farmhouse wiping her hands on her apron and greeted Abby as if she'd seen her only yesterday. 'There you are, love. I told Dan you'd be over, soon as you had some free time.'

'Daisy said he's been poorly.'

'Well, he's not bin himself lately that's for sure. But he's getting about now — helping Wilf with the pigs. They'll be back soon for their tea. Come on in.'

'You sure he's all right?' Abby asked, following Hannah inside.

'It was only a sprain but he couldn't walk for a week. Lucky he fell on to the hay bales so no bones broken. But he's been right fed up.'

'Is he all right now?'

Hannah shook her head. 'And he won't be till he gets news of Joe. He says he hasn't given up hope — no news is good news and all that. But I can tell he doesn't really believe it.'

Abby sat at the kitchen table and put her hands to her face. Her voice choked on a sob. 'Oh, Hannah — what can I say to him?'

Hannah put the cups down and touched Abby's shoulder. 'You haven't given up too?'

293

'Oh, I don't know. I tell myself he must be all right, then ... I dream about him, Hannah. We're walking across the fields together and then — I wake up ... ' She heard voices outside in the yard and brushed away a tear.

Still limping slightly, Dan came in, speaking over his shoulder to Wilf. 'I'm a bit worried about that boar.' When he spotted Abby at the table he broke into broad smiles. 'I wondered whose bike that was. What brings you here, my duck?'

'I've got an afternoon off and it was a nice day so I thought I'd pop over.' Abby tried to sound casual as if she were in the habit of dropping in for tea. But Dan wasn't fooled.

'I suppose Daisy's been telling tales. She do make a fuss, that woman.' But it was said with an affectionate grin. 'As you see, I'm up and about again — no slacking on this farm.'

Despite the cheerful banter Abby could see signs of strain on Dan's face. When she spoke of Joe, he said, 'There's always hope.'

At that moment Polly, the land-girl, came in and Dan introduced them. 'Don't know how I'd have managed without young Polly here,' he said. 'She and Wilf kept things going while I was laid up.'

Polly, a quiet shy girl, smiled and sipped her tea. She pushed her chair back. 'It's getting dark. Better get on with the milking,' she said.

Abby leapt up. 'I'd no idea it was so late. I'd better go.'

'You sure you're all right on that bicycle?' Hannah asked.

Abby reassured her. 'I've got lights.'

'That's just a glimmer. You be careful, girl.' Dan gave her a hug. 'Come and see us again. And don't worry, I'll let you know the minute we get any news.'

Abby could see that Dan did not expect the news to be good.

As she reached the top of the Downs the first stars were appearing. She stopped to fix her lamps, wondering why she bothered when they were only allowed to show a pinprick of light. She hoped that if anything came along they'd see her. There was more traffic on the roads these days.

She started off again and a Jeep passed her, then another, probably on some night exercise to do with the invasion. Despite the secrecy, everyone knew it wouldn't be long, though no one was quite sure exactly when.

Abby carried on pedalling as a voice hailed her. 'Going far — need a lift?' The Jeep drove slowly alongside, keeping pace with her. 'Come on, don't be shy.' The man leaned over the back of the Jeep. 'I know you, don't I

— Cynthia's friend?'

'Larry? Is it you?' Abby couldn't hide her relief. The Canadian servicemen were always polite and friendly. But she was wary of getting into a vehicle with strangers.

The Jeep stopped and Larry lifted her and the bike into the back. 'We're making a detour, Jim. West Chilton Farm,' he said.

'I thought you weren't supposed to give lifts to civilians,' Abby said.

'Hey, you girls aren't civilians. You're in the land army, aren't you? Guess that means you're fighting this war too.'

She smiled. 'S'pose you're right.'

As the Jeep slewed to a stop in the farmyard Larry asked, 'Are you coming to the Christmas dance at the camp?'

'I expect so.'

He laughed. 'Well, Jim, looks like you've got a dance partner.'

Jim blushed. 'Actually, I was wondering if your other friend would be there.'

Abby smiled. 'You mean Cissie? I'll make sure she is.'

'We'll pick all three of you up on the night. See you then,' said Larry as the Jeep roared away.

Abby was pleased that Cissie had found someone. But she wasn't sure if she'd go too. Still, if she was going to convince herself she'd never see Joe again she had to start living once more.

★ ★ ★

They were getting ready to go to the dance when Cynthia, applying her make-up, uttered a soft curse. 'This lipstick's done for,' she said. 'I've tried to make it last but I can't get any more out of it.'

Abby laughed. 'You don't need it, Cyn. You're quite pretty enough without plastering that stuff on your face,' she said in unconscious imitation of her grandmother. She wasn't worried that things like silk stockings and make-up were almost unobtainable these days. She'd never had the money to spend on them anyway. And the one lipstick she possessed had lasted ages.

Cynthia tossed her head. 'A girl can't go out without make-up,' she said.

'I know you don't feel dressed without it, so here — have this.' She passed hers across. 'I know it's not your usual colour but it's better than nothing.'

'Thanks.' Cynthia turned to the mirror and applied the soft pink to her lips. 'There, that's me done.' She stood up to let Abby sit at the dressing-table and picked up a hairbrush. 'Here, let me do your hair. You're so lucky to have these natural curls.'

As Cynthia brushed her hair, she said, 'I'm surprised Cissie agreed to come with us. That sister of hers looked daggers.'

'You know she believes dancing and wearing make-up are sinful — as for sitting in the back of a lorry with a load of soldiers — well!' Abby tried to laugh but she felt a twinge of guilt. Wasn't she too going against her upbringing? But the thought died when she remembered the hypocrite who claimed to uphold those beliefs.

Cynthia gave one last brush to Abby's hair. 'Well, I believe in having fun while you can. So come on. The boys will be here soon.'

★   ★   ★

Paper-chains and streamers looped across the ceiling, totally transforming the drab hut. Holly and ivy covered every window sill and along one wall a buffet table groaned under the weight of heaped plates of delicacies Abby had never seen before. No one would believe that food was rationed, she thought, as Larry handed each of them a glass.

She hardly had time to take a sip before she was whisked on to the dance floor by one of his friends. Despite her initial reluctance, she found herself responding to the music and joining in. She wasn't at a loss for partners and the evening passed in a whirl of strange faces and accents. Larry and Cynthia had disappeared, and whenever she looked round Abby saw that Cissie was deep in conversation with Jim. Good for them, she thought, although seeing her friends so happy increased her own loneliness.

Towards the end of the evening, she felt a tap on her shoulder. 'May I have this dance?' a familiar voice asked.

'Charlie, I didn't realize you were home — how are you?'

'Fine now — the old arm healed nicely,' he replied, taking her hand and leading her on to the dance floor.

Abby ignored the pang of guilt that she hadn't answered his last letter. As they circled the floor, he pulled her towards him, holding her much closer than she liked. 'I've missed your letters. They're the only thing that kept me going out in the desert.'

How could she tell him about Joe, that it was only recently she'd really started to live again? Instead, she told him how busy life was on the farm.

'Not too busy to come dancing,' he said.

She saw that he was upset and felt a twinge of annoyance. Just because she'd written to him a few times, did he think he had a claim on her? She changed the subject, asking how long he was home for.

'I'll be off again soon, God knows where,' he said. 'They've got something lined up for us.'

Abby guessed he was referring to the coming invasion, which everyone knew wasn't far off.

He led her back to her table and fetched drinks for them. He handed her a glass of lemonade and threw himself into a chair next to her. 'You seem to be having a good time,' he said. 'I saw you dancing with that Canadian feller. Thought you were saving yourself for sailor boy.' His voice was bitter.

'Joe's dead.' It was the first time she had really voiced it aloud.

Charlie gasped. 'Oh, Abby, I'm sorry, how could I . . . ?' His face was red and he gulped at his drink.

'You couldn't have known,' Abby said, stifling her irritation. He had no right to be jealous.

'What happened?' he asked.

'What usually happens to sailors in wartime when their ship's torpedoed?' Abby choked on a sob.

'I'm sorry. I know how you felt about him.'

'Yet you practically accused me of being a

good time girl,' Abby said, standing up abruptly.

Charlie grabbed her arm. 'Sit down, Abby. I'm sorry. It's just — I can't help being jealous, although you always said there was no hope. And I've been out with lots of girls too, but it's you I love.'

'Oh, Charlie, I'm fond of you, but — '

'I know — just friends. Look, I'll be off again soon. Who knows what will happen? Please write . . . ' His voice trailed away.

He looked so dejected that Abby smiled and said, 'All right — but don't go reading anything into it, mind.'

When a broad smile lit up his face Abby could see traces of the boy she had known and her heart sank. Did he think there was a chance for him now that Joe was out of the picture? He'd always been presistent but she'd never taken him seriously.

But when the last waltz was announced and one of Jim's friends came over to claim her, Abby was startled at the expression on his face. 'Sorry, Charlie, I already promised,' she said.

She looked over the Canadian's shoulder as the music started to see him scowling, the beer glass clenched in his hand. Maybe she shouldn't have agreed to keep in touch. She didn't want to encourage him with false hopes.

301

The music ended and there was a rush to find their coats. Cynthia and Larry appeared, seemingly from nowhere, both of them a little flushed. Abby took her friend's arm and whispered, 'Don't know why I bothered to lend you my lipstick.'

Cynthia giggled. 'And you — have you had a good time?' She asked, looking over Abby's shoulder.

'This is Charlie, an old friend,' Abby explained, introducing them.

Larry tugged Cynthia's arm. 'Come on, the Jeep's waiting.'

As Abby hurried to join them Charlie caught up with them. 'It was great seeing you again, Abby. Can I see you again before I go back?'

When she hesitated, he took her arm. 'Please?'

She nodded. 'But I don't get many days off you know,' she warned.

The farmhouse was in darkness when they got back. The Jeep dropped them at the end of the track and Abby stamped her feet in the cold as she waited for Cynthia and Larry to conclude their prolonged goodnight kisses. Cissie and Jim were more restrained but Abby still felt a bit left out.

Should she give in to Charlie's pleas? She shook her head. No one could ever take Joe's place. And besides, she didn't need any more complications in her life.

16

One day shortly after Christmas Charlie turned up at the farm offering to help. 'It was in the paper,' he said '*Lend a hand on the land.* So here I am.'

Mr Phillips, who never said no to an extra willing worker, welcomed him.

After that he was there every day of his remaining leave. At first Abby felt uncomfortable with him around. As they worked together, chopping turnips for the cows' feed or mucking out the byre, she would sometimes catch him looking at her intently. But since he'd bared his soul at the dance, he never gave any indication that he wanted more than just friendship.

Gradually she began to relax and even to feel some of the old camaraderie they'd had when they were working together before. It was still a relief when he told her he'd have to rejoin his unit soon.

Abby and Cynthia had finished clearing away the remains of their supper. The others had already gone up to bed. Cynthia lit a cigarette and sat down at the table. 'I expect you'll miss Charlie, won't you?' she said.

Abby sighed. 'In a way, I suppose. It's been fun but I don't want him getting any ideas. I'm not sure if I should keep writing to him when he goes back.'

'It's obvious how he feels about you, Abby. You could do worse.'

'I'm very fond of him. But . . . ' She sighed again.

'Don't tell me — he's not Joe.' Cynthia dragged at her cigarette. 'Joe's dead, Abby. You've got to get on with your life. Besides, who knows what will happen . . . '

'That's what I keep telling myself. That's why I agreed to write. If anything happened to him, at least he'd have something . . . '

Cynthia stubbed her cigarette out and ran her fingers through her hair. 'I do understand. I was engaged once — to an RAF officer. I know now that I didn't love him.' She gave a little laugh. 'I was just caught up in the glamour of it all — the uniform . . . But when he was shot down I was grief-stricken.'

Abby reached out a hand. 'I'm so sorry, Cynthia. But what about Larry — you love him, don't you?'

'Oh, yes. It's the real thing this time. But the point is, I still thought I was in love with Roger until I let myself start feeling things again. It could be like that for you and Charlie.'

'I don't think so,' Abby said. 'I know you're trying to make me feel better.' She arranged the plates on the dresser and hung the cups on the hooks below. 'I'm going to bed,' she said. She didn't want to talk about it any more.

The next day Abby took the tractor and trailer up to the woods to collect the logs that Mr Phillips had cut the previous day. She'd almost finished when she saw Charlie coming up the hill.

Today he was neat and spruce in his uniform, his kitbag slung over one shoulder. With a pang she realized she'd miss him. He'd always been able to make her laugh with his cheeky smile and daft pranks. And she had to admit these last couple of weeks she'd felt lighter of heart than she had for a long time. Was it all due to Charlie?

She waved to him as he came nearer, feeling suddenly nervous.

He waved back. 'Just came to say goodbye,' he called.

'You didn't have to trudge all the way up here. I'm on my way back.'

'Mrs Phillips wasn't sure how long you'd be. Anyway this little hill's nothing to a twenty-five-mile route march.' Charlie laughed.

As Abby bent to swing the tractor's starting handle, Charlie grabbed her by the waist.

Laughing, he lifted her out of the way. 'I'll do that,' he said.

'I can manage you know. I've been doing this for ages now,' Abby said.

Ignoring her struggles, Charlie kept his arms round her. 'I wanted to say goodbye to you properly — not in front of everyone.' He pulled her towards him and lowered his lips to hers.

For a moment she continued to struggle but as his lips caressed hers, she felt her resistance ebbing away. 'I just want a chance, Abby,' he whispered.

'I can't promise, but . . . ' she answered breathlessly.

'That's all I ask,' he said, pulling her towards him again. But this time, despite his resolve to take things slowly, his kiss was urgent, his breath hot, his body hard against hers, pressing her against the huge tyre of the tractor. It was just as it had been before and Abby recoiled, shoving him away and rubbing at her mouth.

He fell backwards and as he struggled to his feet she stumbled away from him. She heard the tractor start up behind her and ran faster.

He caught up with her at the farm gate. Grabbing her shoulders, he swung her round to face him. 'What's wrong with you?' His face was red, his eyes confused. 'It was only a goodbye kiss, for God's sake.'

She stared at him, confusion in her tear-filled eyes. 'I'm sorry, Charlie,' she said quietly.

'It's time you accepted that Joe's not coming back,' he said, grabbing his kitbag from the trailer and walking away.

'Charlie . . . ' Abby's voice was a sob. She should have explained. But how could she expect him to understand her confused emotions, the feelings his rough handling had conjured up? No matter how hard she tried to batten it down the memory of that snowy night when her innocence had been brutally taken away would always be there waiting to ambush her. And then there were the memories of other times and places, happy times with Joe, and that last time when she'd pushed him away — just as she'd pushed Charlie away.

She started to go after him but he'd already turned the corner. Anyway, what was the use? She couldn't tell him what he wanted to hear and she certainly couldn't tell him the truth.

Mrs Phillips came out of the back door, a bowl of scraps in her hand. 'Did you see Charlie?' she asked, scattering the food for the chickens.

'Yes, he's gone. He didn't have time to say

goodbye — had to catch his bus.'

Abby turned away to hide the sudden rush of tears, concentrating on piling the logs in the corner of the yard. Would she ever see Charlie again? And if anything happened to him, would she be able to forgive herself for treating him so badly?

★   ★   ★

There had been no word from Charlie since he'd stormed off and Abby still felt badly about the way she'd treated him. If only she had someone to talk to. She would have confided in Cynthia, but she was upset about Larry who'd been posted away a few days ago. Daisy was the only person who really understood. Maybe she'd get a chance to visit her later in the week.

As she blew on her fingers to warm them before attaching the metal cups to the cow's teats, she glanced across at Cissie in the next stall. She'd been crying. She was obviously missing Jim. Or was it something else? She'd been very quiet since her visit home at Christmas. But Cissie often looked upset after visiting her mother. It couldn't be easy seeing her lying bedridden. Mrs Wheeler had always been so strong — the real boss at The Emporium. But Ethel, who usually seemed unmoved by her mother's illness, hadn't been her usual self either. Something was wrong.

Abby didn't like seeing the other girl so upset. 'Is your mother all right?' she asked.

Cissie sniffed and shrugged her shoulders. 'She's the same — just lies there. Needs everything doing for her.'

Abby smiled sympathetically. 'It must be hard for you all.'

'Father leaves everything to the nurse. Too busy with the shop and his ARP work. And chapel, of course. Always on about duty.' Cissie made a sound between a sob and a laugh, muttering something else under her breath.

But when Abby asked her what she'd said, she shrugged and refused to say any more.

When they went back to the farmhouse for breakfast Bill the postman was there, warming his hands on a mug of tea.

Abby had stopped looking for letters — she'd given up expecting to hear from Charlie and she told herself she'd accepted that Joe was gone.

But when Bill handed her an envelope, she couldn't help that instant flicker of hope, quickly extinguished when she recognized Daisy's writing.

It was only a brief note, hoping that Abby was all right and bewailing the fact that she hadn't been to see her for so long. *'I've got lots to tell you so you'll have to ask your farmer for some time off. I'm on early shift this week so home in the afternoons,'* she wrote, finishing by saying she'd heard from Jimmy. *'He tells me he saw Charlie and they are both well.'*

Abby folded the letter and put it in her pocket.

'News from home?' Cynthia asked as they tucked into the plateful of bacon and fried bread that Mrs Phillips dished up.

'From Daisy. She says she's lots to tell me but she's not much for writing. She always seems to know what's going on — gets all the gossip from the laundry girls.'

'Gossip?' Cissie said, her fork halfway to her mouth.

Ethel nudged her sister. 'Some people have nothing better to do,' she said sharply.

Abby turned to Cynthia. 'It's just harmless stuff, who's getting engaged or married, who's died, you know the kind of thing.'

'That's not gossip — it's news,' Cynthia said. She looked up as Farmer Phillips came in, rubbing his hands. 'I think Abby's due a day off, don't you, Mr P?'

He hesitated and Abby kicked her friend under the table. 'It's all right. I know we're busy,' she said.

'You can have a couple of hours.'

'Thanks.' She'd meet Daisy from work and spend an hour with her. It would be good to catch up with her friend.

★   ★   ★

It was months since Abby had been into town and as the bus rumbled down North Street she gazed sadly at the bomb damage from the previous year. Although the rubble had been cleared away some of the shops were boarded up. In the seclusion of the countryside Abby hadn't realized how bad it had been.

In East Street the shops looked drab and empty, their windows criss-crossed with tape, sandbags piled near the doors. A queue of women in headscarves waited outside Macfisheries, shoulders hunched against the keen wind.

When Abby reached the laundry the shift had just ended and workers streamed out of the gate. She spotted the tiny figure of her friend and ran after her. She tapped her on the shoulder.

'Well, love, you're a sight for sore eyes,' Daisy said, her face wreathed in smiles.

'I've only got a couple of hours.'

'Time for a cup of tea,' Daisy said.

As they walked up the road Abby asked if

311

she'd seen Dan. 'Is he any better?'

'Well, he's not limping now and he's back doing a full day's work. But he's very down. Hannah told me he doesn't see the point of carrying on without Joe.'

Abby nodded agreement. Hadn't she felt the same for months now? 'Pity he hasn't got children of his own.'

'He always thought Joe would take over — even after he joined the navy. He hoped he'd do his time and then settle down on the farm. And then, of course, the war . . . '

Inside the cottage Daisy poked the banked-up fire in the range and pulled the kettle over the flames. 'I've got something to tell you. I couldn't put it in a letter — what with you working with those Wheeler girls.'

'Is it their mother?'

'No — their father.' Daisy's lips tightened as she bustled around, getting the cups out and warming the teapot.

'Daisy — please . . . ' Abby could hardly contain her impatience.

Daisy set the teapot down with a thump and sat opposite Abby. 'I was right all along. I knew you couldn't be the first girl he'd — you know.' She waved a hand and leaned forward. 'And you weren't the last either. Caught in the act he was. Mrs Robinson's girl, only fifteen she is. In the meeting room behind the chapel — Bible instruction it was supposed to be — Bible instruction — huh!'

Abby didn't know what to say. Satisfaction that Ernest Wheeler had been caught warred with pity for Sally Robinson. How many other innocent young girls had been violated while he was spouting fire and brimstone from the pulpit?

Daisy was still ranting on. 'That bloody hypocrite, two-faced swine . . . '

Abby put a hand on her friend's arm. 'Does everyone know about this?'

'They tried to keep it quiet, of course. But he's been thrown out of chapel and you know how gossip flies round this town.'

'I was thinking about Cissie — now I know why she's been crying. I knew something was wrong when she came back on Boxing Day but she wouldn't tell me.'

'Well, she wouldn't would she — her own father?'

Poor girl. Abby knew what Cissie must be going through. Hadn't she too suffered all her life from malicious talk?

Daisy poured more tea. 'I saw your gran in town the other day. She asked about you — if I had any news.'

Abby hadn't seen Aggie Thompson since the day she discovered she was pregnant. The memory of her harsh denunciation, her refusal to believe the truth, still rankled bitterly. It would be a long time before she was ready to forgive her. 'What did she say?'

Daisy hesitated. 'She was upset. She knows now she was wrong to blame you for what happened. I told her you'd had the baby adopted. Of course, she knows where you are from the Wheeler sisters but I think she'd like to hear from you.'

When Abby didn't answer Daisy shook her head. 'She is your gran, love.'

'I don't see why I should be the one . . . ' Abby stood up abruptly. 'She knows where I am — let her visit me, or write. I've got to go. I'll miss my bus.'

As the bus groaned its way up the hill towards Lavant, Abby's thoughts were in turmoil. She was glad old Wheeler had been caught out, but talking about it had dredged up feelings she'd long tried to suppress. She wondered about Cissie. Had she suffered at her father's hands too? It was hard to believe he would treat his own daughter like that but it would explain a lot.

$$\star \quad \star \quad \star$$

When Abby had gone Daisy couldn't stop worrying about her. That poor girl, what she'd gone through in her short life. She still wasn't sure she should have told her about old Wheeler. No sense raking it all up again. It wouldn't change what had happened. But Abby would have heard the rumours sooner or later. At least now Aggie Thompson knew the truth and could try to make amends.

As she sat at the kitchen table, trying to answer Jimmy's last letter, she didn't know what to write. It was hard when there was so much she couldn't tell him. She couldn't risk him passing any of it on to his mate Charlie Simmons.

Daisy was giving herself a headache worrying. If only she had someone to confide in. As if she'd conjured him up there was a knock on the door and she heard Dan's voice.

'It's only me. Got the kettle on, then?'

'Come in, Dan — door's open.' Daisy topped up the teapot, replaced the woollen cosy and got down another cup and saucer, thinking it was a good job she'd made a cake yesterday. Not that it was much to shout about, a fatless sponge that was more like biscuit than the light fluffy cakes she used to make.

'Well, what brings you to Chichester when it's not market day?' she asked, offering him a slice of cake. She didn't dare hope it was only because he wanted to see her.

Dan's round honest face was all smiles but

his eyes held a suspicion of a tear. 'I've got some news,' he said. 'About Joe.'

Daisy sat down and reached for his hand. 'Oh, Dan — is he all right?'

'Well, I'm not sure — but there's a glimmer of hope now, Daisy girl. I think he might have been picked up.' He fumbled in the pocket of his corduroy jacket and brought out a flimsy envelope. 'It's from one of his shipmates. He was wounded and wasn't able to write before. Here, read it yourself.'

Daisy squinted to decipher the spidery writing.

I was picked up straight away by one of our ships. I saw Joe swimming so I know he was OK then. We had to scarper because the U-boat was still around. But I heard that some of our blokes were rescued by a Russian ship. I'm sure Joe was among them. You've probably had an official letter, maybe Joe has even made it home by now, but I thought you'd like to know what happened.

Daisy finished reading and looked at Dan. 'Do you really think he's OK?'

'I don't know. But at least he didn't go down with the ship.' He grasped Daisy's hand. 'We've got to keep hoping.'

316

'Abby will be so thrilled.'

'Do you think we should tell her?'

'Why not?'

'She's got used to the idea he's not coming back. Suppose we raise her hopes and it turns out we're wrong? It's not fair to put her through all that again.'

Daisy nodded thoughtfully. 'She was here earlier and, I must admit, she did seem to have accepted things. Maybe we should wait for more definite news before we say anything.'

'I'll write to the Admiralty — see if they know anything about this Russian ship. Not that I expect them to tell me anything. They're so hot on secrecy. You know what they say: 'Loose lips, sink ships'. Still, they ought to inform next of kin.' Dan ran his hands through his hair and gulped his tea.

'They might not know anything. Still, we've got something to cling on to now.'

'You sure we shouldn't tell Abby? I could bike up to West Chilton and see her.'

'Best wait and see if there's any more news,' Daisy said, cutting another slice of cake and passing the plate to him.

17

When Abby got off the bus and hurried up the farm track to join the other girls in the milking parlour she realized that hers wasn't the only life Ernest Wheeler had ruined. She felt sorry for Cissie and even felt a twinge of sympathy for Ethel. She knew what it was like to be the butt of wagging tongues. But it quickly evaporated as Ethel took refuge in bitterness.

'I suppose your friend Daisy has told you all the gossip,' she snapped as Abby took her white overall off the hook and prepared to help with the cows. 'You don't want to believe all you hear.'

Abby's first impulse was to snap back and she took a step towards the older girl. 'I do believe it — because I know it's true. You couldn't say that when you made remarks about my mother. How does it feel to be on the receiving end for a change?'

Ethel didn't answer but her hands were shaking as she tried to attach the metal cups to the cow's udder.

Abby's elation that Ernest Wheeler had at last been exposed melted away. After all, it didn't change what had happened. That man had ruined her life — spoilt her relationship with Joe and left her with an illegitimate child whose loss was an ever present ache in her breast. And now his family had to bear the brunt of his wickedness.

But when she tried to express her sympathy, Ethel snapped, 'He's ruined our lives. I hate him.'

'Yours aren't the only ruined lives,' Abby said quietly.

Ethel opened her mouth to retort, but Cissie tugged her arm and she turned away.

Whatever she said would only make things worse, Abby thought, going to the furthest stall. Best to leave them alone.

Supper was a subdued affair, even Cynthia for once having little to say. The sisters went to their room early, leaving Abby and the others listening to the wireless. As the news-reader signed off Mrs Phillips rolled up her knitting. 'I'm for bed,' she said.

'Me too.' Cynthia yawned and Abby followed her up to their room, where Cynthia abandoned all pretence of being tired. 'I've been dying to hear — what's their father been up to — pinching from the collection plate?'

Abby sighed. 'I shouldn't tell you — it's not fair on them. There's enough gossip in town without us talking behind their backs.'

'But you hate them. Come on, tell me.'

'Only him. And with good reason.' Abby sat on the side of her bed, clasping her hands across her stomach. 'He should burn in hell for what he's done. I'm glad he got caught. Now he can't hurt anyone else.'

'You mean he . . . ' Understanding dawned on Cynthia's face and came to sit beside Abby, put a comforting arm around her shoulders.

Abby stifled a sob. 'Just when I think I've got over it, something brings it all back.'

Cynthia's arm tightened. 'Now I understand. How dreadful having to work with them — knowing what you did about their father.'

'I don't care about them,' Abby said with a sob. 'But my gran didn't believe me. She admired him. Preaching in chapel — fire and brimstone, punishment for the wicked.'

'He's the wicked one,' Cynthia said. 'He should be flogged. Well, now he's been found out, he won't be doing any more preaching.'

Abby's tears fell as she thought about her lost baby, about Joe and how she'd pushed him away when his eager hands had reminded her of that dreadful experience. Ernest Wheeler getting his just deserts was no comfort.

Cynthia squeezed her shoulders. 'He can't

hurt you any more, Abby. And you mustn't let what happened spoil things. You've got Charlie now. You must look to the future.'

She nodded. But she wasn't convinced. Cynthia didn't know the whole truth and she'd never tell her. As for Charlie . . .

★   ★   ★

Abby was down in the meadow mending a fallen gatepost, making it secure before the cows were moved outside. There had been a few days of mild weather and Mr Phillips had decided to put them out to pasture early.

It was warm work and Abby paused to take off her jacket. As she turned back to resume work on the gate, she glanced towards the house, her heart, leaping into her throat as she saw someone in the farmyard. There was no mistaking the telegraph boy in his distinctive uniform. Her first thought was of Joe — before she realized she wouldn't be the first to get any news. Chiding herself for her selfishness, she ran back to the house. Telegrams in wartime meant bad news and any coming to West Chilton Farm could only concern Tommy Phillips. She couldn't leave the farmer's wife to face it on her own.

By the time she reached the house the boy and his bicycle were on their way and Mrs

Phillips was standing by the door with the telegram in her hand. She didn't look too upset and a parade of names flashed through Abby's head — Joe, Charlie, Larry, Jim.

'It's for Ethel,' Mrs Phillips said before she could ask.

The Wheeler family had no one in the forces. 'It must be their mother,' Abby said. She'd been ill for years and the only surprise was that she'd lasted so long. Maybe the shock and shame of recent events had brought on another stroke. Poor Cissie — and Ethel too — on top of their other troubles.

'Those poor girls,' Mrs Phillips said, echoing Abby's thoughts. She'd heard the rumours about their father although she wasn't one to gossip.

'Shall I call them?' Abby asked.

'It can wait. They'll be back for dinner soon.'

Abby slipped her boots off and joined Mrs Phillips in the kitchen, realizing how hungry she was as she helped dish up the lamb stew and potatoes.

When the other land girls came in Mrs Phillips took Ethel to one side and gave her the telegram. As she read it, her face crumpled and a ragged sob escaped her. Cissie grabbed her arm. 'Is it Mother?' she cried.

Ethel shoved the yellow paper at her and turned away.

As Cissie read the few words her face paled and she swayed. Abby guided her to a chair while Mrs Phillips fetched a glass of water. She tried to think of something comforting to say but the words wouldn't come. Cynthia said what they were all thinking. 'She's been bedridden for years. It must be — '

Before she could finish, Ethel rounded on her. 'It's my father. He's dead.'

'What happened?' Abby asked.

'How do I know? It just says he died suddenly.' She turned to her sister. 'Cissie, pull yourself together. We've got to go — now. We can get the bus if we hurry.'

Mrs Phillips started to protest that they should eat their dinner first and Mr Phillips would take them in the lorry. But Ethel silenced her with a glare.

When they'd gone there was a short silence, then Abby and Cynthia spoke together.

'I wonder what happened.'

'Maybe there was a raid.'

'We'd have heard if there was,' Mr Phillips said through a mouthful of stew. 'No good speculating. We'll know soon enough. Besides, it don't matter how it happened — he's dead just the same.'

'And good riddance from what I've heard,' Cynthia said, tossing her golden head.

'Don't say that, Cyn,' Abby protested. She couldn't be glad Ernest Wheeler was dead. It would be more fitting for him to survive and suffer the shame of pointing fingers and wagging tongues. But she'd have been mortified if her friend could have read her thoughts.

★ ★ ★

The postman was full of the news next day. 'That there preacher, him what owned The Emporium — hanged himself you know. Couldn't stand the talk, I expect. And his poor wife laid up too . . . '

He would have gone on, but Mrs Phillips took the letters without offering the usual cup of tea. He shrugged and got back on his bicycle.

'There's one for you,' the farmer's wife said, handing the envelope to Abby. It was from Daisy and she guessed what it contained. But the single sheet of paper only mentioned the Wheelers in passing with the words '*good riddance*'.

It was the final paragraph which caught Abby's attention. '*I saw your grandmother today. She is truly sorry for doubting you and*

324

wants to see you. Why not pop in next time you're in Chichester. One of you has to make the first move.'

For the rest of the day Daisy's letter played over in Abby's mind as she led the cows out to pasture and cleaned the dairy. Try as she might to harden her heart, she couldn't help feeling sorry for the old woman, struggling alone in her shabby little cottage. Gran had done her best to take her mother's place. Her strictness had been due to her stern sense of morality. For the first time it occurred to Abby how Gran must feel, discovering that the man she'd looked up to was a far worse sinner than those he preached against.

'I'll go and see her on my next day off,' she murmured, scratching the sow's ears as she leaned over the pigsty wall. But if Aggie Thompson once started moralizing, it would be her last chance. She'd go and see Dad too, she decided, even if it seemed he cared so little for her that he hadn't bothered to get in touch. It was time to bury the past and look to the future.

★　★　★

The Wheeler sisters didn't return to West Chilton and the extra workload meant that neither Abby nor Cynthia could have any

325

time off. Spring was their busiest time and gradually the rhythm of farm life took hold. There just wasn't time to worry about what was going on in town. And even the progress of the war sometimes took a back seat.

There was a feeling that something would happen soon and that the war couldn't go on much longer. The roads around West Chilton were often blocked with army vehicles, causing havoc when farmers wanted to move flocks of sheep or herds of cows. Sometimes a Jeep would roar up the track and a soldier would ask directions.

After a while Abby and Cynthia stopped looking up, thinking it might be Larry or Charlie. When Mr Phillips returned from Chichester one day saying he'd caught a glimpse of General Eisenhower going into the Ship Hotel, they knew that something was definitely happening. The invasion of France couldn't be far away and it was unlikely any of the young men they knew would get leave beforehand.

At the end of April Bill brought the news of the worst ever air raid on Chichester. After such a long quiet period it was even more of a shock to hear how many houses had been damaged and people killed and injured.

'Where was it?' Abby asked, holding her

breath, praying that Gran and her father were all right. She'd never forgive herself if anything happened before she had a chance to make up with them. How she wished she'd done it sooner.

'Up the top of St Pancras, over St James's way,' Bill said. 'Not sure exactly, it's all cordoned off, lots of the houses are dangerous, could collapse any minute.'

Abby gasped. St Pancras was where Daisy lived. 'Not the cottages by the river?' she asked.

'Not sure. I think it was a bit further up. I know the school's been hit — lucky the kiddies were moved out — the RAF's using the building now.'

Mrs Phillips saw Abby's distress and put her arm round her. 'Don't worry. I'm sure your friend's all right. But when Perce comes in I'll ask him to let you go into town this afternoon and find out.'

Abby shivered at the thought of anything happening to her dearest friend. 'I'd better get on if I'm to have the afternoon off,' she said.

She and Cynthia worked silently together for the rest of the morning. Abby was glad her friend didn't try to cheer her up and Cynthia seemed to sense her need to immerse herself in her work.

★ ★ ★

As the bus stopped by the Cross Abby decided that after she'd seen Daisy she'd try to find time to visit her grandmother, Dad too. She felt a brief flicker of regret for neglecting him. Did he even care? After all, he'd never tried to get in touch.

In the laundry yard the vans were being loaded with parcels of clean linen ready for delivery. Mr Peterson, who was talking to one of the drivers, saw her and grinned. 'Abby. Come for your job back? Only joking. Daisy told me you're becoming quite the farmer.'

Abby smiled, relief making her legs shake. Daisy must be all right if Mr Peterson was laughing. 'Yes, farm work seems to suit me.' She paused. 'Is Daisy at work?'

'She was here earlier but I sent her home. The housing man was coming to assess the damage to the cottage in case she needs to move out.'

'Were the bombs that close?'

Mr Peterson told her which streets had been damaged and repeated what Bill had said about the school. 'We've been lucky so far,' he said. 'When you think what Portsmouth and Southampton have been through — '

'I'll go along to Daisy's now, then,' Abby

328

said, cutting him off. She didn't want to think about Portsmouth and what might have happened to little Joe, although he must have been evacuated.

★ ★ ★

Daisy was delighted to see her, although she was a bit quiet.

'You sure you're all right?' Abby asked.

'I'm fine. It was the noise — I must have slept through the warning. Those planes sounded right overhead — didn't have a chance to get out of bed before there were flashes and crashes. I hid under the bed.' Daisy gave a little laugh. 'Fat lot of good that would've done. Anyway, when the all-clear went I went outside. You should have seen it — and the noise, the smell . . . '

'It must have been awful.'

'Come and have a look.' Daisy led her into the tiny backyard and pointed to where a row of houses had stood. Now there was a huge gap, surrounded by rubble. Smoke rose from the heap and Abby could hear shouts and the scrape of shovels as the rescue workers searched for survivors.

She shivered and hugged her arms round her body. 'Bill said there were several people killed,' she said.

'Six or seven — not sure yet,' Daisy said, going back indoors. 'The man's been round and said everything's safe — said this cottage will last another hundred years.' She gave a nervous laugh. 'Shook the old place up, though. You should see the front room — load of soot came down the chimney. Suppose I'd better get on with the clearing up.'

'Can I help?' Abby asked.

'I can manage, my duck. You've got better things to do.'

Abby wasn't sure what to say. Daisy wasn't her usual self, hadn't even offered her a cup of tea, and she didn't think it was the shock of the air raid. What was wrong? If she'd had bad news surely she'd tell her? Maybe she was wondering whether to broach the subject of Ernest Wheeler's suicide. Normally she'd have been bubbling over in anticipation of a good gossip.

Abby filled the kettle. 'I've got plenty of time. And you don't need to clean up yet. You've had a shock. Sit down and I'll make you a nice cuppa.' She busied herself with the tea things, sneaking glances at her friend as she did so.

Daisy sat at the kitchen table, twisting her fingers in her apron and biting her lip. The kettle boiled and Abby made the tea. She sat down opposite her friend and took her hand. 'Something's worrying you — and it's not the air-raid,' she said. 'Come on, Daisy. I always tell you all my troubles — surely you can tell me what's worrying you. It's not Jimmy is it?'

'No — not Jimmy.' She hesitated. 'I heard some news and I'm not sure whether to tell you . . . '

'I already know about old Wheeler hanging himself and I can't think of anything else . . . '

'No, it's not that. Oh dear, I promised Dan, but you've a right to know . . . '

'Know what? Is it Joe?' Abby tightened her grip on Daisy's hand.

'Dan had a letter from one of Joe's mates — '

'When, what did it say?' Abby interrupted.

'This mate saw Joe being picked up — might have been a Russian boat, maybe even a German one. The friend was injured, which is why he's only been able to write now,' Daisy continued.

'Why didn't Dan tell me?'

'He reckoned it would be cruel to raise your hopes until he had more definite news. He was thinking of you, Abby love.'

'He should have told me.' She was annoyed — with herself as much as with Dan. How could she have given up hope so easily, have contemplated taking up with Charlie, when all the time Joe might be languishing in a prisoner-of-war camp? She turned to Daisy. 'Does he really think there's a chance?'

'He's not sure — that's why he was waiting for more news before saying anything.'

Abby understood why they'd kept the news from her. But she was still upset. 'Why did you decide to tell me now?' she asked.

'I had a letter from Jimmy. He said you've taken up with Charlie Simmons. At least he seems to think you're his girl now . . . '

'He's taking a lot for granted,' Abby said. 'I haven't encouraged him.'

'I've got nothing against Charlie, he's a good lad. But I didn't want you agreeing to anything if there was a chance Joe might make it back. You'd never forgive your-self . . . '

Abby clasped the cup in both hands, gazing into it as if she was trying to read the future. 'Do you really think he might be safe?' she whispered.

Daisy shrugged. 'You only have the word of someone who saw him being picked up by another boat. But it's something to cling to.'

'I won't give up — I never did really. And when he comes back I'm going to tell him everything. I can't live with these secrets any more.'

'I think that's wise, love. He'll understand, I'm sure.'

'I hope so.'

'Of course he will. None of it was your fault.' Daisy finished her tea and stood up. 'I hope Dan won't mind me telling you. But I'm glad I got it off my chest. Now — let's tackle that soot.'

By the time they'd cleaned the front room to Daisy's satisfaction it was too late for Abby to visit her grandmother. She just managed to catch the bus as it pulled away. She was out of breath, but secretly relieved that she had had an excuse to put off the confrontation.

18

Without the Wheeler sisters, who'd been given compassionate leave, the work at West Chilton was harder than ever. Abby didn't mind. The news from Joe's friend had given her new hope and she went through the days in a fever of anticipation that soon she would — must — hear from him. Everyone said that the invasion was due any day now and then the war couldn't last much longer. At last Joe would come home and everything would be all right.

She and Cynthia were in the pasture fetching the cows in when the gate opened. 'Look, it's Cissie,' she exclaimed.

'She's wearing her land army uniform,' Cynthia said as the girl drew nearer.

'What are you doing back?' Abby said.

'I needed to get away,' Cissie said.

Abby nodded sympathetically, knowing how hard the inevitable gossip and stares must have been. 'What about Ethel?' she asked.

'She's staying to look after Mother — and the shop.'

'I suppose the powers that be wouldn't let

you both leave,' Cynthia said.

'Actually, I asked to come back. Mother doesn't need both of us and I'd rather be here.'

'Good for you. We can certainly do with another pair of hands,' Abby said.

'That's what Mr Phillips said,' Cissie told them, following them into the milking parlour and taking off her jacket. Before long the three of them were working alongside each other in a companionable silence.

When they'd finished Cynthia fetched the lorry. Percy Phillips no longer insisted on loading up the churns himself. He'd long since come to appreciate that the girls were just as capable of doing the heavy work.

When she was out of earshot, Abby paused with the yard broom in her hand. 'Are you all right, Cissie? Sure you're OK to come back?'

'To tell the truth Abby, I couldn't wait to leave. I'm never going back, either. Mother refuses to believe what he did, says his suicide was because no one believed his innocence. Ethel backs her up.' Her voice broke. 'You know the truth, don't you, Abby?' Her voice dropped to a whisper. 'And so do I.'

Abby shouldn't have been shocked. Hadn't she suspected something like this for ages? But — his own daughter. Anger surged and she swallowed hard. When she felt in control of herself she said, 'You must put it behind you, Cissie. I know it's hard but life goes on.' It was a trite sentiment but all she could think of at the moment.

To her surprise, Cissie smiled widely. 'I intend to. I'm staying on the farm and I'm going to learn everything I can about agriculture. And when the war's over, when Jim comes back, I'm going to Canada with him — start a new life.'

'Jim — Larry's friend? I know you liked him but I didn't know it was serious.'

'Since that Christmas dance — we kept it quiet because I knew Ethel would tell our parents. But I don't care now. It's my life.' Cissie looked up as the lorry drew up outside. 'Don't say anything to Cyn. You know how she teases — and I can't cope with that right now.'

'Your secret's safe with me,' Abby assured her.

★ ★ ★

The big job next day was sheep-dipping and, as the weather had turned unseasonably hot, Mr Phillips said they would start very early in the morning to get it out of the way. It was hard work, even with four of them and Jess,

336

the sheepdog. By nine o'clock the girls were exhausted.

When Cynthia stopped to brush her sweat-dampened hair out of her eyes, Mr Phillips laughed. 'You think this is hard, my girl. Time was we had a flock ten times this size — two days it took us sometimes to get them all through.' He paused and gave a piercing whistle as one surly ewe broke away and lumbered up the field. 'Go, girl,' he shouted and Jess raced away, bringing the frightened animal back into line.

The farmer was in his element, working as one with his faithful collie. He loved his animals and Abby sympathized with his frustration as the government forced him to put more land to the plough. She knew Dan felt the same way, although his farm was much smaller than the Phillips's.

Cissie had already left to do the milking and, as the last sheep was dunked in the trough and hauled out dripping wet, Cynthia dried her hands on her shirt and said, 'I'll go off and give her a hand if that's OK.'

Mr Phillips nodded. 'Me and Abby can manage now,' he said. He screwed the lid tightly on the last can of sheep-dip and put it on the cart. 'Reckon we deserve a little breather,' he said, getting out the flask and sandwiches his wife had prepared.

In the shade of the cart Abby closed her eyes, listening to Jess's panting and the steady munching of the horse at his nosebag. The drowsy country sounds were shattered by the noise of engines from the other side of the hill. The sheep scattered and Jess leapt up, barking. 'Those danged fools playing soldiers again,' Mr Phillips muttered.

'I suppose they've got to practise somewhere,' Abby said.

'You're right, my girl. Sometimes out here it's easy to forget about the war — except for the fact that my boy's out there somewhere. But days like this, with life going on as normal . . . ' He shook the last drops out of his cup and screwed the lid back on the flask. 'Better get these animals down to the bottom field. Not so likely to be disturbed by all the noise.'

When the sheep were safely shut in, Mr Phillips went back for the cart, Jess at his heels.

'I'll go and help the girls with the cows, shall I?' Abby said.

'Yes, and after dinner it's hoeing the turnips. This warm humid weather has them old weeds sprouting faster than we can keep up with them.'

Abby didn't look forward to being out in the hot sun all afternoon. But on the farm you couldn't pick and choose. Still, she'd make the most of the cool of the milking parlour while she could. As she crossed the yard the roar of an engine startled her. At first she thought it was the army on exercises invading the farm and she was ready to tell them off before Mr Phillips came back. But it was just one motorcycle, its engine idling now, the rider astride the machine. He raised his goggles and grinned.

'Charlie, what are you doing here? I thought you were in Eastbourne.'

'I can't tell you. Remember, careless talk and all that.' He laughed. 'Pleased to see me?'

She wasn't really. Ever since Daisy had told her there might be a chance that Joe had survived she'd been meaning to write to Charlie. She hadn't heard from him since they'd parted so bitterly just before Christmas but she knew he wasn't the sort to give up easily. Why else was he here today? She ought to have written before, told him in no uncertain terms that they'd never be more than friends. But, knowing he could be sent overseas any day now, how could she do that to him? Still, he was here now and she knew she'd have to be firm.

She smiled tentatively as he dismounted and propped the motorbike on its stand. 'Is there somewhere we can talk?' he asked.

'We can talk here, Charlie,' she said.

'I meant alone.'

The yard was deserted. 'We are alone. Now say what you want to say.' She hadn't meant to sound so brusque but if she was nice he'd take it as encouragement.

'I only came to say sorry about last time. I got a bit carried away . . . ' He scuffed his toe in the dry dirt of the yard. 'I meant to write, but I couldn't find the words. I had to see you, before we go off . . . you know.'

'I meant to write too,' Abby said. It was the wrong thing to say.

His eyes lit up and a broad grin spread across his face. 'You mean it's all right between us?'

'No, Charlie. I was going to say there's nothing between us. We get on well and I enjoy your company. But it's not enough — '

'But I love you, Abby.'

'I'm sorry, Charlie. I don't love you.'

'Bloody Joe,' he muttered. His lips twisted bitterly. 'Time you got over him and started living again.'

Should she tell him Joe might still be alive? Maybe not. It wouldn't help. 'I'll never get over him,' she said softly.

'You say that now but you can't cling on to a dream.'

'I think you'd better go, Charlie. There's

nothing more to say.'

He took a step closer and grasped her hands. 'I won't forget you. Maybe when I come back . . . ?'

Tears trembled on her lashes. 'I'm sorry, Charlie . . . '

Instead of letting her go, he moved closer. 'A goodbye kiss — for luck?'

She didn't reply and he pulled her towards him. As his lips met hers she put her arms round him and hugged him, remembering the fun they'd had, how his clowning around had brightened their days at The Emporium. She'd always be fond of him, so maybe it wasn't surprising that her return kiss was warm, her hug a little more than friendly.

★   ★   ★

From the corner of the barn Joe watched in disbelief as Abby — the girl he loved, who had sworn she'd wait for him for ever — threw her arms round the soldier and kissed him. The passionate embrace seemed to go on interminably and Joe squirmed in agony. This was how he'd pictured himself — him and his Abby, a joyful reunion after so long apart.

Despite the way they'd parted so long ago he'd always felt deep down that she wasn't really rejecting him. There must have been another reason for her violent reaction to his love-making. He'd never dreamed it was because she'd fallen for someone else, though. He had written to her — passionate letters saying he understood, that he'd only acted that way because he loved her. He begged her to forgive him for his clumsiness. There'd been no reply — as far as he knew. The torpedo had seen to that.

Had he been a fool? During all those months in the hospital, listening to the foreign voices jabbering around him, desperate to discover where he was and what would happen to him, he had clung on to one thought. He *would* get home one day. And when he did, Abby would be waiting for him, she'd forgive him and they'd never be parted again.

But everyone had believed him dead — Abby too. When Dan told him, he couldn't wait to see her. Despite still feeling weak from his injuries, he'd grabbed Dan's old bike and set off to West Chilton straight away.

Now, he dashed his hand across his eyes. It hadn't taken her long to find consolation, had it? He wanted to rush across the farmyard, grab the soldier by the throat and take out his pent-up frustration on the man who'd dared to take his Abby from him. He clenched his fists and kicked the side of the barn, his anger turned on her. After all, she looked willing enough. His eyes blurred with tears. When he looked again, the soldier was astride his motorbike, kicking the engine into life. Abby waved, brushed her hand across her eyes, her shoulders slumped.

Joe's anger melted away. She was unhappy and he'd give anything to wipe those tears away, to see the smile he loved flash out — for him. But she thought he was dead. Hadn't Uncle Dan told him how she'd grieved, been the last one to give up hope? How could he blame her for trying to find happiness while she could? And now she was seeing someone else off to war.

A small part of him couldn't help hoping that the soldier wouldn't come back — a guilty thought, immediately suppressed.

Abby had turned away, walking towards the shed from which came the clanging of churns and the lowing of cows. She looked thoroughly dejected and, for a brief moment, Joe was tempted to go after her. But what would that achieve? He grabbed Dan's bike and pedalled slowly down the lane towards home.

★　★　★

Cynthia looked up as Abby entered the milking parlour and grinned. 'Did you see Charlie? He came to say goodbye.'

'Yes. He's just gone.' Abby wasn't in the mood to talk and she went to help Cissie with the churns.

But Cynthia wasn't teasing today. Her face was sombre as she said, 'They'll all be off for the big push any day now. You're lucky Charlie managed to get over to see you. I doubt I'll see Larry again.'

'I'm sorry, Cyn. It doesn't seem fair, does it? I didn't particularly want to see Charlie but he manages to get off and you two . . . ' She sighed, wishing that Jim and Larry had managed to come and say goodbye too. 'Well, we don't know for sure when they're going. You never know, they might get some leave.'

'I doubt it. It can't be long now.'

Cynthia was right. It was obvious from the frenzied activity, the build-up of military traffic and the plethora of different uniforms in the area that something was happening. It was supposed to be top secret but it didn't take a genius to work it out. Abby thought about Charlie, the dejected slump of his shoulders as he'd mounted the motorbike. Maybe she should have told him why she couldn't return his feelings. Even if Joe didn't come back, she knew now she could never settle for second best. But Charlie would have been more hurt to know that that was all he ever would be.

Abby heard the lorry and opened the shed door. Mr Phillips got down from the cab and stretched. 'Had visitors, have we?' he asked.

'Charlie came to say goodbye. He said he won't get any more leave now till after . . . you know.'

'Did you send him away with a flea in his ear then?' Mr Phillips grinned. 'He looked right fed up — pedalling away down the lane like fury. I nearly knocked him off his bike.'

'That wasn't Charlie,' Abby said. 'Not on a bicycle.'

Mr Phillips shrugged. 'Must've been someone lost his way then.'

They were so busy loading the churns, turning the cows out, cleaning the milking machines and hosing down the stalls that it was supper-time before Abby thought any more about the stranger on the bicycle. Why hadn't she seen him when she was speaking to Charlie? She'd been in the farmyard for several minutes and no one had come up the lane then. Maybe it had been the postman.

As they sat down at the table, Abby asked. 'Was there a late post today?'

'No. Were you expecting a letter?' Mrs Phillips said.

'I just wondered.' She carried on buttering a slice of bread and helped herself to pickles. It wasn't important — probably someone who'd taken a wrong turn.

But as she got ready for bed later that evening, she was still wondering. Four and a half years of war had made everyone aware of strangers, people who looked out of place. Not that there was anything of military interest around here, even if he had been a spy.

Cynthia burst out laughing when she suggested it. 'He'd be better off down in the town if he wants to find out anything. That's where all the top brass are at the moment, so I hear.'

Abby laughed too. 'I know — I'm being daft. But it's strange someone coming up the lane and not calling at the farm. It doesn't lead anywhere.'

'Well, at least it's taken your mind off your troubles. That's the first proper laugh I've heard for ages.'

'There's not much to laugh about, is there? I don't know how you manage to keep so cheerful. You must be worried sick about Larry.'

'Of course I am. But it does no good to brood. You have to get on with things.'

'You're right, of course.' Abby finished brushing her hair and got into bed.

Cynthia leaned over to put the lamp out and looked at Abby. 'It's not Charlie is it? I know he wants to get serious. But you're not over Joe are you?'

Abby hadn't told anyone what Daisy had let slip when she'd last seen her two weeks ago. She'd hardly dared let herself believe it. Even if Joe had been rescued after his ship sank, surely she'd have heard something — even if he was a prisoner? Sometimes she woke in the night thinking she might have dreamt the conversation with Daisy. Now, she let it all pour out and Cynthia listened sympathetically.

'I can understand Joe's uncle not wanting you to know about the letter. What good is it if you still don't know what really happened? Daisy shouldn't have told you — you've got yourself all worked up again, just when you were almost ready to settle for Charlie.'

'I wasn't. I thought I might, but last time he was here, he behaved so strangely. I was quite scared, actually. And then when I saw him today I knew it would never work out.'

'Did you tell him that?'

'Yes, I was quite clear. He was upset but I had to do it. It's not fair to keep him hanging on . . . '

'I'm sure you've done the right thing,' Cynthia said.

Abby lay awake a long time, staring at the dim rectangle of the window, until the early May dawn began to streak the sky. She'd just settled into an uneasy doze, when Cynthia gave her a shove. 'Come on, lazybones, rise and shine.'

She staggered out of bed and splashed her face with cold water. Another long day's labour beckoned and she could only be glad that the hard work would serve to take her mind off the disturbing dreams she'd had.

After milking and breakfast, Abby wandered down to the meadows by the stream. Two of the fields had been left to hay and, as there'd been a spell of warm dry weather, Mr Phillips thought they might be ready for cutting. He trusted Abby to make the decision while he checked over the machinery. Cissie and Cynthia went off to feed the pigs and check on the sheep.

Beside the stream, brushing her hands through the grass studded with wildflowers and inhaling their heady scent, Abby was reminded of country walks with Joe, in the first flush of their love, when they'd been getting to know one another and before he'd gone off on his long posting abroad. She'd never been happier. Her father's drinking, the lack of money, her grandmother's stern disapproval, had paled into insignificance as she lived for Joe's rare spells of leave and those carefree moments.

She had dreamed of their life together, certain that things could only get better. The loss of her mother, the disappointments and sufferings of her childhood — none of this mattered any more.

Ernest Wheeler's evil doings had changed everything and she had thought she would never be happy again. She'd convinced herself that Joe would blame her. So she'd rejected him — until sensible, forthright Daisy had convinced her that she should give him a chance. And then . . .

She leaned on the little wooden bridge, gazing down into the gurgling water and recalling how she'd pushed him away with no explanation. How often had she wished she could relive those moments? Would she ever get the chance to make it up to him? Had Daisy been right to give her hope?

She sighed and crossed the stream into the other field, checking the long grasses, feeling how dry they were. The sun beat down on her back. It was time to start haymaking and she walked back towards the farmhouse, more briskly now, knowing there was work to be done. It was useless to keep thinking about what might have been — or even what might be in the future.

19

Joe came downstairs rubbing his gritty eyes, his shoulder and leg aching from yesterday's furious cycle ride. When he was on leave he usually helped on the farm. But he hadn't fully recovered from his injuries and Dan had insisted he should rest and recuperate now that he was home.

He sat at the kitchen table, his head in his hands. Had he been too quick to believe the worst? But he'd seen her kissing Charlie Simmons. What else could he think?

He looked up when the door opened and Hannah came in.

'Want some breakfast, lad?' she asked.

'Not hungry,' he said.

'You must eat. Keep your strength up.' She began to bustle about the cosy kitchen and soon the smell of frying teased Joe's nostrils. Despite himself his mouth watered.

'That's it, eat up,' Hannah said sitting opposite him. 'It's good to have you home. It's been a bad time for your uncle.'

Before she could mention Abby he had finished. He stood up. 'I'll see if Dan needs a hand.'

'He's doing the milk round today. It's Polly's day off.'

'I'll help him. Can't sit around all day.'

'You're supposed to be convalescing,' Hannah said with a laugh. 'Go on then. But take it easy.'

Dan had already loaded the milk churns. 'Want a lift into town?' he asked.

'Thought I'd give you a hand,' Joe said, climbing up beside his uncle.

Dan didn't comment, just shifted over to make room on the wooden seat.

As Gertie ambled up the track to the main road Joe looked about him at the familiar green fields, the spire of the cathedral in the distance. It promised to be another hot day. After the bitter cold of the Atlantic convoys, the bleak months in the Russian hospital, it was good to be home. If only Abby . . . But he refused to let his thoughts go in that direction. It was over and he had to make the best of things.

Dan glanced at him. 'I know you don't want to discuss it, but are you sure you got it right?'

Joe turned on him. 'She was kissing him . . . '

'It could have been innocent. Abby loves you. No one grieved more when she thought you were gone — and for all I know she's still

351

grieving. I didn't tell her about the letter from that mate of yours — didn't want to raise her hopes. I mean we didn't know either — thought you were a ghost when you turned up yesterday.' Dan shifted on the seat. 'You shouldn't have left without talking to her.'

'Maybe — don't know what I would've said, though.'

'You could have told her how you felt, given her a chance, son.'

Joe went over the scene in his mind. That Charlie Simmons had always had an eye for her. And that kiss hadn't been just a friendly peck on the cheek either.

Dan clicked his tongue and Gertie turned down Orchard Street towards Somerstown. 'First stop, the Crocker sisters,' he said.

'Those old dears still around?' Joe asked, glad to change the subject.

'Oh, yes, very active in war work. On this and that committee — given them a new lease of life it has.'

'Do you still deliver to Mrs Thompson?'

Dan nodded, his lips tight. 'She's a hard woman, that one.'

'I'd better keep out of the way. She's never had any time for me.'

'Nothing personal. I try to make allowances for her because of Abby's mother.'

'I know she took it hard when Mrs

Cookson ran off with another man — her being chapel and all,' Joe said.

'There wasn't another man — leastwise she didn't run away with him.' Dan said. His voice grew soft and Joe turned to look at him. 'I told you I was in love with her before she married Wally. It was my own fault — that's why I think you should talk to Abby. Don't lose your chance of happiness through a silly misunderstanding like I did . . . ' His voice trailed off. 'Anyway, she disappeared after that night at Sloe Fair. I think she was frightened of Wally finding out who her lover was. She ran away — to protect me, I always thought.' His voice caught on a sob. 'Silly girl. It's me should have been protecting her.' The sob turned into an embarrassed cough. 'Never heard from her again. I just hope she managed to make a decent life for herself.'

'But why leave Abby behind?'

'Maybe she meant to send for her when she'd got settled. I don't know. All I do know is Aggie Thompson never forgave her for abandoning her daughter and bringing shame on the family.' Dan squared his shoulders and jerked the reins again. 'Better get on. The milk will go off before we get it delivered at this rate.'

Joe made up his mind. 'I'll go up to West Chilton this afternoon,' he said. 'Maybe I can stop history repeating itself.'

'Good lad,' Dan said, getting down from the cart. Within minutes he was whistling as he strode up the path to the Crockers' cottage and knocked on their door. Those moments of confession might never have been.

★　★　★

Joe and Dan had finished the milk round and turned the cart towards home when they heard the plane. It roared low over the town, its engine stuttering.

'Sounds as if someone's in trouble,' Dan said, shading his eyes against the sun.

'It's all right — it's going away,' Joe said. 'Funny, there's been no air-raid warning.'

'It's one of ours, I think.'

When the crash came Gertie's ears went back and she shied a little. 'Whoa, girl.' Dan hauled on the reins. 'Sounded over the market way,' he said, standing up in the cart and looking back towards the town. Smoke and flames leapt into the air engulfing the east of the town.

'Looks bad, lad.' Dan's face was pale and his knuckles whitened on Gertie's reins.

Joe touched his uncle's arm. 'Daisy lives over that way, doesn't she?'

Dan bit his lip. 'Not sure if she's at work

this morning, but I must find out if she's all right.' He turned the cart round and followed the crowd streaming towards East Gate. This was no ordinary air-raid.

As they reached Eastgate Square they saw that several shop windows had blown in, the road now littered with shards of glass. A warden came towards them. 'Can't go through that way,' he said. 'We've cordoned it off.'

Several policemen were trying to hold back the gaping crowd. The clang of fire engines and ambulances pierced the air. Joe tried to reassure his uncle but he was convinced that something had happened to Daisy.

As rumours flew among the crowd they learned that the plane was an American bomber. But no one really knew what had happened, except that the laundry was on fire. Dan turned to Joe. 'Look, lad. I know you're anxious to get up to West Chilton. I'll hang around here until there's any news. I can't go home yet.'

Desperate as he was to see Abby, Joe was reluctant to let Dan face bad news on his own. Comforting himself with the thought that she was safe in the country, he said, 'I'll stay. Abby's not going to run away.'

Dan nodded gratefully. 'Thanks.'

★ ★ ★

The weather forecast wasn't good and at West Chilton they were desperate to get the haymaking finished before it changed.

Abby should have been feeling happier today, the end of the war was in sight, and there was the joyous hope that Joe would be restored to her. But all she could think of was Charlie and how sad he'd looked as she said goodbye. She hated hurting him.

She bent to fork another load of hay, tossing it to Cynthia, who stood on top of the cart, her blonde waves shining in the sun, looking like one of those WLA recruiting posters. Her mood lightened and she couldn't help smiling.

Cissie caught her look and grinned. 'How does she do it?' she asked, glancing at Cynthia, then down at her dusty clothes, brushing at the hayseeds lodged in her hair. 'Be just my luck if Jim turned up now.'

'Come on you two — stop chatting. We want to get done before lunch,' Cynthia called.

'Come down and give us a hand, then,' Cissie said.

'I'm stopping up here — someone's got to do the hard jobs,' Cynthia said.

Abby was glad of the friendly banter taking her mind off things. Since Ethel had left the atmosphere was much lighter. She couldn't believe the difference in Cissie, who'd blossomed since escaping her sister's influence and falling in love.

At midday they sat in the shade of the hedge to eat the pasties Mrs Phillips had made. They couldn't relax for long — haymaking had to be done quickly while it was dry. The weather could change without warning.

'If we finish today, we'll start building the ricks tomorrow,' Mr Phillips said, swallowing the last of his pasty and starting the mowing machine.

Towards the end of the afternoon Mr Phillips stopped the machine at the top of the hill. He stood up, shading his eyes and looking down towards the town.

'What's up? It's not break-time,' Cissie said, abandoning the cart.

'Must have been an air-raid,' Mr Phillips said.

The girls ran towards him and leaned on the gate, haymaking forgotten, gazing silently at the dense column of black smoke billowing up into the blue sky. They hadn't heard the ack-ack guns from the hill further to the east.

'Could've been a hit and run,' Percy muttered.

If it had been a full-scale raid surely they'd have heard something, even in their sheltered valley.

The smoke was well to the east of the cathedral spire, so it was unlikely Somerstown had been affected.

'Maybe Mother and Ethel are all right,' Cissie said. 'Your family too.'

Abby sighed with relief. She still hadn't made her peace with her family and she'd never forgive herself if anything happened before she had a chance to do so. But her eyes remained fixed on the dense column of smoke. Wasn't that near the laundry? Her thoughts turned to Daisy. Was she on the afternoon shift? She had to find out.

Mr Phillips sensed her distress. 'Maybe it's not as bad as it looks from up here.'

She shook her head, fighting tears.

'I'm sorry — of course you're worried. When we're finished you two can get the bus into town and find out what's going on.' He smiled at Cynthia. 'You'll have to manage the milking on your own, lass.'

The short bus journey seemed to take for ever and Abby was conscious of Cissie's sweaty hand clutching her arm all the way into town. Despite her repeated reassurances — as much for herself as for her friend — Cissie seemed determined to believe the worst. Maybe she had guilty feelings about her family too, Abby thought.

The bus reached the outskirts of town and

Cissie jumped down. 'I'll see you later,' she said, hurrying away.

In the town centre Abby stumbled to the door so that she could be first off. The conductor put out a hand to steady her. 'Here, what's the rush?'

'I need to find out about the raid, who got hit,' she said.

'Bad business that. Happened this morning but they still haven't put the fire out,' he said.

'Where?' Abby felt like shaking him.

'Wasn't a raid, you know — one of them big American bombers, crashed on the laundry, nearly hit the petrol depot.'

Her stomach lurched and before the bus stopped, she jumped down and started to run.

Beyond Eastgate the streets were cordoned off and groups of people stood in shocked silence. Abby pushed to the front of the crowd and waylaid an ARP warden. 'Is everyone all right?'

'Do you have relatives working in the laundry or the garage?' the policeman asked.

'A friend,' she stammered.

'Sorry — can't give you any information. You'll have to wait like everyone else.'

A woman in the crowd touched Abby's arm. 'I heard that several people were hurt but no one killed. It could be just a rumour.

No one really knows.'

'The bus conductor told me it was a plane crash.'

'Yes, an American bomber. I think he tried to head out to sea — but something went wrong. Someone said the plane turned back and headed for the city after the pilot baled out.'

The ARP warden addressed the crowd. 'No use you folks hanging around here. I suggest you all go home. Next of kin will be informed as soon as there's any news,' he said.

They began to disperse reluctantly but Abby hesitated. With the road closed she couldn't get through to Daisy's cottage without a long detour. Besides, if she found no one home she'd be even more worried. Maybe she should do as the warden suggested — go home and wait for news. Or perhaps she should go and see Gran. She might not get another chance for ages now they were so busy on the farm.

As she turned away someone called her. 'Abby, thank God. I was trying to remember the name of the farm where you work.'

It took a moment for Abby to recognize Norman Peterson, the laundry manager. His overall was torn and filthy, his normally cheerful red face streaked with soot. One of his hands was wrapped in a makeshift bandage.

'Mr Peterson, you're safe. What about Daisy — is she all right?' Abby's heart sank as the foreman's smile of greeting faded.

'She's been taken to hospital,' he said. 'Look love, I must go. I've got to help the warden — there may be more people trapped inside.'

'Thanks, Mr Peterson,' Abby said, hurrying away.

It was only after she'd turned the corner that she realized she hadn't asked about Maggie, her old supervisor, or the other girls she had worked with — so long ago now, it might have been in another life. She prayed they were all right but mostly her prayers were for Daisy, the friend who'd stuck by her through all her troubles. She couldn't bear it if she lost her too.

The reception area of the Royal West Sussex hospital was chaotic and Abby had a long wait before she was told that visiting was limited to close family only.

'But there's only her nephew in the army and her cousin in Norfolk.'

'I suppose we could make an exception — but not today. Why not pop in tomorrow for a few minutes.'

Despite her pleading that she had to get back to the farm and couldn't get any more time off, the ward sister was adamant.

Abby choked back a sob at the thought of her friend lying there with no one to care. She wondered if Dan knew what had happened. He must have seen the smoke but would he have realized that the laundry had been hit? She'd have to let him know — Jimmy too. Perhaps he'd get compassionate leave.

★   ★   ★

Dan hung around for hours but there was no news. The scene of the crash was chaotic and no one seemed to know anything. But he refused to go home. Eventually he persuaded Joe to take Gertie and the cart back to Applegate. 'Go and see Abby. The longer you leave it, the harder it'll be.'

When Joe reached the farm Hannah was waiting by the gate. 'Dan phoned,' she said. 'Daisy's in the Royal West. Not badly hurt, they say — but he's hanging around in case they let him see her.'

Wilf came out of the barn and took Gertie's reins. 'You look whacked, son. I'll see to her. You go and sit down.'

Joe followed Hannah into the house and sank into a chair. 'It was awful, Hannah. The noise and the smell . . . '

'Dan said you're going to see Abby. But you must have a bite before you go. Don't forget you're still convalescing. You've got to keep your strength up.'

He managed to eat a little and gulped down two cups of Hannah's strong brew. Ignoring the old woman's protests he got Dan's bike out of the barn and set off. Cycling would probably be quicker than getting the bus.

As he came up the hill towards the hospital he spotted Dan by the bus stop.

'Did they let you see her?'

'Only for a minute. Close family only they said. But I told them I was her fiancé.' Dan grinned. 'She'll have to say yes now.' He ran his hand through his hair. 'She's asking for Abby.'

'I'd better get a move on then,' Joe said. 'Maybe her boss will let her off.'

Dan shook his head. 'She was at the hospital asking for Daisy. I must have just missed her.'

Joe's heart began to beat faster at the thought of her being so near. He still wasn't sure what he'd say. Of course, she still thought he was dead, but once she'd got over the shock, would she be pleased . . . or sorry?

As he got back on the bike the wail of the siren pierced the air. 'Not a raid on top of everything else,' Dan said. 'Let's hope it's a false alarm.'

But as the siren's last notes died away the guns started and they heard the heavy drone of bombers. They were still some distance away from the shelter when a bomb dropped nearby.

Joe's nails dug into the palm of his hand. This was nowhere near as bad as the ship being torpedoed. But it wasn't fear for himself that made him tremble. He prayed that Abby had gone back to the farm.

20

Abby had been standing at the bus stop for ages. Maybe the buses had stopped running. The plane crash had disrupted everything.

On impulse she decided to call on her grandmother as she was so near. It was time they were reconciled.

As she turned the corner by the Sun public house the piercing wail of the air raid siren set her heart hammering. The door flew open and she shrank back against the wall as she recognized her father. He was the last person she wanted to see.

His eyes widened as he spotted Abby. 'Is that my little girl?' He staggered towards her. 'So, you've come to see your old man at last. Been a long time, gel.' He clutched her arm and she recoiled at the smell of stale beer on his breath.

She pulled away. 'I'm on my way back to the farm, Dad.'

'Won't be no buses now,' he said as the wail of the siren died away and the noise of the anti-aircraft guns started up. 'Better come home with me.'

'We should go to the shelter.'

'No — if I'm going to die, it'll be in me own bed.' He staggered towards Tanner's Court.

Abby heard the drone of planes above the chatter of the guns and sighed. Better get him home. When the all-clear went she'd walk down to the bus station to see if the buses were running.

Holding Wally's arm, she stumbled along George Street, down the dark twitten into Tanner's Court. As she opened the cottage door, the sour smell of neglect hit her — a combination of damp, unwashed clothes and spoilt food. Taking shallow breaths, she helped her father into the battered armchair in front of the fireplace where he immediately flopped down and began to snore.

Making sure the blackout was firmly in place, Abby lit the gas lamp and looked round the tiny room, her gaze coming to rest on her father sprawled in his chair. It was a sight familiar from her childhood, yet something was different. With a pang she realized he'd aged. His hair, once dark and thick, now hung in lank grey strands, his face was threaded with broken veins and his clothes were shabby and unwashed.

'Oh, Dad, I'm sorry,' she murmured. He was still her father after all and, as so often in the past, she made excuses for his behaviour

— his experiences in the last war, the loss of his wife. Since she'd been away it had been easier to remember the drunken beatings, the housekeeping money frittered away, his refusal to stick at a job so that they could leave this hovel and find a decent home.

Now, all she saw was a pathetic, broken old man and her soft heart was moved to pity and the familiar guilt. Surely he wouldn't have deteriorated so badly if she'd been here to look after him?

But, as she tucked a blanket round him and started cleaning the room, she told herself firmly it wasn't her fault. He'd begun to slide into dissipation long before she was old enough to do anything about it.

She was hardly aware of the drone of planes, the rat-tat of the guns until a loud crash nearby shook the little cottage. The cupboard under the stairs was supposed to be the safest place. She shook Wally's arm. 'Dad, wake up.'

'Leave me alone. Can't a bloke sleep?' he mumbled, lashing out at her.

'There's a raid, Dad.' Sobbing, she managed to rouse him and they stumbled across the room. She pushed him into the cupboard, squeezing in beside him.

Wally came fully awake. 'Need a drink,' he muttered, pushing the door open and falling back into the room.

'Dad, come back,' Abby screamed as a louder crash shook the little cottage to its foundations. All went quiet, except for the buzzing in her ears. She shook her head. 'Dad, are you all right?' Her voice sounded faint and tinny.

She couldn't move. In the pitch darkness she felt the weight of a beam across her legs. Her fingers scrabbled on dusty brick. She was trapped.

Gradually her hearing returned — a sharp scream, running footsteps, shouting. And the sinister creaks and rattles as the debris settled. Her leg throbbed and she felt blood oozing from the wound. Her throat was parched, her nostrils clogged with dust. She tried to shout but the sound came out as a croak.

Surely someone would rescue them? She listened intently. Nothing. Had Dad escaped? Was he even now summoning help? It was a forlorn hope and Abby gulped back a sob. She shifted her position and a trickle of dust rained down. Enfolded in pitch blackness she willed herself to keep calm and began to pray.

★　★　★

As Joe and Dan reached the shelter, an ARP warden approached. 'We need some men. We think someone's trapped,' he said.

Joe clutched Dan's arm as they turned the corner and saw the ruins of Tanner's Court, the gaping hole where Number Four had stood.

'Don't worry, lad. She'll be back at the farm by now.'

The warden stopped. 'You know who lives here?'

'My girlfriend's father.'

'Was he at home?'

Joe shook his head. 'Don't know.'

The warden glanced at the women standing nearby. 'Anyone know how many people were here?'

'We all went to the shelter except Mrs Jones — she refused to leave. And I think Wally Cookson was at home,' one of them said.

'Probably drunk again,' another said.

'He had a visitor. I heard voices.' The woman shrugged. 'The walls are so thin.'

'Right — three people possibly trapped. We'd better get to it.'

They started to remove the rubble. As darkness fell they stopped to allow a glimmer of torchlight to play over the ruins. When the rescue squad arrived, Joe and Dan were pushed aside and could only watch helplessly.

'Get off home, you lot. Can't do any good

hanging around here,' said the warden.

But although Joe told himself that Abby wasn't — couldn't possibly be — trapped, he couldn't tear himself away. After a few minutes he began to scrabble at the debris.

'Hang on a minute, son. If you're going to help, do it right.' The warden showed him how to remove the rubble without disturbing what was underneath. He worked steadily for hours, careless of his cut hands, the pain in his recently healed wounds.

The warden held up a hand for silence and Joe's heart started thumping painfully as they lifted someone out. One of the waiting women said, 'It's Mrs Jones.'

'Did you get the others out — Wally and his daughter?' Joe heard her say as they laid her on the stretcher. 'I saw her go in, just after the siren went.'

Joe began to dig with his hands again. 'Abby, please be all right,' he muttered, shrugging off those who tried to stop him. 'I've got to get her out.'

★　★　★

Dawn was streaking the eastern sky when they pulled Wally Cookson's broken body from the wreckage. But he lapsed into unconsciousness before he could tell them if his daughter had been with him.

'We must carry on, lads — just in case she's there,' the warden said.

They soon stopped again and someone peered into the hole they'd excavated. 'Look, there she is.'

Joe pushed the man aside, catching a glimpse of dark hair and a scrap of blue cloth before the warden grasped his shoulder. 'Leave it to us, son. There's nothing to be done for this one.'

Sobbing, Joe leaned against a crumbling wall, covering his face with his hands. 'Why didn't I speak to her yesterday?' he moaned. Now, it was too late.

Dan's words of comfort lodged in his throat. Abby was gone — his last link with the woman he'd loved and lost. Anger burned in his chest and he longed to man one of the guns, to fire again and again at the threatening sky.

He became aware of a muffled exclamation from one of the men. 'Oh, my God — what have we got here? Hey, Bill, come and look at this.'

Something in his tone caught Dan's attention and he followed the warden across the cobbles, looking down at the body they'd brought out. His vision blurred. No, it couldn't be.

'Looks like she's been down there a long time — whoever she is,' the man said.

Dan gasped. The hair — so like Abby's — and that blue dress. He remembered that. She'd been wearing it the last time he saw her.

His knees buckled and he gave a stifled groan. 'Carrie — no . . . '

Someone thrust a cup at him. 'Here, drink this, mate. I told you to stay away. Not a pretty sight if you're not used to it.'

Dan pushed the hand away. He looked at the body again. 'It is Carrie, isn't it?'

'You know her, mate? You sure?'

Dan explained and the warden decided they needed a policeman. While they waited, the workmen leaned on their shovels, drinking the tea that someone had brought from a nearby cottage.

Joe took no notice of the murmuring voices. They'd get her out and take her away. But he had to make sure it was her. He stood, his legs shaky, noticing how pale his uncle was. Of course, Dan loved Abby too.

'It wasn't her,' Dan said, his voice breaking. 'It was — '

'But they've stopped digging,' Joe interrupted.

One of the men spoke up, still leaning on his shovel. 'They said there was three and we've got three out. No point carrying on. We can't hear anything and we don't know for sure the girl was there.'

'Dan, tell them — they must be sure . . . ' Tears streamed down Joe's dirt-streaked face as he fell to his knees once more, tearing at the debris.

21

Abby moaned, pain shooting through her as she tried to move. Had she been unconscious? Did anyone know she was there? She began to push at the rubble covering her legs but the rattle of falling debris forced her to stop. She didn't want the whole lot caving in on her.

She realized that her legs were crushed but apart from that she didn't seem to be hurt anywhere else.

Turning her head warily, she noticed a pinprick of light. It had been dusk when she arrived at the cottage. She must have been here all night. Had the rescue workers — if there were any — given up already? And what about her father? Was he safe?

She tried to shout but her voice was a hoarse croak. A sob caught in her throat as she realized that no one knew where she was.

After a moment she rallied. In that case, she'd have to get out by herself. A beam was wedged at an angle an inch above her head, creating the air pocket that had probably saved her life. The light came from a small hole. If she could move some of the debris, maybe she could wriggle round and make the hole bigger. Even if she couldn't get out, she could shout.

In minutes, the tiny space was filled with choking dust. She stopped, holding her hand over her mouth and nose and taking shallow breaths.

'I can't give up,' she murmured. 'Take it easy, one piece at a time.'

Engrossed in moving the small pieces of plaster and brick, trying not to stir up more dust, she was scarcely aware of the sounds above her head.

The joist above her moved, and a lump of plaster fell on her. Someone was out there. She tried to shout but no sound came from her parched throat.

'Is anyone there?' The voice seemed to come from a long way off.

Abby coughed and tried again. 'I'm here — don't leave me.'

'I heard something. Come on, lads, don't give up now.'

Thank God. She'd soon be out of here — Dad too.

The voices of the rescue squad rose and fell and she thought she heard Joe calling her. Was she dreaming?

Suddenly, the weight on her legs lifted, sending waves of pain through her body.

Everything went dark again.

When she came to someone was holding her hand and she heard Joe's voice again. 'It's all right, Abby — you're safe now.'

She smiled drowsily. She must have died and dear Joe had come to meet her, she thought. She'd heard of people being greeted by loved ones who had gone before.

When she opened her eyes again, she was lying on a stretcher and Joe was there, gripping her hand as if he'd never let go.

'Is it really you, Joe? I thought you were — '

'As you can see — I'm alive and well.' Despite his attempt to sound jaunty, Abby could see lines of strain around his eyes.

'I never gave up hope,' she said.

A shadow crossed his face and Abby thought he was remembering the ship being torpedoed. His grip tightened. 'There's so much I want to say, Abby.'

The starched figure of a nursing sister appeared. 'You'll have to say it later, young man,' she said. 'We must get that leg seen to. You can come back later.'

Reluctantly, Abby released Joe's hand. 'Don't go away,' she whispered.

Joe watched as Abby was wheeled into the operating theatre before returning to the waiting room where Dan and Mrs Thompson were sitting.

The old woman jumped up. 'Is she going to be all right?' she demanded.

Joe had always been nervous of Abby's grandmother but now her look of anguish made her seem less formidable. 'She'll be fine. They're going to operate on her leg but otherwise she's not badly hurt.'

Aggie Thompson dabbed her eyes with a damp handkerchief. 'I'll never forgive myself. I judged that girl so harshly and all the time . . . ' She turned to Dan. 'I called her a liar. Daisy tried to tell me I was wrong, but I wouldn't listen . . . ' She began to cry, harsh dry sobs.

As Dan tried to comfort her Joe grabbed his arm. 'What's she on about?'

'It's a long story, son,' he said.

Before he could continue, the door opened and a police inspector and a sergeant came in. 'Mrs Thompson?' the inspector asked.

'This has all been a terrible shock,' Dan said. 'Can't you leave it till later?'

Aggie blew her nose and pushed Dan's arm away. 'I'm all right. What do you want to know, Inspector?'

Dan had told Joe that the body found under the floor of Number Four Tanner's Court was Abby's mother. He was still shocked as he listened to Mrs Thompson's account of her daughter's last day on earth.

No wonder Abby had been so unhappy.

She didn't yet know that Carrie had been killed in a drunken rage all those years ago. But surely it would be a relief to discover that her mother hadn't abandoned her after all.

Aggie's voice, stronger now, broke into his thoughts. 'I often wondered why that no-good drunk decided to do that work on the house just after Carrie went. He said the flagstones were all broken up and the landlord wouldn't fix them.' She gave a harsh snort of laughter. 'Claimed he was worried little Abby would trip and hurt herself.' The laughter turned to sobs. 'I should have guessed.'

Dan patted her shoulder. 'You couldn't have known. At least now we know why Abby was left behind.'

'I disowned her, called her an unfit mother — and worse.'

Joe couldn't help himself. 'You disowned Abby too — and all because she fell in love with a sailor . . . ' His voice was tinged with bitterness.

'That wasn't the only reason,' Aggie snapped.

Before she could continue, Dan interrupted. 'You know the truth now. Best leave it.'

The inspector stood up. 'I don't think we'll need bother you again. Mr Cookson con-fessed before he died. He killed his wife in a jealous rage, hid her body under the floor, then told everyone she'd left him.'

'What about Abby?' Joe asked. 'She's already gone through so much . . . '

'I doubt she saw anything. Besides, she was so young — probably doesn't remember anything significant.' The inspector nodded to the sergeant, who snapped his notebook shut and followed him out of the room.

'Poor Abby — to lose both her mother and father. How are we going to tell her?' Joe asked. He put aside the way he'd felt when he saw Abby with Charlie Simmons — was it only two days ago? All he wanted now was to assure her of his love — to comfort her through this dreadful time.

★ ★ ★

Abby opened her eyes to bright sunlight streaming through the high window. She was in a tiny room with bare walls painted white. After a moment of confusion she realized that she was in hospital and it all flooded back, the bombs, the darkness and the terror.

She couldn't move and her throat was parched. Someone gently lifted her head and held a glass to her lips.

'Here, drink this. Not too much now.'

She gazed into Joe's dear face. So it hadn't

been a dream. He was really here. 'Joe, you came back,' she whispered.

He put the glass down. 'Thank God you're safe. When they pulled you out I thought . . . '

Abby tried to move once more and a spasm of pain crossed her face. 'What happened?'

'Your leg's broken but it'll mend. You'll need lots of rest — no driving tractors for a while.' Joe gave a short nervous laugh, then looked away.

Abby was puzzled. 'I suppose Dan told you I'd learned to drive.'

'I saw you,' Joe said abruptly. 'At the farm the other day.'

'But why?' Understanding dawned. 'Oh, Joe — surely you didn't think . . . ?'

'You were kissing. What was I supposed to think?'

'Charlie's a friend. I was saying goodbye.'

'It looked more than friendly to me.'

She began to protest and he took her hand. 'Sorry, I had no right to say that. You thought I was dead and after all these months it's only natural you would — '

'Charlie did try to convince me you weren't coming back. But I never gave up on you, Joe.'

'So why didn't you write? And why did you say you didn't want me?'

Now that he was here, sitting so close,

holding her hand as if he'd never let go, Abby asked herself the same question. He loved her. Surely he'd have understood if she'd explained how his passionate embrace had brought it all back to her — that dreadful night stuck in the snow? She realized that if they were to have any future together she'd have to tell him now. But where to begin? As she searched for the right words, the door opened and the ward sister came in.

'That's enough, young man. Can't have you tiring our patient. You can come back at the proper visiting time.'

Joe reluctantly stood up but Abby pulled at his hand. 'I feel awful for not asking before — what about Dad? Did they get him out all right?' She knew the answer before he spoke. 'He's dead, isn't he?' Tears welled up. He hadn't been the best father in the world but she'd still loved him.

The sister pushed Joe out of the way. 'Come on, my dear, no use getting upset,' she said, straightening the counterpane. 'We'll take you down to the main ward and you can have a nice rest. Things will look better then.'

★   ★   ★

Aggie leapt up when Joe came out of the ward. She'd been unable to face her granddaughter after thinking badly of her for so long. And how could she tell her what had really happened to her mother? She hoped Joe had broken the news.

'Does she know about Carrie?' she asked.

Joe shook his head. 'I told her about her dad but she got upset and the nurse made me leave.'

'I should be the one to tell her,' Aggie said. But she didn't know how she'd find the words. It was still hard to believe her daughter was dead. And she was ridden with guilt for slandering Carrie all these years.

'Plenty of time when she's a bit stronger,' Joe said. 'Where's Uncle Dan?'

'He's visiting Daisy Hill — I didn't realize they were such good friends.'

Joe smiled at the tartness in the old lady's voice. 'A bit more than friends if you ask me. He was frantic when he heard she'd been hurt. I expect he wanted to reassure her about Abby too. Mrs Hill's been like a mother to her.'

Guilt washed over Aggie. She should have been the one supporting Abby in her trouble. But she'd refused to listen, called her a liar and disowned her — and all because of that hypocrite who called himself a Christian. She bit her lip. It was wicked to be glad he was dead and could no longer corrupt innocent girls. She reminded herself that forgiveness was part of what she believed in — but it was hard.

Joe was looking at her strangely and she forced a smile. 'Abby's lucky to have Daisy as a friend — and you, young man. I misjudged you — I'm sorry.'

Did he know about the baby, she wondered, and would he stand by Abby when he found out — as he was sure to in a small town like this? Men were funny like that. It wasn't the poor girl's fault — at last she was willing to face up to that.

Joe shrugged and looked relieved when Dan returned, beaming. 'Daisy's being allowed up this afternoon,' he said.

'Was Mrs Hill badly hurt?' Aggie asked.

'Her hands were burnt helping one of her workmates and she breathed in some smoke. It could've been worse. I hear there were more than twenty people injured but only three were killed — one was a special constable. It's a miracle really.'

'I'm glad she's all right,' Aggie said, forcing a smile. She'd always resented Daisy's interference in Abby's life. But she was determined to bury the past — and that included old grievances. She had a lot of making-up to do with her granddaughter and accepting Abby's friends was part of that.

She stood up and tucked her handbag under her arm. 'There's no point in hanging around here any longer. Come along. I'll cook you both some dinner and then you should both go home and rest.'

22

When Abby woke up in the main ward Daisy was sitting at the bedside, a concerned expression creasing her forehead. She took in her friend's bandaged hands and struggled to sit up, frustrated at the cage holding her injured leg in place. 'Daisy, what happened . . . ?'

Her voice trailed away as it all came back to her — the plane crashing on the laundry, that pall of smoke over the city, then the air-raid and being trapped in the ruins of her home. A sob welled up as she remembered that her father hadn't survived the blast.

Daisy smiled. 'You do know it was Joe who got you out?'

So, it hadn't been a dream, his voice calling her, his hand holding hers as she was brought into the hospital.

Daisy was still speaking. 'What possessed you to go to the house instead of the shelter? And what were you doing here? I thought you were safe up at the farm.'

'I heard you'd been hurt but they wouldn't let me see you. Then the siren went and I saw Dad. I wanted to make sure he was all right.' Her eyes filled with tears.

Daisy patted her arm with her bandaged hand. 'Dan told me. It's a good job someone saw you go in — otherwise they'd've stopped searching once they found the bodies.'

Abby gasped and Daisy's expression grew troubled. 'They haven't told you, have they?'

'I know Dad was killed but . . . You said bodies. Who else . . . ?'

'I don't know how to tell you. I think your gran or someone should . . . '

'Daisy, tell me. I'll go mad if you don't.'

'It was your mother, Abby. She didn't run away. She was . . . '

Abby's face paled, the room swam. She put a hand to her throat. But she'd always known really, hadn't she? When people had slandered her mother, accused her of abandoning her daughter for another man, she'd known deep down that the woman she remembered would never have left her behind. Mingled with the shock and horror was relief. At last she knew the truth.

'I thought she'd abandoned me — but she was here all the time,' she murmured, vaguely aware of Daisy calling for the nurse, of being made to drink something. Then she was falling into a dark well, followed by merciful oblivion.

★   ★   ★

386

Much later she opened her eyes to see Joe and her grandmother at her bedside. She smiled to see Gran, upright on the hard chair, black hat firmly pinned to her head, clutching the big bag on her knee with one hand, while the other was firmly clasped in Joe's. It seemed strange to see the little woman, who normally disdained displays of affection, accepting comfort from the young man she'd always referred to as 'that sailor'.

Joe realized she was awake and leaned forward, taking her hand in his free one. 'How do you feel now?'

'I'm fine,' she started to say, then it all flooded back to her. 'Is it really true?' she whispered.

Joe nodded and Aggie said, 'You mustn't upset yourself. It all happened a long time ago.'

'Of course she's upset,' Joe said indignantly.

To Abby's surprise, Gran nodded meekly. 'You're right. What a silly thing to say. What I meant was — you must concentrate on getting better, keep your strength up and . . . ' Her voice trailed away.

'It's all right, Gran. I understand,' Abby said. She knew how hard it must have been for Gran to admit she was wrong. 'It's the future that's important — not the past.' She looked at Joe as she said it. But she knew she had to confront the past. If only they were alone.

The bell rang for the end of visiting and Joe stood up, still clinging to her hand. He bent to kiss her — not the sort of kiss she wanted. But what could she expect with Gran looking on? As it was Joe's face and ears were bright red. 'I'll come back this evening,' he whispered.

Gran leaned over and pecked her on the cheek. 'I'll pop in tomorrow,' she said.

When they'd gone, Daisy came over. 'Just a quick word before they make me get back in bed. I'm so glad you and your gran have made up,' she said. 'As for Joe — I told you everything would be all right.' She looked closely at Abby. 'It is all right, isn't it?'

Abby flushed. 'He saw me with Charlie but I explained and he's accepted it. He thinks everything's all right now but I'm not so sure ... I don't like the idea of keeping things from him. I lied to him about why I left Wheeler's and went to Southsea. Suppose he finds out — about the baby and everything.'

'Well, I've always thought you should tell him. It'll be harder for both of you if he found out later.'

'You're right. I'm going to tell him everything. If he doesn't want to know me after that, well he isn't the man I took him for. I'll be well rid of him.' It was defiantly spoken but Abby knew it was easier said than done. When Joe came for evening visiting she would need all her strength to find the right words to convince him that, whatever had happened in the past, she had always loved only him.

⋆　⋆　⋆

Abby's heart leapt as the ward doors swung open. Joe reached her bed in a few strides and she struggled to sit up, holding out her arms.

The kiss took her breath away. It certainly made up for that little peck earlier on. She pulled him as close as she could, careless of the flimsy hospital gown and the stares of the other patients, prolonging the kiss, revelling in his closeness, the smell and feel of him after so long apart. She had to make the most of it, knowing what she must do now.

'Joe, I do love you so.' Her voice caught and she gently pushed him away. She had to do it, even if she lost him for ever. There could be no more secrets between them. 'Sit down, Joe. There's something I must tell you.'

'It's about Charlie isn't it?' He took her hand. 'I do understand . . . '

'Joe — just listen — please. This is so hard.'

Gripping his hand she took a deep breath. 'Remember when you came to Daisy's house that time . . . '

Joe nodded. 'I got a bit carried away and you pushed me away. But I said I was sorry . . . ' He reached for her, but she leaned away from him.

'Let me explain, Joe. It wasn't because I didn't love you, or want you. It was just — it all came back to me and . . . '

Once she started it poured out — Ernest Wheeler's taunts and insinuations that she was 'just like her mother', she was leading him on, tempting him into wickedness. 'And then, in the car, he . . . ' She couldn't go on. She buried her face in the pillow, sobbing as if she'd never stop.

Joe grasped her shoulders and she could feel his anger. 'He didn't . . . ?'

She nodded and his grip tightened. She pushed him away, sitting up, her eyes blazing. 'I knew you'd blame me. But I tried to stop him . . . '

Joe pulled her to him, stroking her hair. 'I don't blame you, Abby, my sweet. It's him I'm mad at, the wicked bugger.'

Abby blew her nose and hiccuped. 'You haven't heard the worst yet,' she said, her voice subdued.

'What could be worse?'

'I had a baby, Joe,' she whispered. She looked at him through her tears, expecting to see disgust, condemnation. But his eyes were wet too.

He took her hand, kissed it, held it against his cheek. 'Oh, Abby — you went through all this alone? Why didn't you trust me?' He stood up, pacing the small space beside her bed. 'If he wasn't dead already, I'd kill him myself,' he muttered. He sat down abruptly and took her hand again. 'Abby, I love you. I would have stood by you — I *will* stand by you.'

'I'm sorry, I should have trusted you,' she whispered, feeling as if a great weight had been lifted from her.

'I just wish I'd known about it. What happened to the baby?'

'I had him adopted. Daisy's cousin Ivy arranged everything. I don't know what I'd have done without her.'

The bell for the end of visiting went before Joe could ask more questions. If she'd had any doubts, his goodbye kiss told her that everything was all right. She clung on to him, not wanting to let him out of her sight. But the nurse rang the bell again.

Daisy was having an equally hard time letting Dan go. 'You two were very engrossed,' she said when at last she'd waved him out of the door. 'You hardly said hello to Dan.' She leaned over and lowered her voice. 'Did you tell him?'

'Everything.'

'He obviously took it well. And I'll bet you feel better for getting it off your chest.'

Abby nodded. 'I wish he didn't have to go — there's so much I still wanted to say. I was going to tell him I called the baby Joe and pretended it was his.'

'Perhaps it is as well you didn't. It's time to put the past behind you and start living for now. You and Joe will have your own children one day.'

Abby hugged the thought to herself. They hadn't talked of marriage yet. But Joe had a few days before going back to light duties in port. Maybe they wouldn't have to wait till the war was over. Best of all, he'd promised not to sign on again. He would fulfil Dan's dream and settle down at Applegate Farm. Abby couldn't imagine a more blissful future.

★   ★   ★

The nurses had settled the patients for the night and the lights were out but Abby couldn't sleep. She should have been able to relax now that she'd unburdened herself. But the pain in her injured leg made sleep impossible. To take her mind off it, she relived Joe's every loving word and gesture. But she couldn't rid herself of the thought that she probably need not have given her baby away after all. She choked back a sob and wiped her eyes with the sheet. It was too late now.

She'd just closed her eyes when Daisy leaned over and whispered, 'I'm going home tomorrow.'

'Good,' Abby said, closing her eyes. She didn't feel like talking but Daisy whispered again.

'There's something on my mind, love. You said no more secrets. And I'm beginning to think I should've told you before. It's about little Joe.'

Abby sat up, trying not to attract the attention of the night nurse. 'What do you mean?'

'Ivy deceived you, saying he'd been adopted. She didn't want you to know, but . . . ' Daisy paused.

'What happened to him?' Visions of her baby killed in the bombing made her tremble. Why tell her now just when happiness seemed in sight? She was shaking so much she hardly heard Daisy's next words.

'She kept him — she and Sid took him to Norfolk with them.'

When she realized what Daisy meant she was furious. How dare they keep her baby?

Before she could speak the nurse appeared. 'Can't you sleep?' she asked.

Abby didn't want the pill but she swallowed it. As sleep overcame her, the anger receded, replaced by gratitude. If her baby had been legally adopted she'd never know where he was. Ivy must have had a good reason for what she did. A smile crossed her face. One day she might even get to see him. She pictured a rosy-cheeked toddler with fair hair and brown eyes — just like Joe.

When they were woken at six o'clock the next morning, Abby's first thought was of the shocking news Daisy had given her. 'I must see him, I must know,' she said tearfully.

Daisy was doubtful. 'Wouldn't it be best to let him go — start a new life with Joe, put the past behind you, love?'

Abby shook her head. 'I just feel bad that I abandoned him . . .'

'You didn't abandon him. You thought he'd been adopted — that he'd be loved and wanted. Well, he is — Ivy and Sid dote on him. And they kept him safe from the bombing.'

'You're right.' Abby was silent, thinking what might have happened if she'd kept him. Suppose she'd been at home with her father? They'd have been in the house when the bomb fell. Yes, things had turned out for the best.

Daisy interrupted her thoughts. 'Why not write to Ivy in Norfolk? She'll tell you how little Joe's doing — they kept the name, by the way. She might even send you a photo.'

'But she didn't want me to know she kept him.'

'I'll write too,' Daisy said.

Writing the letter took Abby a long time, but it filled the long hours between visiting times and distracted her from the pain.

Daisy had gone home but Gran came every day, bringing little treats and trying to make amends. She had even attended Wally's funeral as Abby was still in hospital. He'd been the only casualty of the raid.

As Aggie said in her forthright way, it had been for the best. 'Saved the cost of a trial,' she said grimly, not sparing Abby's feelings.

The scandal over the discovery of Carrie Cookson's body had been a nine-days' wonder in the town, quickly eclipsed by the excitement over the build-up to D-Day and the invasion on 6 June.

Abby, secure in Joe's love, couldn't really grieve for her parents — she had lost her mother long ago and Wally had never been much of a father. There was relief, too, that at last she knew she hadn't been abandoned after all.

Now she lived for Joe's visits and longed to

be discharged from hospital so that they could start their life together. Sometimes thoughts of little Joe would bring a tinge of sadness but Ivy had replied to her letter saying that, when the war was over, they planned to return to Southsea. They'd arrange a meeting then. It was something to look forward to.

A few days after the D-Day landings Abby was discharged from hospital. Her leg was still in plaster but beds were needed to cope with the invasion casualties.

Joe, still convalescent from his spell in the Russian hospital, hadn't been fit enough to take part — he was safe, at least as much as anyone was these days. Abby refused to feel guilty for feeling grateful, although she spared a thought for her friends as they waited anxiously for news of Larry and Jim.

There was no question of Abby going back to West Chilton and Gran took it for granted that she would live with her. But she couldn't bear the thought of passing Tanner's Court every day with all its unhappy memories.

It seemed natural to return to Daisy's riverside cottage where they'd be able to look after each other.

'I could do with the company,' Daisy said to an indignant Aggie, 'and besides, we have a double wedding to plan.'

EPILOGUE

1950

Abby straightened her beret and pulled the green jersey down over her hips, amazed that the uniform still fitted her after the birth of two children. She smiled at Cissie and Polly, straightened her shoulders and stepped into her place, her heart lifting as the band of the Irish Guards started up and she took her first step on the march from Buckingham Palace to St Paul's Cathedral. How proud she was to be part of what had been called the forgotten army — an army that was at last receiving recognition for the vital part it had played during the war.

As she marched she wished Cynthia was with them. But her friend was expecting another baby and couldn't make the journey from Canada. Still, Cissie and Jim were there.

And there was Joe holding little Danny on his shoulders and waving like mad. And Daisy and Dan, holding hands with Caroline. She wanted to wave back but sternly faced front, her eyes blurring as she said a prayer of thanks for her lovely family.

The war had been over for five years and those dreadful hours trapped in the ruins of her childhood home, as well as the traumas that had gone before, now seemed like half-remembered nightmares. On their wedding night she had been torn by her emotions — joy at being reunited with her darling Joe warred with trepidation as he began to make love to her. Would those dreadful memories rise up and overwhelm her as they had before?

She needn't have worried. Joe's tenderness, swiftly turning to passion had swept away the dark fears and she had melted into his arms. It was as it had always been meant to be. And, true to his word, Joe had never once referred to her ordeal at the hands of Ernest Wheeler.

The past seldom intruded, except when she and Daisy occasionally took the train to Portsmouth to spend a few hours with Sid and Ivy and their son. Joey loved his Auntie Abby and she, despite her vow to have no more secrets or lies in her life, could see how harmful it might be to upset the lad's stable life by telling him about his real parentage. He was happy — that was all that mattered. Maybe one day he could be told the truth.

In the cathedral, Queen Elizabeth praised the girls — women as they were now, although they'd always be known as the Land-Girls. She spoke of their courage, their willingness to face hardship in all weathers. 'By their hard work and patient endurance they earned a noble share in the immense effort which carried our country to victory,' she said.

Abby felt a swell of pride, but deep down she knew that for her it was no hardship. It was a life she loved and now, sharing it with Joe, she had found true happiness. She glanced over her shoulder and caught Joe's eye. His smile warmed her heart and she stood to sing the harvest hymn, '*Come ye thankful people*,' reflecting on how much she had to be thankful for.

As she sang, she treasured the moment, storing it away in her memory. Danny and Caroline were too young to remember this momentous day and she wanted to be able to tell them about it when they were older. She resolved that they at least would have no dark memories, no secrets or lies in their lives.

We do hope that you have enjoyed reading this large print book.

Did you know that all of our titles are available for purchase?

We publish a wide range of high quality large print books including:
Romances, Mysteries, Classics
General Fiction
Non Fiction and Westerns

Special interest titles available in large print are:
The Little Oxford Dictionary
Music Book
Song Book
Hymn Book
Service Book

Also available from us courtesy of Oxford University Press:
Young Readers' Dictionary
(large print edition)
Young Readers' Thesaurus
(large print edition)

For further information or a free brochure, please contact us at:
Ulverscroft Large Print Books Ltd.,
The Green, Bradgate Road, Anstey,
Leicester, LE7 7FU, England.
Tel: (00 44) 0116 236 4325
Fax: (00 44) 0116 234 0205

Other titles published by
The House of Ulverscroft:

A BLESSING IN DISGUISE

Pamela Fudge

When Alex Siddons becomes pregnant after twenty-five years of childless marriage, her life is turned upside down and her relationship with her husband, Phil, hangs in the balance. A child at their time of life is the last thing either of them wants or needs and yet, despite pressure from Phil, Alex cannot bring herself to terminate the pregnancy, even if it is the only thing that will save her marriage. Facing the prospect of life as a single mother, Alex finds unexpected support from within the Siddons family. Now she finally learns the true meaning of family and love.

VOICES OF THE MORNING

June Gadsby

Patrick Flynn doesn't want another mouth to feed, so he endeavours to ensure that his newborn son Billy does not survive. But, helped by a warm-hearted prostitute and Laura Caldwell, the daughter of a wealthy local family, Billy does . . . Patrick deserts his family, leaving Billy to struggle for a living and to look after his alcoholic mother. He becomes obsessed with Laura, but she has other ideas, and it is with Bridget, the prostitute's daughter, that Billy joins the Jarrow crusaders marching to London to demonstrate against unemployment. Neither of them, however, is prepared for the reappearance of the evil Patrick Flynn . . .

1	26	51	76	101	126	151	220	310	460
2	27	52	77	102	127	152	227	312	461
3	28	53	78	103	128	153	233	317	478
4	29	54	79	104	129	154	234	324	479
5	30	55	80	105	130	155	237	331	486
6	31	56	81	106	131	156	238	341	488
7	32	57	82	107	132	157	241	355	499
8	33	58	83	108	133	160	242	357	500
9	34	59	84	109	134	164	243	363	509
10	35	60	85	110	135	166	244	375	511
11	36	61	86	111	136	167	249	380	517
12	37	62	87	112	137	168	250	383	519
13	38	63	88	113	138	172	252	393	523
14	39	64	89	114	139	174	257	396	529
15	40	65	90	115	140	175	259	400	534
16	41	66	91	116	141	180	262	403	538
17	42	67	92	117	142	182	268	405	544
18	43	68	93	118	143	183	269	413	552
19	44	69	94	119	144	188	272	417	565
20	45	70	95	120	145	189	273	435	570
21	46	71	96	121	146	192	274	440	575
22	47	72	97	122	147	195	279	447	583
23	48	73	98	123	148	203	285	451	595
24	49	74	99	124	149	208	288	452	619
25	50	75	100	125	150	212	299	453	624